TAP TWICE FOR REVENGE

TAP TWICE FOR REVENGE

A NOVEL

GREG HEIST

For my wife, Diane.

SOLEMN OATH COLLECTION

BOOK ONE

"Beware the fury of a patient man."

—JOHN DRYDEN

TAP
TWICE
FOR
REVENGE

ONE

THE SILENCE WAS DEAFENING. A man of such strength wept like a child. He was overcome with emotions that he didn't recognize. There seemed to be a combination of joy, guilt, and resolve. A pent-up tension that exploded like shrapnel in the form of tears.

"I'm sorry I haven't done anything," he said as his crying gradually subsided. "My rage is clouding my brain. I can't seem to think about anything else. I can't reason. I can't get that letter out of my mind."

The silence came and went, between each spoken word. Each moment of pain escaped, briefly, through the tears that choked his soul.

"I finally came to a decision. I thought I would feel some relief. I am so goddamn crazy. What am I about to do?"

He walked back and forth, around in circles. Looking to the sky for answers. Looking to the heavens for some sign that he was about to do the right thing. He paced some more, staring down at the grass. The grass was tall. He wondered why the men didn't take better care of this place. After all, this was the place his wife and only child rested. It's where he came once a week, every Sunday, to cry, laugh, shout, regret, and wonder. What would life have been like? How would things be if it had not happened? Where would he be every Sunday had things been different?

"I've got to go now my sweet ones," he whispered, "but I'll see you both again. Soon."

He walked away, looking back over his shoulder. He never wanted to leave them. He would turn, walking backwards, and then walking straight again. When he reached his old pickup truck waiting by the fence, he opened the tailgate and grabbed a weed trimmer lying in the bed. He turned back and fixated on the two headstones bearing the names of Ellen and Kristine Steele. They rested in the most peaceful part of the cemetery. The morning sun bounced off the marble like a ship's spotlight bounces off a moonlit ocean. His wife and daughter were right next to each other, where they should have been, under a beautiful oak tree that protected them like a sentry at the door of a castle. They were sheltered from the rain. Shaded from the sun. Now, protected from the evils of an unjust world.

His wife had turned fifty-one when she was taken from him by the indiscriminate violence of cancer. Porter was never a man to wallow in self-pity, but losing Ellen began to change him. He began to dwell on the loss of his parents, his grandfather, and fellow Green Beret soldiers that fought by his side. But Ellen, her loss to cancer was unfair. Death seemed to surround him like a smothering blanket.

While coping with his wife's death, he lost his only child. Kristine was twenty-eight and was taken from him by her own hand. A beautiful, thoughtful soul, seemingly in the grip of a depression. It would not stop squeezing. No one knew the pain she was unable to purge from her body. A pain that was born in her mind but jabbed at her heart. Jabbing night and day, day, and night, until she halted the madness with a bottle of pills. The only two people left in life that depended on Porter Steele were gone. He was alone. There was nothing that could heal his heart. Ellen was the innocent victim of a terrible disease. Kristine died by suicide. Nothing would bring them back.

He walked over to their headstones, started the weed trimmer, and began to clear away the tall grass. Within minutes, the small parcel of land that sheltered his two blessed loved ones, was cleared. Just for that moment, he felt he had made them smile. Life would not change. The pain would never cease. His heart and soul simply would not release him from this self-imposed exile. An exile that barricaded him from the joys of the outside world. For Porter Steele, self-indulgence of any kind would be a form of betrayal. He threw the weed trimmer back in the bed of his truck and drove away from the cemetery. Six miles to go, down a brown dusty road, toward his ranch.

PORTER STEELE'S RANCH was beautiful. It sat on over five hundred acres in the northwest region of Arizona. The land was rugged. Peaceful. Vast, yet secluded. It was not the type of home generally occupied by a retired police captain. It was a rustic log home, handcrafted decades ago by his grandfather. Grandpa Parker Steele, whom Porter simply referred to as Papa, was larger than life. Papa Steele raised Porter from the age of eleven. He could do no wrong. Both of Porter's parents were killed in a private plane crash. They were flying to Papa Steele's ranch to pick up Porter after one of his week-long summer visits. After the funeral, he continued to live and work on the ranch with his grandfather. He learned everything there was to know about ranching, working hard and becoming a strong man. Not just physically strong, but mentally strong as well.

The next several years quickly passed. When Porter reached the age of nineteen, he decided there was more of the world to be seen. He began to feel isolated on the ranch. Perhaps his youth, and a disconnect from his own generation, caused this feeling. He signed up for the Army to fulfill his sense of patriotism. This too was inherited from Papa. With his grandfather's rugged individualism flowing through his blood, there was still more to accomplish. He was selected for the

Army Special Forces, Green Beret. This was a sense of accomplishment. A sense of pride. He knew his grandfather was proud and that was all that mattered.

After a five-year stint in the Army, Porter returned to work in the southern Nevada area. Not too far from Papa's ranch. He eventually became a police officer with the Las Vegas Metropolitan Police Department. His career began, as did a whirlwind relationship with Ellen, who was slightly older than Porter. He had no problem with that. She was a young, smart, beautiful grad student at the University of Nevada Las Vegas. She soon became his wife. His life was beginning to take on a sense of true meaning. He was building a solid foundation for the future. Something tangible, like Papa Steele always taught. He was creating commitments. Porter was becoming a man that others depended upon. He was a man that other men looked up to. Those duties and commitments made him feel worthwhile.

Porter Steele was not an ordinary man, by any means. He spent over thirty years in law enforcement when he decided that it was time to retire. Retirement wasn't easy for a man with such strong character. A man with integrity and a sense of justice. A man people depended upon. Porter kept busy. The ranch was a place to work. There was no doubt about that, but his life was not what he expected. Not what he had hoped.

He was a man of great intellect, but even greater humility, which concealed his creative mind. Throughout his career as a criminal investigator, there were many things he wanted to achieve. He flew a private plane, just as his father and his grandfather before him. He loved riding his motorcycle and horses. He loved doing anything that allowed him to touch the land and be part of the fabric of nature. He had the gift of foresight. An ability to plan far ahead. Porter learned the skills of strategy, logistics and a keen sense of organization. Not just from running the ranch with his grandfather, but also from the survival tactics he was taught as a Green Beret.

He also learned how to compartmentalize all his emotions after the death of the only two people he loved more than life itself. When it came to money, he had no worries. Porter had a nice pension after three decades in police work. His grandfather left him the ranch, a 1970 Cessna, and a significant trust fund, which Porter was uncomfortable to receive.

When it came to happiness, it had died with Ellen and Kristine. He had no idea how to find it again. He wasn't sure if he wanted to. The ranch he loved was becoming a reminder of loneliness. A place that forced him to recall the memories he swore he would bury forever. A place that made him regret those times he failed the people he loved. A place that challenged him to face those memories and regrets head on. He needed to wake up one day and do something about it. Porter could not live the rest of his days doubting, regretting, and ultimately failing. Something had to change.

DRIVING UP THE DIRT ROAD to his ranch house was always familiar. It was his routine. His property was huge. Porter allowed a friend, Jose, his daughter, Esmerelda, and his granddaughter, Roseanna, to live in the guest house. Jose's family was struggling since Esmerelda's husband was killed in a farming accident the year before. Jose sought out his trusted friend, Porter, for help. Jose was in charge of the work on the ranch. He tended to the animals, outbuildings, and issues with the main ranch house. Esmeralda helped with the cooking and cleaning while Roseanna focused on school. Porter felt it was a way of giving back to an old Army buddy down and out at the time. Jose wanted to do what was best for his family and help them get back on their feet again. The plan was to have them move back to Albuquerque, where Jose originated. They were paid well for their work. They were able to stay in the guest house for free, as long as they took care of the two-bedroom log cabin like it was their own, maintaining the small problems that arose.

As Porter approached the house, he noticed a large man standing in the driveway. It wasn't Jose. At first, he couldn't tell who it was. As he got closer, it brought a smile to his face. Sean Wallace stood there, amused, as big as a tree. Sean was an old flying buddy, whom Porter had not seen for at least a year. He lived in southern Utah and had been sick for several months. When both men weren't working their properties, they flew together for fun. They talked about planes, the construction business, the ranch, and the ills of a changing society. Porter pulled right up beside him as he stood near the driveway. He rolled down the window of his truck.

"How the hell are you, Sean?" Porter got out of his truck and shut the door, immediately reaching out for Sean's renowned vise grip handshake.

"I'm a hundred percent better than I was this time last year, bud." Sean breathed deeply. "Thought I was a dead man walking."

"So, the surgery worked?"

"Yes, and some radiation and chemo. But I'm alive my friend."

"Thank God." Porter leaned in for one more handshake, and a man hug, shoulder to shoulder. "You drive or fly down?"

"I flew," Sean said. "That's okay, I hope?"

"Hell yes, it's okay. That's great!"

"Hoped you wouldn't mind. Pulled the plane off the end of your runway and parked it near yours."

"Perfect...," Porter hesitated, taking time to look Sean over. Up and down, like readjusting to the sight of an old friend that had come back from the dead. "Damn, I can't believe you're standing here. I thought the next time I saw you would be at your funeral. Let's go inside."

Both men walked inside the ranch house and Porter pulled up a couple wooden dining room chairs. The table was eight feet long, four inches thick and as solid as stone. It was made from a thick white oak tree that had died on the ranch. Papa Parker had the tree cut down and turned into a table and chairs by an old timer in town who was a true wood artisan. He often bragged that it only cost him five hundred dollars for a piece of sturdy furniture, which would last a lifetime. He imagined it would cost five thousand dollars in one of those highfalutin furniture stores in New York City.

"Sean, how 'bout a beer?"

"Sounds good."

Porter walked to the fridge and grabbed two dark specialty beers, sliding Sean's bottle down the long oak tabletop, right to his waiting hand.

"You always have to serve something different," Sean said as he raised the special brew to toast a long friendship that had been placed on hold for a while. "Sláinte."

"Sláinte," Porter toasted.

The two men talked and laughed like young boys, reminiscing about days gone by. Happier times. Porter had been thinking a lot about Sean for the last several months. But, as many men do, he didn't reach out. He waited. Porter regretted that but did little to change it. It wasn't like Sean reached out to anyone, either. He had been sick with cancer for a year. Several of those months he never told anyone. Sean Wallace was a private man. He never married, had no children, and spent his adult life running a luxury home construction business in southern Utah for over thirty years. He had socked away quite a fortune. He sold the entire business after getting sick. That move doubled his fortune. Sean had one love, but few friends. His best friend was Porter, and his first love was flying. Now healthy again, and having enough money to do as he pleased, Sean began to fly regularly.

"Porter, you have to see the new gift I bought myself."

"You finally got one?"

"It's brand new. After surviving cancer, I pulled the trigger. I'm getting old. I have to spend my money on something."

"Cessna?"

"What else?"

"Citation?"

"No, no. I'm not a Citation kind of guy," Sean winked. "Caravan, of course. Eight-seater. And I got some luxury options on the interior."

"You have it here, with you, today?"

"I want you to go up with me."

"Let's do it."

The two men headed toward the back of the ranch house. A hundred feet away sat Sean's new Cessna Caravan. It was gleaming white with blue striping. Sean took Porter on a quick walkaround, explaining some of the new options on his plane. At the same time, he was making sure his Cessna was ready for a short flight, to let Porter enjoy the feel of his new purchase. Porter climbed up into the passenger side and got himself belted in.

Sean entered the pilot's seat. "Ready for takeoff?"

"Ready as I'll ever be," Porter smiled. Just for a moment he forgot about everything. He forgot about the pain, the loss, the regret. He forgot about death. He forgot about the tall grass. Porter hadn't felt this relaxed in a long time. He focused on his good friend, and his new plane. Sean hit the throttle and got the plane storming down the runaway. Then, they gently lifted off the ground like a feather in the wind. The sense of initial weightlessness caused Porter to close his eyes.

He smiled, soaking it all in, like a happy child on a roller coaster. He knew it wouldn't last. For a brief moment this was the closest he had been, in a very long time, to finding true peace.

TWO

SIX-THIRTY IN THE MORNING, in a small apartment just outside Milwaukee, Jen anticipated another day from hell. Her job as branch manager at a local bank was necessary, but far from her dream job. She just turned thirty-eight but felt like she was fifty-eight. Where had all the time gone? Why did everything she ever wanted to do fall by the wayside? She knew why in her heart but couldn't say it out loud. Facing the truth was too painful. Blaming something or someone else was not her style. No matter how wrong she was, she could not come to grips with the truth, the past.

Sixteen years ago, she graduated from Arizona State University's W.P. Carey School of Business with a degree in finance. She was going to take Wall Street by storm. She dreamt of start-ups, investments, IPOs, and being the CEO of a Fortune 500 company. She could never have imagined being a bank branch manager in Wisconsin. She was an excellent student who excelled in the area of finance. Numbers came easy, stock analysis was her forte. Partying came in a close second, though. Jen was not much different than any other student when she attended ASU. She studied hard throughout the week, and when Friday came around, she was ready to let loose. Jen had friends that did the same, so it wasn't as if she stood out from the crowd.

After she graduated, she did make it out to New York, working for an investment firm. She loved her job, the lifestyle of Wall Street, and also a young investment banker that swept her off her feet. Head over heels in love, she felt that two salaries were better than one. When he asked her to marry, she didn't hesitate. Only twenty-four at the time, him being twenty-nine, she was ready to take on Wall Street and married life. So, she thought. His model good looks and Hollywood personality were too good to be true. There were always a handful of young ladies that loved him as much as Jen did. After two years of sharing him, it became too much to handle. Jen was young, strong-willed, and competent. She learned quickly that New York could be cold and harsh, as well as glamorous. To make matters worse, after their quick divorce, his connections at the company got him a promotion. She got fired. She convinced herself that since they had no kids, the divorce was much like breaking up with a boyfriend. No harm, no foul.

Jen didn't get anything from this guy, and he never got anything from her, so they went their separate ways. She decided to chalk it up as a minor failure in the marriage department and decided it was not the end of the world. Unfortunately, Jen's sense of right and wrong got in the way of her happiness. She tucked that failed marriage away into the recesses of her heart. Reaching deep within, now and again, pulling it out, examining it, analyzing it, torturing herself. For no reason, other than she could not figure out how to stop repeating her behavior.

Jen moved to Chicago and took a job with another large investment company. She needed the change. She felt as if she was starting over. She was still young, smart, willing, and able to succeed. Jen was also not so interested in the male species, so she believed this would help her stay focused on her career. For the next six years she was on top of the world, at least for most of the time. The money was great, she loved her apartment in the loop, and the weekend partying reminded her of the good old days at ASU. Her relationships with men were brief, shallow, often personally exhilarating, but without commitment. They were hardly emotionally fulfilling. Jen's days were filled with work, some yoga, dining out and drinking wine. A lot of wine. Too much wine.

Jen could not get enough money or enough wine, so when she met a businessman, ten years her senior, at a wine tasting party, she quickly fell in love. He had money, drive, and a gorgeous three-bedroom condo, fifty stories up in the sky within one of the most prestigious buildings in Chicago. She loved it and began to spend more time in his condo than in her own. The wine flowed, money flowed and lust flowed at a pace neither one of them could sustain. The only way to slow down their passion was to get married. This guy had already been divorced, with two young children, whom he rarely saw. But marriage suited him better than long-term dating. Jen decided to give it another try. Perhaps, this was the one.

She was now in her early thirties, he forty-two, but she never thought for a moment that she may have been searching for a father figure to protect her from the evils of the outside world. She never considered that perhaps he was the man to make her forget about the past, the pain, and the thoughts that crept into her head, late at night, only to be washed away with that sweet red juice. It helped her sleep. Jen no longer looked at bottles of wine through the eyes of the connoisseur, as a collector of the prized grape. Even though her husband studied wine as a hobby, Jen began to look at the reds and whites as simply bottles of medicine. One more secret to hide. One more crutch to perpetuate the illness. One more failure to embed itself inside her thoughts. Ripping away at her soul and reason to live.

No new man, no new marriage, no new job, no new city, no new outlook on life, was ever powerful enough to quash the inner turmoil that ultimately led her down the road of self-destruction. She knew why. She knew exactly why. She just didn't know how to destroy the reason. How to bury the memories that haunted her every waking moment.

Jen was able to drink herself through the next three years of marriage, but her husband simply could not tolerate it any longer. One bottle of wine turned into two, then three, then Jen being carried into bed. When he told her that he had taken a job in New York, she told him that she could not return to that hell on Wall Street. That was the answer he was hoping for. That was exactly what he wanted her to say. The divorce was simple. Once again, no children and a solid prenup that held up through all court proceedings. Jen left the marriage the same way she came in. She was broke, alone, and now, starting all over again. She also had a drinking problem she had to attend to if she expected to keep pace with her job.

Unfortunately, like many alcoholics, Jen failed at trying to control her drinking on her own. After several missed days of work, and even more days of going to work, but not being all there mentally, her lack of dedication cost her a good job. Jen had no choice but to move again and start all over. The one thing she didn't ever want to do was go home to Milwaukee, to her father's place, and feel like a reject from the world of business.

Her father was a successful high-level executive with a Fortune 500 company in Milwaukee but had very few hours in the day to know what was truly going on with his daughter, or his own wife for that matter. After Jen's mother and father divorced, her seemingly distraught mother quickly remarried another executive from a rival company. Her mother's goals seemed to be focused on money, self-absorption and relishing the luxuries that could be bestowed upon her by a well-paid man.

Essentially motherless, and now in the incapable hands of her father, Jen seemed to have the worst of both worlds. He believed anything

Jen told him, because it was easier that way. He assumed she would eventually get her act together after a few months. Although he took her in willingly, he had not changed very much over the years, which was what Jen expected. He was still too busy and still too absent from her life, even after they began to live under the same roof. His house was over five thousand square feet, so at times it was as if they didn't live with each other at all.

Jen was now in her mid-thirties, and her father didn't have enough energy, or the motivation, to try to play father of the year. Truthfully, she knew that he had his own issues with alcohol. He just had a good way of ignoring it, while continuing to function. Being a good, concerned loving father wasn't in his DNA. It wasn't in him and she knew it. He was able to land her an assistant manager position at a local bank, because the president was a very good friend of his. Jen knew that getting acclimated to this lifestyle was going to be more than a challenge.

After her life in New York and Chicago, adjusting to living with her father, at age thirty-six, in Milwaukee, was like being dropped from an airplane onto a remote island. This was more than starting over. This was like being reborn into a world she did not recognize. Jen was hardly able to get through this process without a few drinks and a few mental breakdowns.

After a year with her father, Jen moved to her own apartment, alone again. He decided to retire, now spending six months in Florida. Once again, she was left behind. The men she dated came and went. The days and weeks passed. The desire for fulfilling relationships waned. How did this happen? This was a question Jen asked herself daily. Life was harder, much harder. This was a woman that needed help. This was a bright, talented woman that needed renewal. Two years as a branch manager, and living alone in Milwaukee, this was a broken woman that needed a major epiphany in her life. Jen needed some sort of psychological recalibration, perhaps even retribution. She needed to be healed from the wounds of a vicious crime that occurred to her in the middle of a deep, dark, moonlit night within the four walls of a cold, dilapidated, abandoned motel on the outskirts of Las Vegas on March 6, 1999.

ANGIE WAS A STUNNING woman to behold. She was thirty-nine years of age with the fit, sinewy, body of a woman half her age. This look came from years and years of hard work in any gym she could find to workout. Angie was always athletic. While a student at Arizona State University, she was a runner on the track team. She loved the outdoors, the desert, the mountains, and canyons. She loved her teammates and school. Her dream of becoming a physical rehabilitation specialist was solid, achievable. Angie was bright, outgoing, a people-person, with ambition. Her friends couldn't keep up with her. She wanted things in life and wanted them now. Waiting was not an option for Angie. She had the ability to succeed. Her parents were very proud of her. They showered her with unconditional praise and rarely said no to any request. They believed supporting their only daughter, in any adventure she tried, was required for doting parents.

When Angie graduated from ASU, she went back to her hometown of Lawrence, Kansas and received her master's degree in athletic training from the University of Kansas. At twenty-five she took a job with a prominent physical rehabilitation group. She was familiar with her surroundings, near old friends and willing to dedicate herself to her company. For eight years Angie worked as a rehabilitation specialist and worked out at the local gym even harder. She relished the life of a young, single woman, which is exactly what she wanted. She spent every waking hour either at work or in the gym. Other than meeting men at the gym, she didn't have the time, or the desire, to date anyone seriously. These men were more like work-out partners than anything else. Many of those men found her to be simply one of the boys than a girl they would ask out. Her beauty and brawn were both intimidating, which kept many men at bay. While in her presence, her preoccupation with fitness and self-fulfillment was palpable. The psychological shell she developed around her physical being was almost as visible as her physique. She would not let anyone inside that shell to find out who Angie truly was. You had to accept what you saw. You had no choice.

At the age of thirty-three, Angie decided it was time to step up to a challenge she gave herself some years earlier. She promised herself that she would open a modern CrossFit Gym. But this meant quitting her career as a rehabilitation specialist. This was a frightening adventure, but she knew that she wasn't getting any younger. After months of planning, and borrowing money from her father, she finally put in her letter of resignation to the rehabilitation group. This was a bittersweet decision, to say the least. Angie always won though. She knew she would be successful. Her dream was to expand and open several gyms. This was possible if, and only if, she could fight off one major roadblock. There was a secret, vicious, demon that she battled daily. One quiet, but powerful force, which buried itself so deep into her psyche that she was not smart enough, strong enough, brave enough, to battle against its power. This failure haunted her, because she did not think anyone, or anything, could conquer her.

Angie had fought against an eating disorder that went hand in hand with her Type A personality. She was determined to sculpt the human body into perfection. The thought of gaining weight drove Angie to purge frequently. She viewed it as a simple and fast way of remaining exactly where she wanted to be, eight percent body fat, which was on par with professional bodybuilders. Angie was consumed by perfection at the same time she was consumed by guilt. A guilt that covered her like a blanket in a cold, unforgiving storm that would not subside.

There was no such thing as downtime, or quiet time, for Angie. Her mind would not allow it, and her body would not accept it. The years passed and she grew her company to five separate and successful CrossFit Gyms throughout the Midwest. Her nest egg grew substantially, but so did her struggles with anxiety, depression, eating disorders, and a sense of failure. Angie was in her late thirties and had never married or had children. In her relentless drive to have it all, she realized that on cold, dark, quiet evenings, in front of her fireplace, she sat under a soft, cozy, warm blanket all by herself.

At the age of thirty-nine, Angie realized that there wasn't a single person to turn to, look into their eyes and ask one simple question: *Do you remember when?* Life had been all about Angie. Perhaps this was a question she avoided for the last sixteen years for one good reason. Perhaps the answer was too excruciating. Perhaps the crime that occurred to her on March 6, 1999, was the sole reason for her life spinning out of control. Even though it appeared to others that she was on top of the world, they couldn't have been so wrong.

LYNN WAS UP EARLY getting her youngest of three children off to school. It was a typical morning. She was a single mother and had been for the last five years. Lynn had a daughter who was in the third grade, one son in middle school, and her eldest son was a sophomore in high school. It was very difficult for her to be a single parent for three children who were at stages in their life where two parents were a must. Having one son in his teens, and a second almost there, was a next to impossible task without a father figure in their lives. She cherished her youngest, a beautiful seven-year-old girl, who never really knew her father. It was difficult to raise an innocent, loving child, who could not relate to conversations about her absent father. Lynn struggled daily to keep up her job as a registered nurse, where she dedicated herself to a career in medicine. The hours were often long, but with kids in school, she had very little choice.

Lynn's life was not always this complicated. She had a plan and up until five years ago it was coming to fruition. When Lynn graduated from Arizona State University, she set out to find a career in the field of medicine. She started out as an emergency room nurse at a medical center in Denver, where she met the love of her life. He was a young attractive doctor with a sharp mind and even sharper wit. Lynn loved his sense of humor and his dedication to his patients. Even though he was seven years older, she knew that he was definitely Mr. Right. Lynn was focused on her career as well, but she saw the potential for a great relationship with this successful doctor. They secretly dated for six months, until he changed locations and began to work at a hospital twenty miles away. Lynn thought that the change made it easier for both of them to date, so she became very open about their relationship. A couple years went by, and Lynn decided to seek employment, as well, at the same hospital. Even though she was anxious to work at the same location as her boyfriend, she feared having to go back to keeping their relationship hidden. She had no intention of pressuring him into taking their relationship to the next level. Lynn was hopeful about the potential outcome.

He began to speak of marriage so they would not have to date any longer, under the radar, while they both worked together at the same hospital. He wasn't getting any younger and he was well aware that Lynn knew the ups and downs of being married to a busy physician. She was beyond thrilled and waited for him to pop the question.

Within six months of her new employment at the hospital, he asked her to marry him, which she quickly agreed before he could even finish the final words of his proposal. They soon married.

When she was twenty-five, they had their first son. Lynn was ecstatic and so was her husband. She doted over their child and spent the next three years becoming a wonderful mother. This prepared her for their next child. At the age of twenty-eight she had their second son, who became the lucky beneficiary of a woman that had mastered parenting. Lynn and her husband were still hoping for a daughter. They decided they would eventually try one more time. But if they were to have another son, they both agreed he would be their last. At the age of thirty-two, Lynn had their final child, the daughter they had hoped for. That was Lynn's plan, and it was playing out exactly how she and her husband had wanted.

Lynn's husband was now thirty-nine years of age and a well-respected surgeon at the hospital. Their life was very comfortable. She no longer worried about the future. Lynn had someone that was dedicated to her, loved her, took care of many of her needs, and was on the same page when it came to parenting. There were no financial struggles. There was a happiness that Lynn strived for and thought would last forever.

Unfortunately, two years later Lynn's world came crashing in and destroyed her perfect life. Her loving husband was killed in a tragic car accident while he was attending a medical convention in California. She could not accept the news. She could not release the anger that encapsulated her being. How could she explain his death to her children, who were much too young to understand the consequences? How could she look into the beautiful blue eyes of daddy's little girl and speak about her father's death? How could she explain to her sons that their caring father, their rock, was not coming home again? Lynn did not have the strength to speak the words; *Daddy is now in heaven.*

Lynn knew that someday her daughter, a mere toddler, would not even remember her father's face. This caused her immense heartbreak.

Now, at the age of thirty-eight, Lynn was surviving, but that was all she was doing. Suffering from depression and hiding her severe pain, oxycodone became her drug of choice. Lynn got skilled at stealing the medication from work, any way she needed. She now realized that her broken dreams had turned her into a broken woman. This was also the first time that she admitted it to herself and came to grips with the fact that it was also pain pills that relieved her misery back in her early twenties. That was a secret that she hoped would fade away, but now again it raised its ugly head.

No one knew but her parents. Lynn had stolen many bottles of oxycontin in her early twenties to battle an agony that was not visible. It was an agony that she never wanted her future husband to ever know about. For her, it was a secret worth hiding. She knew that it was her strong, protective husband who rescued her from an ongoing psychological battle. A battle forced upon her by one crime that she tried so hard to bury. It was a crime that tore at Lynn's soul, like a cat scratching at a screen door. Lynn needed her husband. She needed her kids. She needed her job. She needed her pills. Lynn also needed a life so perfectly prearranged that there would never be one single second in the day for her tortured mind to wander back to that dark, fateful night on March 6, 1999.

THREE

AS THEY FLEW NORTH, Porter caught himself gazing out of the window of Sean's new Cessna Caravan. The sun broke free from between two clouds. Sean smiled as he piloted his new plane. He could tell that Porter was relaxed and taking it all in. Porter smiled as he thought of Ellen and Kristine. It was as if they knew he was flying today and had just offered him a gift of sunlight from heaven. He accepted it as a sign of the promise he made to them so long ago. It was the promise of justice for two women that held his heart like a sick child holds a well-worn teddy bear. Although Porter was smiling, Sean noticed that he was quiet, pensive, and withdrawn.

"Porter...are you okay?"

"Yeah, I'm fine," he replied. "For the first time in a long time, I'm okay."

"If you don't mind me asking, is this about Ellen and Kristine?"

"It's that obvious?"

"I know how much you loved them," Sean answered. "I'm sorry I haven't said anything. I'm not very good at showing my emotions, or the right etiquette, I guess."

"Listen, my friend, I've kept myself inside this shell. It has nothing to do with you, Sean."

"You know I'd do anything for you," he stated, "and when it comes to Kristine and Ellen, I'm not sure what I could do, but if there is anything..."

Porter raised his hand to interrupt and smiled. "I know you'd do anything for me. That's kind of you and I do appreciate it."

"Anything. I mean it, Porter. Anything."

"I might just take you up on that offer one of these days."

The men flew and talked and laughed for the next two hours. Sean flew northeast toward his new home, which was near Durango, Colorado.

"I want you to see my new vacation home. I've been building it for a while now. It's finally done."

"You're kidding me...a new home and a new plane?" Porter shook his head.

"Hey, my friend, you only live once, right?"

"I thought this was going to be a quick trip out and then back to my place."

"You're stuck up here in the air with me now," Sean said. "One night at my new place...c'mon buddy, live a little. You gotta see this log home I've been working on."

"You never mentioned this house."

"I know I never did, because I was building it for a client."

"What happened?"

"Honestly, I never once thought of having a vacation home in Durango."

"How did it come about?"

"It's a long story, but I'll try to give you the short version."

"That'll be hard for you."

"I'll try," he laughed. "I was building this gorgeous log home for a retired dentist out of Boston. These guys must make a fortune. It sits on fifty private, beautiful acres just south of the San Juan National Forest."

"God, it sounds beautiful."

"The guy was only in his sixties."

"And?"

"He wanted to have a place for his family and grandkids."

"Don't tell me..."

"The guy drops dead of a heart attack."

"Goddamn..."

"His family just couldn't bear going to this place without him. Too many memories."

"You let them out of their contract, didn't you?"

"I felt I had to. The home was about eighty percent finished."

"You finished it just the way you wanted it, right?"

Sean grinned. "It's sweet, Porter."

"You go from never thinking about having a vacation home in Durango, to having a log home there...just like that?"

"That's how it happened."

"Where do you fly into?"

"We'll go to the county airport. I keep an old Land Cruiser there to run back and forth from the house to the plane. It's not too far of a drive to my place."

"If it's as nice as you say, you may not be able to get me to leave."

"Stay as long as you'd like, buddy."

The flight was smooth. The weather was beautiful. Calm winds and blue skies. The men talked about their lives and their pasts, and their futures. There was a clear acknowledgment that time had literally flown by, and life was not an endless adventure they once believed, as young men. There was an ending to all of it. There was a finish line that seemed to be creeping closer and closer, quicker, and quicker, as the years passed. Sean thought about this more and more since surviving cancer. Porter felt this way due to his loss of Ellen and Kristine.

It caused even the toughest of men to stop and reevaluate their lives. To decide how they should move forward the rest of their days on earth. For Sean, it was all about him. He had no one else. A new home, a new plane, and a new outlook on life after his illness. This was how he viewed his future. Sean ignored his age. He felt it was just a number. Porter couldn't blame him, but he was not Sean. He couldn't look inward after the loss of Ellen and Kristine. He could not bring himself to focus on his own personal well-being. He had too much guilt. No man is ever the same after burying his wife and only child. For the first time in his life, Porter began to understand the pain his grandfather felt when his son and daughter-in-law died in that horrible plane crash.

"About thirty more minutes and we'll be on the ground."

"Your Caravan is something special."

"You like it?"

"It's smooth," Porter said. "How many people will it carry?"

"I can take six passengers comfortably with the capacity to store more luggage and cargo than those people could haul for a month's stay."

"I see," Porter pondered. "What a beautiful ride."

The men spent the last twenty minutes of their flight enjoying the peace and quiet of a silky-smooth sky and the sounds of a flawless flying machine. Sean landed at the county airport with the skills of a commercial pilot landing a Boeing 777. After getting the Cessna into Sean's hangar, the men found their way to his waiting Land Cruiser. They still had a fifteen-minute ride to Sean's new home. There was nothing to carry. Because of Sean's surprise trip for Porter, he had no time to pack a bag. There would be one night at Sean's place, get dressed in the same clothes and fly back home to Arizona. Porter shouldn't have been shocked. This was a classic Sean move. This is exactly something his old flying buddy would try and pull off. Porter should've known.

AFTER A SHORT DRIVE, the men arrived at the front steps of the largest log home that Porter had ever seen. Seven thousand square feet of white oak and natural stone seemed to go on forever. An endlessly expanding roof covered in beautiful cedar shakes veered one direction for fifty feet, and then off in another direction for another fifty. The entrance was protected by what appeared to be two thirty foot Arizona white oak trees, meticulously handscraped and preserved for a beautiful hue. Porter noticed that the trunks of the oaks were easily three feet in diameter. The builders were able to keep much of the exposed root growth at the bottom of each trunk. It gave the impression that the trees were growing straight out of the ground. They stood guard on each side of the covered entrance, leading to the massive mahogany double front doors. It took Porter a while to take it all in, as Sean opened the sculpted wooden doors and led him into a massive foyer, which was as enormous as most small log cabins. The foyer was vast, with huge slate floor tiles that stretched each direction, twenty feet by twenty feet. The stunning beamed ceilings rose up to their inner peak at least thirty-five feet, expanding outward like the inside of an enormous circus tent.

"Enjoy the view," Sean welcomed, as he headed to the kitchen to look for something to drink for the men.

"How can I not enjoy this view," Porter replied. "This is beyond unbelievable, Sean."

"That dentist knew what he wanted...or at least his wife did. I just continued with most of their plans."

Sean returned with a couple of beers. "Follow me." He led Porter into a Great Room that was magnificent to behold. Two full stories of sheer glass, thirty-five feet high and forty feet wide, spanned the northwest wall, framing a stunning panoramic view, which looked like a long-lost Albert Bierstadt painting. The men sat down on two dark reddish-brown leather highback chairs, built overly robust for the hardworking rugged taker.

"My God," Porter gasped. "I don't know whether to curl up and fall asleep or stare out these windows until my eyes hurt. When the sun strikes that red rock, it is absolutely incredible."

"If you can't relax in this place, Porter, you can't relax anywhere." Sean took a long swig of his beer and looked around the Great Room. "I want you to know, you can use this house whenever you feel like it."

"Thank you."

Porter began to think about a time when he would have gladly used Sean's vacation home. He thought about Ellen's love of the outdoors. He wondered if Kristine would have married and had children. In his mind, he pictured grandchildren outside running around, enjoying the beautiful outdoors. Being kids, being Grandpa's kids. He knew that he would never get to be the grandfather to his own grandchildren, as Papa was to him.

"There was a time, once, but there's no sense in going back there, Sean. It's too painful."

"I'm just saying. It's yours if you ever want it."

"I might take you up on your offer." Porter leaned forward, toward Sean with a raised bottle. Sean leaned in, also raising his bottle, until the two clinked together. "To continued good health my friend."

"To your health as well," Sean smiled, eager to have some good company. "I'm just glad you didn't make me force you to get in my plane and fly here."

"I'm too old to resist."

"You're in better shape than guys I know who are half your age."

"Now you're blowing smoke."

"How does a good steak dinner sound tonight?"

"Sounds like a plan."

Sean downed his beer, stood up, and invited Porter out to his garage. He had all kinds of interesting toys to show him. Besides Sean's old Land Cruiser, he also had a John Deere Gator he utilized for chores and getting around his property. Porter noticed a dirt bike for riding trails, and a beautifully restored 1967 Corvette, Ermine White with a red leather interior. Porter straddled a black Harley Road Glide, noticing it had less than two thousand miles. Sean didn't like to drive the Vette and Harley around the property too often, because it was always dusty and he wanted to avoid having to clean them. Just owning all his toys was good enough for Sean. Porter knew that was how he operated. He also knew that Sean was happy as a kid just possessing things. He was more of a collector than a user.

Some people would say that Sean was somewhat shallow, when it came to his possessions, but Porter also knew that he was the type of guy that would give you the shirt off his back. All you had to do was ask. He would be there for Porter if need be. He would have his back if the shit should ever hit the fan. Porter felt this was the most important attribute that Sean offered as a friend. It was an imperative personal characteristic that would be a necessity if Porter had the courage to ask one special favor of Sean.

Porter had been considering doing something in his life that took a lot of guts, and he realized he needed someone like Sean to help. It was the type of favor you shouldn't ask of good friends, unless you knew they would be all in. He had been contemplating taking a serious, even dangerous, turn in his life. Only men like Sean would be able to understand Porter's dedication and desire to fulfill a promise. He decided he would open up to Sean during their steak dinner tonight. He would either be all in or all out, but one thing Porter knew for sure was that no matter what Sean decided, this special request would never be revealed to another living soul. In one hour or so, Porter would have his answer.

BOTH MEN SAT UP to the table for dinner. Porter admired his friend's hospitality.

"This steak is great."

"Thanks. I've learned to become a pretty good cook over the years," Sean smiled. "I guess if I want to eat, I have to cook. Going to restaurants alone gets pretty old after a while."

"I miss Ellen's cooking."

"I'm sure you do. She was like a chef."

"I've been thinking about something for the last several weeks, Sean, and your offer to use your home here in Durango has caused me to seriously reconsider it."

"I told you this home is yours whenever you want it." Sean leaned toward Porter as if to press his point. "Anytime. Anything. Whatever you need, I'm here for you."

"I have some people I would like to bring here, just for a few days. Maybe longer. Some special friends."

"Go on. I'm listening."

"I know you'll wonder what in the world I'm doing, but I want a reunion of sorts with some important women."

"Okay, you're piquing my interest now. What in the hell are you thinking about?"

"Three women."

"Three? You're not getting weird on me, are you?" Sean laughed. "This doesn't sound like the Porter I know, so I must be letting my mind wander to the places it seems to want to go on its own. What's up?"

"These ladies were best friends with Kristine back in college."

"That was a long time ago."

"All these years, since Kristine died, I've wanted to reach out to these girls and see how they're doing."

"But I take it you've been afraid? They're not girls anymore."

"Afraid? I suppose I have been afraid. That's an understatement."

Sean was tiptoeing on eggshells. He knew since Kristine's death there was a raw emotion that Porter didn't want to stir. There was a time when he treated these three girls like his own daughters.

"Could you handle seeing them again? After all this time, I mean. Wouldn't it tear you apart?"

"I keep thinking of them as girls. It's hard to believe they are pushing forty."

"My God, Porter, where has all the time gone?"

"I think about those girls every Sunday when I go over to the cemetery to visit Ellen and Kristine. I remember them vividly as young vibrant college students, preparing for life, ready to take on the world."

"All I can tell you is my home is your home my friend. If you want them to come here and visit, they're more than welcome."

"Thanks, Sean."

"I guess my next question is how are you going to pull it off?" he asked. "How will you reach out?"

"Good question. Frankly, I'm not even sure if I have the guts to get them all together in one place. I get nervous just thinking about it."

"You have the courage, I know. I just wonder if you have the emotional strength?"

"I think I do now but talking about it and actually going through with it is two different things."

"I hear ya."

Sean thought he heard Porter whisper, *March 6, 1999,* as he lowered his head.

"What's with that date?" Sean asked.

"What occurred on that date killed my Kristine." Porter threw his napkin onto the table next to his plate. He leaned back, and grabbed his bottle of beer, taking a long slow drink. He emptied the bottle. "I couldn't imagine what it has done to Jen, Angie, and Lynn."

"Sounds like you're about to find out."

"I have to. There's no way around it."

FOUR

(SIXTEEN YEARS EARLIER)

IT WAS SPRING 1999, and the Arizona State University campus was bustling with a tangible sense of relief. Students were done with their classes and the itch to get going on spring break was palpable. Some students were heading to Florida, some to Colorado, and some would take this time to go across the country to do charity work. Jen, Angie, Lynn, and Kristine were best friends. Over the last four years they had grown to be a close-knit group, usually doing something fun together over spring breaks. They were seniors now and looking forward to graduation. They had all begun to realize that the reality of life after college was about to set in.

All four were going different directions in life, seeking their own challenges in the job market. Some were heading for their hometowns and some seeking new places to call home. They were not interested in a trip to the beach this year, deciding to stick close to where they were. Kristine had suggested three or four days in Las Vegas and the other three girls thought that sounded like a plan. This was going to be their last fling as ASU girls.

IT WAS WEDNESDAY, MARCH 3rd and the weather was beautiful. Angie agreed to drive her car. She was the oldest of the group and more mature than the other girls. She was undoubtedly the leader. They all joked about going to Las Vegas and winning the big bucks. *Gamble until we drop* became their motto. It was an amusing, yet ironic aphorism used to tease each other. Even though all four girls enjoyed having a good time, they were far from risk takers. The bright lights of Las Vegas were not the atmosphere that matched up with their personalities. They were all conservative when it came to spending their own money, so gambling it away was not in their DNA.

They all talked about graduating and having to seek new careers, rent apartments, and buy cars. Figuring out how they were going to pay for it all would be a first. They joked about winning millions of dollars at the casinos and meeting that high roller that would pay their tabs. Enjoying a few nights on the strip, before having to face the so-called real world sounded fun.

"How far is this drive?" Lynn asked Angie.

"Around three hundred miles."

"So, it's less than four hours with your lead foot," Kristine joked.

"I can make it in five."

"That'll get us there in time to check in and have a late lunch," Jen said.

"How much money did you guys bring?" asked Kristine.

"I brought three hundred," Jen said.

"Two-fifty," Lynn shouted.

"Oh my God...I brought three-fifty," Kristine winced.

"Good, because I only have two hundred bucks on me," Angie laughed.

"You aren't gambling much are you?" Lynn teased.

"I figured you guys would be giving me some cash for gas. Remember? If you pay up, I'll have some more gambling money on me, thank you."

"Works for me. Break out the snacks, Kristine. I'm already hungry," Jen laughed.

"I'll take something to drink. Non-alcohol, please," Angie ordered.

"Coming up. Diet Coke or Diet Pepsi?" asked Kristine.

"Either one will do."

"My God, Angie, how can you drink either one?" Jen asked. "Real Coke lovers can't stand Pepsi."

"I like Pepsi," said Lynn.

"Whatever you have, I'll drink it," Angie replied. "I really don't care. I drink either one."

"Keep your eyes on the road. I'll open it for you."

"Thanks Kristine. You're such a sweetie," Angie teased. "Did you hear that, Jen? Lynn?

"We heard it, Ange. Everyone knows Kristine is the sweet one in this car."

The girls were settled into the drive. Only a few more hours to go and they would be pulling onto the famous Vegas strip. They spent a lot of time talking about school, exams, grade point averages, and career prospects. And, sometimes, even young men. Kristine seemed much more relaxed than she was before they left ASU. She was beginning to leave the gnawing memory of her last classes behind her. There was nothing she could do about it now anyway. Angie kept telling Kristine that she was going to do just fine. Angie was always the group cheerleader, uplifting and positive. Kristine looked up to her. She seemed so strong, not just physically, but mentally strong as well. Kristine wanted that for herself but struggled with her insecurities.

Her friends couldn't understand, since Kristine was bright and well-liked by everyone she met. She knew she was going to have to develop more confidence, a stiffer backbone if you will, before taking on the real world. Kristine appeared to be envious of all her friends. Lynn seemed to have her entire life pre-planned, and Jen was intelligent when it came to business and finance. Kristine figured none of them would have any problems finding jobs and being successful. But she worried about finding those things for herself.

Lynn and Jen eventually fell asleep and Kristine stayed awake, keeping Angie company. There was only about an hour left to Vegas. Angie enjoyed Kristine's friendship. It was obvious they were polar opposites, which is probably the reason they got along so well. They were best friends throughout college, starting the day they became roommates as freshmen.

"I hope those two don't get too wild this trip," Kristine said, as she nodded back toward Lynn and Jen, who were now sound asleep in the back.

"Stick close to me girl, we'll be fine."

"I'm such a worrier about other people," Kristine said. "I can't help thinking about all the bad things that could happen to us when we're out having a good time."

"I'd have to agree with you on that one."

"Why aren't you that way?"

"I can be," Angie revealed. "I probably just keep it inside more than you. But I still worry, believe me."

"I know I get it from my dad."

"Hey, having a cop for a dad will do that to you. I'm sure as a kid every time you walked out the front door your dad had a list of dangers you needed to watch out for, right?"

"How'd you know? That's so true."

"Don't get me wrong, Kristine, I love your dad," Angie smiled. "He's a great guy and he cares a lot about you. He cares a lot about all of us. He treats the three of us like his own daughters."

"That's for sure," Kristine replied. "Dad does worry about all of us. I guess I get it from him."

"My dad never seems to worry about me," Angie said. "I'm the youngest of four, so by the time I came along he had no fears left in him. My three brothers totally drained him of any worry."

"Oh my God, your brothers are so cute, but they are such bad boys."

"Remember Kristine, you're an only child. That gives your mom and dad just one person to place all of their hopes, dreams and worries on."

"I suppose you're right. I never thought of it that way."

The two slumbering bodies in the back seat began to stir. Jen yawned, then spoke out first. "I've got to pee really, really bad you guys."

"That makes two of us," Lynn groaned.

"Alright, I get the picture you two. Hold it for just a few more minutes. It's time to stop for some gas anyway," Angie said. "I'll pull over at the next station."

"Cross your legs if you have to," Kristine laughed.

Angie pulled into the gas station, got out, and stretched. A slow-moving old-timer shuffled out, tipped his ball cap to the girls, and filled up the tank. All four went to the restroom, checked their hair and makeup, and hopped back in the car for the final stretch of driving.

"I'd say we only have about fifty miles to go," Kristine announced.

"Great, I can't wait to get there," Lynn said. "Do you want me to drive for a while, Angie?"

"You're kidding me, right? I just drove two hundred and fifty miles and with forty-five miles to go you want to take over?"

"You're right. I was just kidding."

"I don't want Lynn to drive anyway. She scares me when she drives," Jen snickered. "You keep driving Angie. I feel safe riding with you."

Angie continued to drive and with only thirty miles to go the girls began to perk up and feel more energetic. They anticipated their brief vacation, which pumped more vigor through their blood. Their sense of humor was re-energized, and it was obvious to all of them they were due for a little excitement over spring break. After all, it was their last one together. Angie even began to get a little giddy, which was rare.

"Hey ladies, look over there. A roadside bar we need to remember on our way back home," Angie declared, as they drove past a hardcore biker bar just off the highway.

"Oh my God, the Hard Times Tap. We have to stop there on the way home," Jen said. "We can find some real men in there."

"Not happening," Kristine whispered to Angie.

"I'm up for it," Lynn said. "That'll be our final stop on the way out of town."

"Oh, for sure. It can be one of our what happens in Vegas stays in Vegas moments," Jen giggled. "Places like that are the reason they call Las Vegas sin city."

"The Hard Times Tap. Could you imagine us in that bar?" Angie asked. "That would certainly be on your dad's list of things we should never do while we're here, Kristine."

"That's why we have to do it," Jen proclaimed.

Lynn started laughing. "Bikers are just your type, Jen. You love the bad boys, don't you?"

"It's not their motorcycles I like. It's those faded blue tattoos on their knuckles."

"The ones that spell out such touching messages, all in eight little letters," Angie joked.

All the girls were laughing out of control now. Jen could hardly breathe and Lynn was snorting, which made everyone laugh even harder.

Kristine shouted, "I'm about to pee my pants."

Angie had a difficult time keeping the car on the road. A bar like the Hard Times Tap was completely out of character for all four of these girls. But being out of character was what spring break was all about, right? Being someone other than yourself was the joy of letting loose. Stories could be told. Memories could be made. Risks could be taken. Secrets could be hidden. People could get hurt. But young students on spring break never think about getting hurt. They are so invincible. So naive.

WHILE THE FOUR GIRLS were primed to have a fun weekend in Vegas, Kristine's father spent his weekend working the afternoon shift at the Las Vegas Metropolitan Police Department, fighting the never-ending war on drugs. Porter Steele was just the man to battle the criminals who dumped drugs onto the city streets. He was intimidating to look at. Just over six feet tall and a hundred ninety pounds, Porter always appeared ready for combat. His Green Beret roots had stuck with him. His powerful physique was not brought about by weights in a gym, but by chores on the ranch. His was a natural strength, perpetuated by years of military and police training.

There was one characteristic that stood out above Porter's physical prowess, and that was his mental strength. He had a reputation of being tenacious, persistent, and patient. Porter simply refused to quit. He had now been working roughly twenty-one years with the agency. He had spent several years in the patrol division, but when he made it into investigations he felt as if he was finally doing what he was meant to do. Porter loved fighting drugs, gangs and solving the peripheral crimes that attached themselves like barnacles on a boat.

This work made him feel alive, worthwhile, and motivated to make a difference. He felt as though the beauty that surrounded him in nature was being tainted by the realities of the filth, violence and suffering that occurred in the shadows. The remains of broken lives, which seemed to peek out from the darkness, wore on his soul. He had to find a way to make a difference. It was propagated through him like the muscular lines of a thoroughbred. His sense of duty was evident to those around him. Porter's dedication often tested Ellen's patience, but she was a resilient and strong woman. She knew exactly who she married.

The undercover unit he supervised at the time witnessed the birth and rise of the meth trade. Southwestern states, Nevada, Arizona, and southern California, were hit hard. The nineties were a decade of misery for so many police agencies fighting the battle to rid the southern states of the meth epidemic. Porter knew he was just a very small cog in that massive wheel of justice. A wheel that turned painfully slow, torturing its victims at every turn. Methamphetamine had wreaked havoc for several years now and was still going strong. Exploiting ephedrine had morphed over the years. Biker gangs always seemed to figure out ways to avoid being detected.

Violence was one of their most prevalent methods of controlling members, and rivals. Intimidation ruled the streets. When it came to the members of biker gangs, they had an unspoken creed; you're either with us or against us. If one gang member hesitated to choose, there was no doubt he'd be introduced to a ruthless beating. In some cases, execution. Porter knew this was the reason it was difficult to develop solid confidential sources, or snitches. This made it next to impossible infiltrating any of these gangs with an undercover officer. Embedding a cop within this environment was not only difficult, but it was also dangerous. And sometimes, deadly. But things were about to change. At six o'clock, Porter's boss paged him to call into his office.

"Porter, I need to meet with you in my office, pronto," Captain Ryan directed.

"Yes sir, I'll be right there." Porter hung up the phone and headed to the captain's office. These meetings could be bad news or could be good. It was a flip of the coin. With the constant stress of police work tearing down morale at every level of law enforcement, those in upper management felt a special obligation to stay on top of every negative issue. But even more so, regarding the investigations into the violent meth trade. Drugs damaged so many lives. Porter knew this and tried to keep his supervisors apprised of all events regarding the biker gang problems that were seemingly growing. Vigilance became extremely important.

"Have a seat, Porter."

"Thank you, Cap."

"I have some important information that hopefully will bring some much-needed relief for you and your unit."

"Sir...?"

"There are going to be some changes. I know that's a terrible word to say out loud around here, but I think these changes will help us tremendously."

Porter sat back in his chair and crossed his legs. With his elbows resting on the arms of his chair, and his hands folded as if to begin a prayer, he listened.

"And...?"

"We're going to participate in a new undertaking with the SAFE Streets Gang Task Force."

"Why is the Gang Task Force interested in us, now, if I may ask?"

"Hey, don't sound so surprised," the captain said, tilting his head as if to ask him why he is so shocked. "This is something that came up over a year ago, and now it's going to happen."

"What's the plan?"

"They're bringing a guy over from New Mexico to go undercover."

"New Mexico? Really?"

"We're going to infiltrate the Hell Riders," said Ryan.

"It's finally going to happen. After all these years of begging? Sorry...I mean, requesting."

"This agent is good, Porter,"

"He's done these operations before?"

"Yes, once. Successfully."

"Where at?"

"Albuquerque."

"You ought to see this guy. He has biker gang written all over him," Ryan hyped.

"It's not just about looks. Looking the part only goes so far..."

"I understand," he interrupted, "but when it comes to getting in, he has to look the part."

"He needs the smarts, too," Porter strongly noted, without challenging his boss too outwardly. "He'll get himself killed if he's not smart."

"I'm told by the Gang Task Force he has the resume. West Point grad some years ago, but you would never know it by looking at him."

"West Point? Okay, I'm starting to like him more and more."

"Don't fall in love too quickly."

"Let me guess, he looks more like he graduated from University of Harley Davidson?" Porter grinned.

"He has more than a few tattoos. I know you hate that crap."

"I'm just too fucking old for that wannabe bullshit, pardon my French."

"I get it. I'm just like you, but this guy is for real and I think he'll have a great chance of infiltrating those assholes in the Hell Riders."

"I take it there is a meeting coming up, soon? With the G.T.F.?"

"Next Thursday...0900...conference room."

"I'll be there."

"By the way, the guy's name is John Rocker, or Rockwell. Something like that. Hold on a minute." The captain sorted through some paperwork on his messy desk.

"I think its Rockwell," Porter smiled, implying he had some inside information on this guy already. "Word gets around."

Captain Ryan picked up some notes. "You're right, it's Rockwell. John Rockwell."

"Got it. Thanks, boss."

PORTER WALKED OUT of the meeting. On the one hand he was kind of pissed, because he felt it was a slap across the face regarding the progress of his own unit. On the other hand, he felt a sense of relief. This was something he practically begged for a year ago. No one seemed to listen then. Perhaps this John Rockwell character could penetrate this ruthless biker club. Only time would tell. There was a long learning curve for a new undercover detective. Especially one coming here from New Mexico. Unless the Gang Task Force has been feeding this guy inside information about the Hell Riders, he wouldn't have the sufficient intelligence to work his way inside this gang. Porter couldn't be certain. He didn't know John Rockwell from Adam. Even though he viewed the last year as a waste of precious time, maybe Rockwell had been spending the last several months educating himself on the entire club membership and criminal histories of the Hell Riders. Porter could only hope. The violence was rising. The meth was flowing. There were certain members of the Hell Riders getting brazen. Something new had to be tried.

Porter entered his office and dialed Ellen.

"Hi Porter. How are you?"

"Fine."

"What's going on today?" Ellen asked. "You don't sound fine to me. I hear it in your voice."

Porter hesitated. "Just the usual confusion around here."

"Oh really? You sound like you're down." Ellen could always sense the slightest change in Porter's mood.

"I'll talk about it when I get home. I'll be home by ten tonight."

"I'll be up."

"Ellen?"

"Yes."

"Have you heard from the girls at all?"

"I did. Kristine wanted me to tell you they are safe and sound. All checked in and just relaxing by the pool."

"Good to hear. Where are they staying again?"

"You know right where they are staying," Ellen laughed, knowing how much Porter worried about his only child.

"She is fine. The girls have each other. They are in a very nice hotel. It's still quite new and they are all together. They never leave each other. You know how they are. Don't worry about them, okay?"

"I won't. I was just curious if they were all settled in."

"Just curious? I'll bet you were. I know you, Porter."

"You know me too well, then. Love you, Ellen."

"Love you," she said, "and I'll see you when you get home."

FIVE

SPRING BREAK IN VEGAS was about to come to an end. It was Saturday night, March 6, 1999, when the girls decided they would head for home. After all, it was only seven o'clock and a five-hour drive. Maybe less. They would be back to the campus before one a.m., Arizona time. They considered it their last late-night adventure. It was their road trip home. Their gambling exploits were nothing to brag about. Lynn lost fifty dollars. She was happy it wasn't any more than that. Kristine was up twenty. She felt like a real winner. Angie basically broke even and laughed at how little she really spent. Jen lost the most. Over a hundred dollars down the drain, but she didn't care. She just looked at it like spring break money well spent.

They enjoyed most of their time by the pool during the day, drinking wine and beer, and splurging on dinners in the evening. They found time to take in a couple shows, one of them their favorite singer, Céline Dion. With Angie's car packed and almost a full tank of gas, they headed back to Tempe. It wasn't too dark out yet. The strip made it feel as though there was a night light left on somewhere in the sky. That gave an unrealistic sense to the girls that heading home to Arizona was a safe thing to do.

They were less than twenty-five minutes into the drive when they came upon the location. It wasn't even seven-thirty, so what could one last drink hurt? All the girls were sober, so one bottle of beer or glass of wine would not change things. They'd be okay.

"There it is!"

"Are you serious, Jen?" Angie asked.

"We kind of promised ourselves it would be our last hurrah, right?" Lynn laughed. "Kristine, are you up for one last stop before we head for home?"

Kristine leaned forward in her seat and looked out the side window of the car as Angie slowed way down. There it was. The Hard Times Tap.

"Oh, yeah. Our dream tavern we promised to stop at on the way home."

"Remember, this was where Jen was going to meet the man of her dreams," Angie joked.

"Let's stop for one," Lynn dared the group.

"C'mon gamblers," said Jen, "it's our last Vegas treat. We won't be in there for any more than fifteen minutes, then back on the road again."

"You call the Hard Times Tap a Las Vegas treat?" Kristine shook her head. "Right up there with the Riviera and the Mirage."

"Just one drink? Is everyone in agreement?" asked Angie.

"I'm in."

"I'm in."

"I'm not in," Kristine announced, "but who am I to ruin the party. It'll be something crazy to talk about."

"You can tell your dad all about it," Jen teased.

"Speaking of my dad," Kristine said. "I need a promise from every single one of you that the words Hard Times Tap will never pass through any of your lips, while in the presence of my father. Just during my lifetime."

All the girls laughed. In perfect unison Kristine received her answer. "We promise, Krissie." All four girls were cracking up now as Angie slowly pulled off the roadway and deliberately coasted toward the far corner of, what appeared to be, a parking lot in front of the Hard Times Tap.

"One more promise," Angie said. "I don't want any of you falling in love while we're here."

"You really are a sick woman," said Lynn.

All four of the girls opened the doors to the car and exited. They looked at each other and began to walk toward the front door of the tavern. They were thinking to themselves that this place was a real dump.

"One drink," Kristine reminded. "Just one. Got that?"

The parking lot of the Hard Times Tap was dusty, unpaved, with potholes. It appeared to be the type of place that welcomed few customers. Especially ones that looked like college girls. There were seven motorcycles parked like a row of dominoes directly outside of the front door. They were all Harleys and all filthy dirty.

"You got your wish, Jen," Lynn said. "There has to be at least one man in there with those beautiful tatted up knuckles that turn you on so much."

"Oh yeah, I can just imagine it now. H.A.R.D. on the left knuckles and T.I.M.E. on the right."

"In that deep dark blue ink you love so much," Angie snickered as she reached for the door handle to let the other girls walk in.

"I will remind you guys one more time," Kristine said. "One drink and we're out of here."

They entered the front door of the tavern. As they stepped through the door, they watched seven men all turn at the exact same time, as if they were a well-choreographed Broadway dance group trained with synchronized precision. The bartender was opening a bottle of beer for one of the men, and the other six had looks on their faces that appeared to be a rare combination of utter confusion and an unexpected sense of contentment. The girls' brains were delivering to their bodies the proper natural warning signals, but they seemed to be fighting the instinct to turn around and walk back out just as quickly as they arrived. They were young and foolish. They were naive, but they were just having fun. If they thought they were safe, they were sadly mistaken. This was the wrong place. The wrong time. The wrong people. The wrong decision.

"Well, look who's here," a large man with a long white beard said loudly. "You ladies look lost."

"Hey, Bear, maybe these fine young girls need directions," a short, stocky, thick, powerfully built young man joked.

"Did your car break down?" the bartender asked. He was sure these girls would not have walked into the Hard Times Tap intentionally, unless there was an emergency of some kind. The only women that deliberately set foot in this bar didn't look anything like these college girls. Women that entered this bar looked like the female version of the men that entered this bar. Black leather vests. Black leather pants. Black leather hearts.

"Give them a hand, Hammer," Bear shouted out as he turned to grab his beer off the bar. Hammer was over six feet tall. He was lean, but wiry, muscular, and sickly vascular. It was the kind of muscularity that was almost revolting to look at, as if his body was depleted of all water. The skin drawn inward, forming around every nook and cranny of his lean, long, lanky frame. His knuckles were scraped and boney. They were the knuckles of a fighter. He sauntered toward the girls, sneering, while he reached for the front door.

"We're here for one drink," Angie quietly announced, before Hammer opened the door outward to the parking lot, just to take a quick look around.

"I see," Hammer said with a disingenuous grin, looking out over the girls toward the men at the bar. A look on his face as if they all just hit the lottery.

"Well then, come on up here and put your order in," Bear invited, as if he were a nice guy. It was an obvious ruse. The other men laughed.

"Hey Stump, buy these ladies a drink."

Stump was a squat, stocky young man, with a child's face and a grown man's chest. Angie knew bodies. Stump played football at one time. It was clear to her that when he was younger, he spent a lot of time lifting weights. Heavy weights. He was no more than five-six but was over two hundred pounds. He was not fat though. His forearms were freakishly thick. They looked like the fat end of a Louisville Slugger. He had a leather band of some kind on his left wrist that was so tight it caused a severe indentation. He was missing the ring finger on his right hand, revealing several scars that made it seem the amputation was one of violence, not one of surgery.

It became evident, rapidly, that the guy called Bear was the leader. He directed Stump as if he were a new member of the group. Hammer had been around, but he clearly respected Bear's seniority in the gang. Bear was beyond intimidating. At least six-five and over three hundred pounds, he was frightening in his movements. Bear stood and turned from the bar, barking out orders to the others. The men that went by Stump and Hammer responded to his every word, as if they were either loyal soldiers, or simply obedient followers. The other four members of the biker group drank, watched, laughed, and behaved with curiosity. They were surprised that these four girls were brave enough to walk into their bar, let alone stick around for a drink.

The girls noticed that all seven men at the bar were wearing leather vests, sleeveless, patched up. The most distinguished patch on the back of each vest contained the words, *Hell Riders*. The letters were black as midnight and under the words was a bright mixture of deep red and orange flames. It looked like hell. They looked like hell. The Hard Times Tap looked like hell. Dark and seedy, dirty, with the pungent odor of booze and sweat.

The girls were handed their drinks by the bartender. His hands were shaking. Beads of sweat forming on his forehead. Detached, lost in his own world of failure, deceit, and loathing. His ill will was not directed at the girls, but at the world in general. He had no feelings toward these girls. They were just there. They were just taking up space. They were just the ones that stepped into the wrong place at the wrong time. They were just, next. He knew it and had no intention of doing anything about it. Perhaps, because he knew he couldn't. The bartender did make one comment, which showed a small fraction of empathy for the girls. Maybe he had a daughter, somewhere, of his own?

"Here are your drinks," he said as he handed them each one beer. "One drink, and then get out of here," he whispered. Was this his warning? Was this his one act of kindness? Was this one last minuscule drop of empathy that arose from his withered black heart?

"Jesus Christ, Ray!" Bear yelled in feigned anger. "Is that anyway to welcome the girls into your bar? Hand 'em a drink and tell them to get out?"

"Yeah, Ray," Hammer responded. "Don't be an asshole."

"They can have as many drinks as they want," Bear said. "Am I right, ladies?"

Angie thanked Ray. She knew what he was trying to do. "One drink is all we want."

The girls began to drink their beers, as quickly as they could. They walked over to a table to try and create some distance between them and the bikers. It didn't work very well, considering there was not a lot of distance between anything in this place. It was too small of a tavern.

Jen was almost done with her beer, Angie and Lynn were halfway through with theirs and Kristine slowly nursed hers, although not intentionally. The girls kept watching Kristine. She was slow. She was not a big drinker. They crinkled their eyebrows, communicating their desire for her to speed it up and finish her beer. She never planned on finishing anyway. Kristine knew that she was not a heavyweight, when it came to the consumption of alcohol. She gently slid her glass over toward Angie. While the girls finished, Stump nodded his head toward Ray, as if to demand another round of drinks for the young ladies. He did as he was told. Before the girls could stand to leave, he came around the end of the bar and brought four more beers to their table.

"After this one, you'll be able to go. You need to just get up and leave."

Ray seemed to be anticipating something that he knew all too well happened with these men. He knew that whenever members of the Hell Riders got drunk, something bad happened. Ray couldn't imagine a situation where these men got drunk, had four attractive college-aged girls under the grip of their immediate power, then didn't take advantage.

The four girls tried to remain calm. They began to drink their second beer, hoping that Ray was right. Angie was able to calmly drink hers, while Jen and Lynn struggled to get half of theirs drank. Angie could see Kristine was having trouble.

"Kristine, pour some of your beer into my glass," Angie demanded.

She slid her beer toward Angie and tipped the edge over, pouring a good portion of her beer into Angie's glass. Kristine still had some of her beer left. She was shaking too much by now to drink it. Angie chugged hers down, as did Lynn and Jen.

Ray spoke up. "Okay ladies, the bar is now closed for you. Time to get outta here."

The girls noticed that the four bikers that seemed to be ignoring the entire chain of events stood up and walked out. The only people left in the tavern were Ray the bartender, the men called Bear, Stump, and Hammer, and four extremely scared college girls.

"Hey Ray, I'll tell you when this goddamn bar is closed for these girls," Bear shouted. "Now, get the fuck behind that bar and serve the drinks I order you to serve." Bear was aggressive. Ray didn't hesitate.

Bear walked over to the table where the girls were sitting. They shrunk in the presence of this immense human. They felt tiny, weak, almost as if they had shriveled physically in the presence of this huge man. He pulled up a chair, quickly swung it around, slammed it to the floor and put both elbows up on its back.

"Now, young ladies. College girls, I presume. Daddy's little princesses. I want to formally apologize for Ray over there. He is being very rude. I've never seen Ray try to throw somebody out of this bar before. I want to apologize on his behalf. Ray has bad manners. You are more than welcome to drink here."

Bear looked over at Hammer and nodded his head hard to the left, ordering him to go to the front door. Hammer knew what that meant. He walked over to the front door and locked it from the inside. The girls shook when the deadbolt slammed.

Hammer went back to the bar, drinking a line of shots that Stump had poured for them.

"Stump. Give Ray a little break behind the bar. He seems tired of fixing drinks. Take a break, Ray."

"What do you want me to fix these young ladies?" Stump asked.

Bear looked one at a time at each of the girls, as if to make them a deal. "Here's the plan. Stump is going to fix you one last shot. I can tell you don't like the beer anyway. After you finish your shots, Hammer is going to unlock the front door and let you leave."

Angie looked at her three friends and spoke for them. "One shot and we're gone. Out of your hair."

"Stump. Did you hear that? Fix the girls a shot."

"I heard it," Stump said. "What's the shot, boss?"

"Give them the Hell Riders' special."

"With or without?"

"With, of course. And make it a double."

Stump raised his eyebrows, shrugged his shoulders, then fixed four double shots and brought them to the table.

"We call this drink Hell Fire. The ladies that usually come into this bar and ride with us love this drink."

The four girls sat silent.

"You'll like it. Tastes like hell but goes down like fire." Bear laughed out loud.

Angie grabbed her shot first and looked at the other three, nodding. Her eyes spoke for her. *Let's get this over with.* All four of them took their shot glasses and raised them slowly to their mouths. At the same time, they drank their shots. At the same time, they felt the burn. At the same time, they felt the kick. At the same time, they felt the Hell Fire. At the same time, they felt the drug. At the same time, they felt the ensuing calm. It worked quickly.

Everything turned into slow motion. The room began to gradually spin. Voices were deep, out of sync, words falling to the floor like molasses dripping from a shattered jar. Puddling below onto a dusty wooden floor. The girls tried to stand, but their minds and bodies had abandoned them. Coordination was lost to the chemistry hidden within the hot liquid. Angie tried to get to the door, but raising one foot after the other became cartoonish. Hammer and Stump chuckled.

Sociopaths had a strange, and sick sense of humor. Their lack of empathy even sickened Ray. Bear grabbed onto Angie pretending to help her back to her seat, as if he were a true gentleman caring for his ill date. Lynn fell from her chair to the dirty floor. Hammer went over and could barely help her back to her seat he was laughing so hard. Stump walked over behind Jen and grabbed her by the hair. He pulled every strand tightly behind her head and then leaned over and kissed her on the neck. He acted like an animal marking his prey. The men were like foolish boys attending a middle school dance, daring each other to choose a girl to take to the dancefloor. Bear chose Angie. Hammer chose Lynn. Stump chose Jen. Kristine sat alone, engulfed in a chemical fog.

Ray was not the type of man to take advantage of a young woman. He was shallow. He was angry at the world, yes. Even so, Ray knew he was not a rapist. But he also knew that deep down he was a coward. He feared Bear's volatility. Ray stood by and did nothing. What could he do? He became invisible.

Right next door to the tavern was an abandoned motel. It was the former Roadside Inn. It had been abandoned for years, but the Hell Riders found ways to use it. The gang felt they had become the rightful owners of this place, like squatters. All they had to do was leave through the side door of the tavern and walk south for fifty feet and they were at the rear of the motel. Padlocks had been conveniently cut off of the doors. Entrance was easy.

This place became quite convenient for the bikers. Some alcohol, drugs, then over to the motel for sex and back to the bar to continue partying. Most of the women these guys partied with had lost their morals a long time ago. The abuse was mutual. Meth deals were also taking place inside. The Hell Riders became brazen about their criminal behavior, and the Roadside Inn was just one small, but valuable, perk of membership.

Bear grabbed onto Angie's arm and stood her up from the chair. Stump picked Jen right up from her chair as if she were a small child. Hammer got Lynn to her feet. They all began to walk toward the south side door, when a loud knock came on the front door of the tavern. The knock got louder and harder. Soon a recognizable voice rang out.

"Open the fucking door!"

Bear knew that voice.

"Jesus Christ! Get the door, Stump," Bear ordered, "it's D.T."

Stump quickly laid Jen on the floor and ran to open the door.

"What the fuck is going on?" D.T. demanded. As he entered, he saw Bear, Hammer and Stump staring at him, just feet away from the girls. Ray was still behind the bar. Both hands gripped the stained oak bar top. He waited for D.T.'s response. Ray knew that D.T. was unpredictable. When he wanted to party there was no one that could control him. If he decided he didn't want to party, no one else was allowed.

"Just having a little fun, that's all," Hammer replied.

"Shut the hell up, Hammer," Bear ordered. "I'll do the talking."

"So, what's up Bear?" D.T. asked.

"These young ladies came into the bar to party."

"And?"

"And we've been partying with them," Bear said. "They seemed lonely."

Bear was a big man. He feared no one. He never acted like he was scared of D.T., but he did know that D.T. was more powerful within the Hell Riders, so he showed him respect.

"We're just having some fun, Double Tap," Stump yelled.

"Shut the fuck up, Stump," Bear demanded.

D.T. walked over to Stump and pulled him over to the bar, near Ray. "You're having some fun?"

"Yeah, just a little fun, that's all," Stump repeated. "Just having some fun with these college girls."

"Don't ever call me Double Tap," the man demanded. "Call me D.T., or Danny, or better yet, Mr. Trask...never Double Tap. Understood?"

"No problem."

Danny Trask looked into the eyes of each man, one at a time. "I don't want any of you to ever call me Double Tap."

DANNY TRASK WAS the boss, and not someone to take lightly. He gave the appearance of a man who took the decision-making process seriously. Some in the gang considered him a thinking man's man. He had a rare mixture of high intelligence and common sense. His street smarts were legendary. For those who truly knew him, he was more violent than he appeared, and that is the reputation he wanted. He was not rough around the edges. He was a man who shunned the scruffy, hardcore biker look. This was intentional. Danny Trask considered himself a businessman. He could often be seen without his leather vest, sporting a more business casual look. Some of the other bikers in the Hell Riders didn't appreciate it but could do little to change it. Trask always had an ulterior motive. Everything he did had a purpose.

He often reminded other members that his business dealings always benefited the club. For that reason alone, he thought they should accept his false demeanor.

Danny Trask's business acumen as their leader was well-respected. He was a dealmaker. He dealt in meth and he dealt in guns. Guns were his passion. The drugs gave him the money to fulfill that passion. It was because of the guns that the nickname Double Tap was born. It was a nickname he tried to avoid, but it stuck with him for years. The primary reason he shunned the nickname was because of four separate murders that he was suspected of committing. Four opposition gang members were murdered over a five-year period and Danny Trask was the primary suspect in all four. The victims were bikers, from two separate rival clubs, killed with the same modus operandi.

This was a difficult time for law enforcement. Drug turf was valuable and staunchly protected with a vengeance. The M.O. of the murders was always the same. The killings were no doubt drug related and the manners of death were eerily similar: One bullet to the chest and one bullet to the forehead. Each dead biker was found alone, in a location where it appeared the killer either lured them there or set up a time to meet them there. Perhaps the victims were doing drug deals on the side. Maybe the victims had a side business going on. Buying and selling of firearms? Either way, the murders were quick, clean, and accurate. The killer was precise, and his intentions were communicated with a violent simplicity. The unspoken message delivered to his rivals was one of clarity: *Never try to muscle in on my territory.*

Not only did some gang members refer to Trask by using the nickname Double Tap, but there were police officers that enjoyed using that moniker for him as well. Even though the evidence to convict Trask was not trial solid, those in law enforcement close to the investigation knew he was the killer. One of the cops that knowingly referred to

Danny Trask as Double Tap was his fiercest enemy on the Las Vegas Metropolitan Police Department. Porter Steele had a loathing for Danny Trask that had gnawed at him since he was a detective.

What was about to occur at the Hard Times Tap was pure evil. There was no other way to describe it.

Trask smiled at his three soldiers. "Hey boys, I'm just pissed off that you didn't call me before the party started. Looks like you were going to leave me hanging."

Hammer and Stump seemed as relieved as two young boys that had just got their hands slapped for getting into the cookie jar, instead of getting grounded for two weeks. Bear was less surprised at D.T.'s sudden revelation that he had four extremely intoxicated and drugged college girls at his fingertips. Bear knew Trask would come around after realizing there was one cute girl left for him. That was Kristine. The forces of the planets could never have been more aligned for Danny Trask, even though he was clueless as to whom Kristine was. At least for the moment. There was no way he could have known that Kristine was the daughter of his most hated rival. His most despised enemy.

As depraved as Danny Trask was as a human being, there was no doubt that what was about to happen to Kristine was only a fraction of what would have occurred had he known she was the daughter of Porter Steele. There is no solace in that revelation, but when violence is perpetrated on the helpless luck of any kind for the victim is welcomed.

"Is the Roadside open?" Trask asked Bear.

"Yeah, it's open."

"Let's get it on then boys. Time's a wasting."

Hammer, Stump, Bear, and now Danny Trask, began to drag their unknowing prey south toward the side door of the Hard Times Tap. Just fifty feet to the dark, abandoned motel. They each chose a separate room and anticipated committing crimes. Crimes for which men with any sense of right or wrong would have hesitated committing. But these were not ordinary men. Something inside them was missing. Something inside them was broken. Something inside them was polluted with wickedness. The kind of wickedness only found in the black heart of the devil. Ray closed the tavern and quickly left the area to get home. He had to live with himself. But he had to live with himself on many occasions.

The four men carried the girls to separate rooms. The motel was dilapidated. The wallpaper was pealing from the sheetrock in patches. The carpet was stained and torn, and the furniture was broken and destroyed. There were beds, which had yellow and brown worn-out mattresses. That was all these men needed. They wanted a place to fulfill their sick fantasies. Forcefully dominating young, attractive, yet helpless, college girls.

All four of the perpetrators had the same thoughts: *How dare they walk into the Hard Times Tap? How dare they play their little spring break games and think they could get away with it? How dare they look down their uppity noses at us? How dare they think they would walk out of this bar without giving it up?*

These were the kinds of men that convinced themselves that spring break girls loved to party, loved to drink, and take drugs, and loved to give it up. As far as these animals were concerned, Angie, Jen, Lynn, and Kristine had walked into the right bar, at the right time, to satisfy all of their fantasies.

"When you guys are done, make sure all of their belongings are right next to them," Danny Trask demanded. "When they all come out of it, I want them to grab their stuff and get the hell out of town."

Bear found Angie's car keys inside her purse and threw them toward Stump. "Make sure their car is parked right outside the motel, unlocked. Put the keys in the ignition, so they're ready to drive away."

"Will do, boss."

Four separate doors, which led to four separate rooms, slammed shut. Their collective nightmares had begun. It was roughly nine o'clock at night and for the next several hours, these men had their way with four innocent victims. Four young ladies in an intoxicated state of mind, with no capability of consenting to what was happening. Being victimized by the ruthless acts of men who, somewhere along the way in their miserable existences, lost their souls to the devil. GHB was a powerful drug. Gamma Hydroxybutyrate was the Hell Riders drug of choice, at least when it came to their women. The women they partied with knew it though. They wanted the drug. They consented. It wasn't surreptitiously slipped into their drinks, and the dosage was welcomed.

The Hell Riders thought it was funny to make it a double in the shots they forced the girls to chug. The shots they called Hell Fire. The girls were powerless. They might as well have been hit over the head with a sledgehammer. If there was one, just one, miniscule amount of saving grace, there was a chance the girls would have little, if any, memory of the horrific crimes. The violence would be incomprehensibly entangled with dreamlike hallucinations, disjointed illusions and out of body deliriums. But if there was no saving grace bestowed upon them by a higher power, there was a chance their lives would be forever tortured by the unrelenting memories of the rapes.

ANGIE WOKE FIRST. It was six-thirty the next morning and she sat on the side of the bed. Feelings of dread overwhelmed her senses. She knew she had been raped but did not know how badly she was injured. She tried to remain calm. She looked around the room and thought she was still in a nightmare. She caught a glimpse of herself in a shattered mirror that still hung over a cracked sink in the corner of the room. This was the first time she noticed that she was totally naked. Her bra and panties were on the floor at the end of the bed. Her jeans, socks and blouse were strewn over the top of a three-legged chair, which was leaning against a closet door. Angie's thighs were scraped and stinging from abrasions. She felt like she had run a marathon. She looked down, bruises were noticeable on both legs and blood covered the inner part of her right thigh. *Oh my God, I'm going to be sick.* She ran over to the sink in the corner of the room and vomited. The cracked mirror distorted her face. She thought to herself that she looked exactly how she felt. Misshapen, disjointed, and broken. *Where's Lynn, Jen, and Kristine? God, please tell me they're okay.*

Angie was able to gather the strength to get dressed. On the floor next to the door sat her purse. She looked inside, but no car keys. Now, she was in a panic. Angie tried hard to remember what happened to her, but her mind would not go there. At least not yet. When she went to bend over to pick up her purse her legs began to shake, almost giving out. Her back was hurting, too. Angie felt as though she had been beaten to a pulp. She feared opening the door to the outside world. What would be on the other side? Who would be on the other side?

Angie turned the knob and slowly pushed the door outward. The sun was rising and provided a fair amount of light to the parking lot. Directly in front of the door, was her car. She felt some relief, although her friends were still nowhere to be found. She opened the driver's side door and noticed her keys in the ignition. She leaned in and removed them, placing them in her purse.

"Where are you guys?" she yelled.

Suddenly, the door right next to the room Angie had been in was kicked open by Jen. "I'm here. Come help me, Ange."

Angie ran over to her. Jen was weak. After kicking the door open, she fell to the floor and had a hard time getting to her feet. Angie grabbed her under the arm and helped her up.

"I'm messed up, Angie."

"I know how you feel."

"I feel like I was hit by a truck."

Jen was only wearing her bra and panties. Angie gently guided her back into the room to seek out her other belongings. She helped Jen with her pullover and jeans. Jen grabbed her purse and shoes and began to carry them. She didn't have the strength to try and put her shoes on.

"Jen, your wrists are bleeding."

"I don't know what that's from."

As Jen was beginning to walk toward the front door, Angie looked over at the bed and noticed two leather straps still attached to the headboard. She knew what that animal had done to her, but for the time being Angie kept that information to herself.

"Where are Lynn and Kristine?"

"I'm still looking for them."

"There's Lynn. By the car."

Lynn was in shock. Somehow, she had gotten herself dressed, at least partially, and wandered out into the parking lot. Lynn didn't even notice Jen and Angie walking toward her. She was trapped in a fog of confusion and disbelief. Her mind was working hard to protect her from the truth of what had occurred.

Angie gently held on to her. "Where is Kristine?"

"No clue." Lynn was just steady enough to open the back door of the car and crawl in the backseat. After Angie helped her get into the car, she went to look for Kristine.

"Kristine, where are you?" Angie shouted. She looked around the parking lot. There were no other cars. There were no people. Next door, at the Hard Times Tap, there was nothing but silence. It was as if the tavern was abandoned. The motorcycles that lined the front of the bar last night were gone. All that was left was swirling funnels of dust, a gloomy brown morning haze, weed-filled cracks in the concrete and a tangible pain, radiating from the bodies and souls of four innocent young women. Survival was a foreign word to these girls, until now.

"Angie, I'm in here," Kristine moaned. Her voice was weak, delicate, struggling to be heard.

Angie walked toward the sound of Kristine's voice and gradually opened the door to the northern most end room, the one closest to the tavern. She noticed Kristine still on the bed; still on her stomach, unable to move her body. A belt was wrapped around her left ankle, strapped to the corner of the steel bed frame, while her right ankle was tied down with an extension cord that had been used to plug in a window air conditioner. Her legs were still spread. Her panties torn away. Her vagina exposed. Her wrists were tightly bound with her own bra. She was alive. At least part of her. It was her self-worth that was barely hanging on.

"Lynn...Jen...get in here. I need your help!" Angie screamed. She prayed, *God, help us. Please help us.*

Lynn and Jen forced themselves from the car and went to the room to help Kristine. Angie had her untied and up on the side of the bed. Kristine could not sit upright on her own, so Jen and Lynn held her from each side. Angie was able to get her pants and blouse on her and then grabbed her shoes.

"See if you two can get her up on her feet."

Lynn and Jen tried, but they were not strong enough to hold her up. Kristine was not stable enough to stay on her feet without assistance.

"I'll be right back," Angie said and quickly ran to the car. Her adrenaline was beginning to pump. Something inside began to click, which gave her the power to perform. Perhaps it was her instinct to survive and get her friends out of harm's way. She threw Kristine's shoes and purse in the trunk and returned to Kristine. "Listen up. I'm going to get behind her and grab her under the armpits. You two each grab a leg. We're going to have to carry her."

When they got to the car, Jen lowered one of Kristine's legs gently to the concrete and opened the rear passenger door. "Slide her in there. Jen, you sit up front with me." Once the girls got Kristine situated, Angie got behind the wheel. She took a deep breath. A tear trickled down one side of her cheek. She turned the ignition and was relieved that her car started. Angie looked at Jen, and then back at Lynn and over toward Kristine. She shook her head. "We are going to be alright. I promise you."

Lynn sluggishly lifted her aching head. "Let's get out of this godforsaken place."

Angie drove. Jen and Lynn cried. Kristine moaned. They withheld the remnants of their disgust and shame. They did not talk for the next several hours. Their silence was deafening, but it came so easy. At least for now. For a while. It had to be that way. There was such a distance between the dreams they shared three days earlier and the reality of this morning. The gap between the emotions of happiness and despair had closed within those darkest hours.

Which emotion would eventually take over? Which emotion would destroy the other? Only time would tell. The answers to those questions, unfortunately, would be vastly different for each girl. But for now, getting as far away from Las Vegas, the Hard Times Tap, and the Roadside Inn, was Angie's one and only objective. The cracked concrete passed under her tires, milepost after milepost, telephone pole after telephone pole, billboard after billboard, cloud after cloud, and tear after tear. They arrived at campus in shock, shattered, with broken spirits and violated souls simply striving to keep their secret pain hidden.

As the scabs formed over their psychological wounds, it was time that turned them into scars. Scars that made it impossible for the outside world to penetrate their gristly barrier and shine a bright light on the truth that struggled to be free.

SIX

IT WAS THURSDAY MORNING, five days after Kristine and her three best friends were drugged and raped. They had not told a single soul. Unfortunately, it was just another workday for Lieutenant Steele. Today was his meeting with Captain Ryan, William Jennings, a supervisor from the SAFE Streets Gang Task Force, and an undercover detective named John Rockwell. Porter was uncertain about the meeting. On the one hand, he was set in his ways and wasn't thrilled about taking on new people. On the other hand, he knew this could be the break they needed to build a solid RICO case on the Hell Riders. The Racketeer Influenced and Corrupt Organizations Act was an excellent tool for federal prosecutors. This was proven time and time again with organized crime and was being used on gangs more frequently. Porter knew these investigations could be successful without someone on the inside, but with an undercover detective embedded within the Hell Riders there could be a lot of criminals put away for a long, long time.

"Porter, this is Special Agent William Jennings. He leads the task force," Captain Ryan began. Porter reached out for Jennings' hand.

"Call me Bill."

"And this is Lieutenant Steele," Ryan announced.

"Just call me Porter."

"I'll let you introduce your man, Bill."

"Thank you, Captain," Jennings replied. "This is Detective John Rockwell."

"Nice to meet you," Porter said, shaking his hand.

All the men sat. These were all the people attending this meeting. This would be their first. There would be many more to come, but Captain Ryan had already made the decision prior to this meeting to assist Detective Rockwell, in any way possible, to infiltrate and build a long-term RICO case against the Hell Riders.

"John has already been studying extensively about the Hell Riders, gentlemen," Jennings said.

"So, you're learning curve has been greatly reduced?" assumed Porter.

"I feel like I'm ready to go when you say the word, Lieutenant."

"I like that attitude," said Porter. "I take it this isn't your first infiltration of a motorcycle gang."

"That's correct, sir."

"Tell me a little bit about yourself."

"I'm thirty-five years old. West Point grad. Divorced. No kids. I spent eight years in the Army. Special Forces."

"You can stop right there, John," Porter said. "That's all I needed to hear." The men laughed.

"Yes, sir." Detective Rockwell didn't know if that was a good sign or bad.

Captain Ryan laughed and leaned forward in his chair. "Lieutenant Steele is former Green Beret. Excuse me...not former...just Green Beret. Porter gets pissed when I say former."

"Aha. I see now, sir. Thank you."

S.A. Jennings leaned across the table and slid a thick folder toward the center, which held the resume of Detective Rockwell. "Here's everything you need to know about John."

"I'm sure it's more info than I will ever need to know."

"You got that right," Jennings smiled. "We have bigger files on our own cops than we do the bad guys."

"No doubt."

"Let's talk about our strategy here, gentlemen," said Captain Ryan. "Perhaps Detective Rockwell could start off with some general information."

"That works for me," Jennings agreed. "You have the floor, John."

Rockwell stood and began to present a roadmap of how he perceived the next several months would play out. "Once I feel comfortable with the players inside of the Hell Riders, I'll begin to find a subtle way to start connecting with one of their weak links."

"To build a friendship, so to speak?" Porter asked.

"You could say that. The word friendship is rarely tossed around within their circle, but they are working relationships. Like fragile alliances. They're usually based on the old fashion tit for tat. You scratch my back and I'll scratch yours. All these pricks may be gang-oriented, but they all look for some sort of illegal gig on the side, where they're able to profit some on their own."

"Sometimes they look for praise from their boss. Especially the weak links," Jennings added. "Sorry, for the interruption. Continue, John."

"You're exactly right. Sometimes they just want to make an impact on the club. Do something that will appear good for everybody else and advance the criminal enterprise. It helps them move up the ladder."

"Have you identified any of those weak links yet?" Porter wondered.

"I believe I have, but I have some names that I want to run past you, to see if you and your people are in agreement with me," Rockwell said. "Your people are going to have a perspective that I haven't been able to uncover. A weak link to me may turn out to be way too risky for your taste. A guy like that may be too much of a loose cannon for me to waste my time on."

"Got it. I understand what you're looking for," said Porter. "What approach have you considered in order to get a hook into one of these guys?"

"Excellent question. As an example, there's a guy they call Hammer."

"Ah…Nick Emerson. He's a fighter."

"He is. But Emerson is more than just a fighter. He's a Harley nut. All these guys ride bikes, but Emerson could tear one down and put it back together in a day. Give this guy a few beers, listen to his stories about the bikes he's worked on, and maybe even surprise him with better building skills in the garage. If I do that, I won't be able to get rid of this guy. I learned a lot about Harleys during my first go around. Not only that, but I also have a connection. I have a guy that would open up a shop for me in a moment's notice. When I want. Where I want. He's a good friend of mine. Lonnie Stickler. He's willing to help me out when I say the word. This guy can build a beautiful custom bike from scratch."

"He'd get compensated, of course," Jennings added.

"Nick Emerson is not the brightest Hell Rider in the group. That's for sure. But he does like to fight. He's a hothead. Dealing with him could be a bit risky," said Porter.

"What if he thought he would end up with a beautiful chopper… for free…if he was able to get you into the club?" Captain Ryan asked. "After all, you'd convince him that riding with the Hell Riders would be an honor for you. That's if he had the pull to get you in."

"That's what I'm talking about. Access."

Porter summarized: "A guy like Emerson fulfills the profile. He's stupid. He's angry. He wants something for himself, like a vintage chopper. He does something for the club, by introducing you to the boss, helping to build the membership."

"And he also can't shut his mouth," Rockwell said. "He spits out more information on other members, their crimes, their victims, and their organizational structure, than anybody else would risk doing. You'd be surprised what this guy would tell me if he thought he was going to get a new custom Harley out of the deal. That could be worth four to six months of Intel."

"How long do you expect this initial phase of the investigation to take?" Porter probed.

"I think we're talking at least two or three months to get in good with a guy like Nick Emerson. I'll have to read him as we go. A solid RICO case could take one and a half, or maybe even two years."

"It's a massive undertaking, gentlemen," S.A. Jennings said. "I'm lending you a wonderful asset in John Rockwell, but it's a dangerous assignment. John's safety is paramount, at all times. Captain, I have to have the authority to pull him out at any time, without being second-guessed."

"Understood."

"Who are the current players that you have on your radar, Lieutenant?" Rockwell asked. "I'd like to compare them to those I've been studying up on."

"Here's the core group we would want to focus on. First, there's Mike Carlin. He's called Bear and is their enforcer."

"Huge guy. And batshit crazy," Rockwell said. "Scares people just looking at him."

"That's him. He's intimidating. Carlin actually had several offers to play college football, if you can believe that. He has to be every bit of six-five and three-thirty, but just like everything else in his life, he managed to screw that up. From what I hear he created havoc at one of the college visits."

"Most of his criminal history involves assaults, firearms and drugs," Rockwell added.

"He was a big steroid dealer at one time," said Porter. "Then we have Joe Sterns, Sam Wiggins, Nate Thomas, and Willie Morrison. Within the Hell Riders, this group of four seems tight knit. They hang together frequently."

"I'm familiar with this group," said Rockwell. "These guys really like their meth."

"Especially selling it," Porter responded. "They try to lay low. They concentrate on building clientele."

"Whatever it takes, right?"

"Then there's Jake Severs," said Porter, "or as some refer to him... Stump."

"Good nickname for him. He's not much over five- five."

"He's as dumb as a stump, too," Porter smirked. "Severs will absolutely follow any direct order from Carlin or anyone above him. This kid is the perfect soldier. If they told him to kidnap his own grandma and force her to make the Hell Riders a batch of chocolate chip cookies, this ignorant prick would do it in a heartbeat."

"Totally obsessed with impressing those above him," Rockwell said. "His juvenile record was rife with crime after crime where he was basically showing off for the other guys he ran with. Peer pleaser."

"The guy has never produced an original thought."

"Talk about our weak link, Hammer, again," Rockwell said.

"Good ole Hammer. As I've already mentioned, Hammer's real name is Nick Emerson. A real bad boy. He's a big fighter. Has several assault and battery charges on his record. Doesn't care if it's men or women. He's an equal opportunity asshole. We have one case on him where he punched his own mother in the face. Apparently, she didn't make him dinner fast enough. His DNA is messed up. Dad liked to fight, too. His father got killed in a bar fight back in the late seventies. Ran into a guy at a pool hall that didn't like to fight fair, either. The old man took a knife to the side, just under the ribcage. Caught his liver. Daddy liked the ladies, too. Hookers, mostly. When the condom broke, Nick Emerson was conceived. Emerson is the kind of guy that would never use meth. His body is a temple, so he thinks. And all that bullshit, but he has no problem selling it to others. As you have already explained, Emerson loves his motorcycles. That is all he loves."

"This is the guy I'm going to focus on. He's dangerous, but he's a major weak link into this gang," said Rockwell.

"Then there's Danny Trask. Or D.T. as some refer to him," Porter stated. "If there's one man we need behind bars, this is the main guy."

"The leader?"

"Yes. A very unusual leader at that. There's never been a record of this guy ever being in a physical confrontation with anyone. Yet, I'm convinced he has killed at least four rival gang members. He's the opposite of all brawn, no brain. This guy is all brain, no brawn."

"Never been arrested for any of the murders," Captain Ryan opined.

"That is true. Thanks for reminding me, Cap. That's why some of my people say the nickname D.T. does not stand for Danny Trask. It actually stands for Double Tap. All four victims, if you want to refer to rival gang members as victims, were shot once in the chest and once to the forehead. We believe that was, and still could be, Danny Trask's calling card."

"It may be hard to believe, but Trask was raised in a well-respected home. He spent two years at Stanford University," Rockwell shrugged. "He apparently gets bored. School came too easy for him."

"That's a true story. And his father was a successful businessman, in real estate development. His mother, a high school math teacher. Trask has the smarts, but he lacks the motivation to do things the right way.

He is not a rule follower. He saw no reason to get into any business that took a lifetime to build. He wanted money, now. He wanted power, now. I think he's a classic sociopath. He loves his firearms. Although, for Trask, just shooting into a paper target was as boring as being at Stanford. Nailing Danny Trask on those four murders would be icing on the cake."

"My records show he had a personal beef with you, Lieutenant," S.A. Jennings cautiously revealed.

"I don't know how that info got into your meeting prep file, but it is a fact," Porter admitted. "Years ago, I arrested Danny Trask on some firearms charges and had him dead to rights. At least I thought. He shot a guy during an argument. There was alcohol involved, along with a drug deal. The guy survived. He ended up testifying for the defense. Said he had befriended Trask and that he was shot accidentally. No harm. No foul. He testified it was his own fault. Not intentional. Turns out the guy says the gun was in fact his and he should have never let Trask handle it drunk. What bullshit. Trask would've done a couple years at least but skated altogether. When you have weak eyewitnesses, weak co-defendant statements, and rival gang members, they all end up ruining your case. It didn't help that this guy had a record of his own the prosecutor couldn't minimize during testimony. When we walked out of the courtroom Trask approached me. He not only told me that the trial was a waste of his time, but he also told me that I should stop messing with him. He said that I should seriously consider his reputation for accidentally shooting people. That's when he gave me that stupid-ass grin of his and flipped me off."

"Sounds like Trask is made of Teflon," Jennings replied.

"It's best to keep Porter away from this chump...as you can see," said Captain Ryan.

"Thanks for pointing that out, boss. So, who will John be reporting to, directly?" Porter asked as he looked over at both Ryan and Jennings.

"That will be me, Lieutenant," Jennings answered. "I don't want there to be any Intel kept from you, whatsoever, so I want you to have supervisory authority on par with mine. I want John to feel free to go to you with any decisions."

"Let's do it this way," Captain Ryan proposed. "Detective Rockwell will report directly to you for official purposes. But any issues operationally, he will seek authority from Lieutenant Steele. When it comes to the sharing of intelligence, investigative updates, and progress reports, John will consider you both equals. Then, I would like you, Porter, to be in frequent contact with S.A. Jennings, so you are both on the same page at all times. I cannot have any of these behind the back games. People picking and choosing who gets to know what. I've seen too many times when one agency doesn't find it necessary to share Intel with another. Trust has to be mutual and paramount. Just so you guys know, the Federal Prosecutor handling this case is a woman named Gabriela Sanchez. She's bright, but she's young. From what I'm told, she knows the law. Especially RICO. Don't underestimate her. She wanted to be at this meeting but ended up covering for a colleague in court today. You will get a chance to meet with her soon. She wants to be completely in the know here and wants me to assure her that we will accommodate. More than likely, Porter, you will be her eyes and ears. She's a go-getter. You'll like that. I've been told she's a rising star in the Federal Prosecutor's Office. I would like to help her keep it that way. If she's successful with this case, that means we all win."

Porter looked down at his watch and then looked over at his boss. He tapped his watch, as if to say he had to leave. Captain Ryan remembered that Porter had another very important meeting to attend.

He nodded his head, telling him to go ahead and take off. Ryan turned back to Detective Rockwell and S.A. Jennings to wrap up the meeting.

Porter stood to go. "Gentlemen, it's been a pleasure. I have to get to another important meeting, so please excuse me."

Captain Ryan ended the meeting. "What I would like to do is schedule another meeting in the near future and start putting a timeline together for this operation. There are a lot of details to get through. I know Porter is going to want a lengthy one-on-one with you, John, so we need to get that set up soon."

"Thank you, Captain," S.A. Jennings said. "I'll wait for your call."

"It will be within the next few days. Nice meeting you Detective Rockwell. I have a lot of respect for your dedication. I know Lieutenant Steele does as well. Your enthusiasm for such a dangerous assignment is highly commendable."

"Thank you, sir. And please thank Lieutenant Steele for his time. I consider this a great opportunity."

PORTER MADE IT OUT to his car and drove as fast and safely as possible, so he could make it to Ellen's doctor's appointment before it was over. This was one appointment that she would not forgive him for missing. He arrived at her doctor's office and trotted in without trying to make a scene. Porter looked at his watch and knew he was twenty minutes late. Once there, the receptionist pointed him in the right direction. She knew Porter and Ellen and knew exactly why he was in a hurry. He found the exam room and immediately entered, trying to remain calm. When he walked in, he saw Ellen sitting in a chair, the doctor was there, but about to leave. He noticed that Ellen had been crying but was trying to wipe her tears away prior to Porter's arrival.

"Ellen, what's the matter?"

The doctor stopped for a minute to greet Porter. "I'm glad you were able to make it. I'll let you speak to Ellen for a minute and then I'll be back shortly."

"Thank you, Dr. Stevens."

"Sit here with me," Ellen said, her voice shaking.

"What's the matter, honey?"

"I can't believe this…"

"Ellen, please tell me what's going on."

"It's cancer, Porter. She just told me those tests I took last week show cancer in my left breast."

"Oh my God, Ellen. That can't be."

"Dr. Stevens wants to talk to us about what she thinks needs to be done."

"I'm sorry I wasn't here sooner. I was in that goddamn meeting with the captain."

"Wouldn't you know that on the one day I want you here, Dr. Stevens would be the one on time," Ellen smiled through her tears. "Usually, I sit here in this godforsaken exam room for at least a half hour before anyone shows up."

Porter sat right next to her, placing her hand in his and putting his arm around her shoulders. He hugged her, kissing her cheek.

"I know, I know. I was still too late. I'm sorry I wasn't here with you."

"You're here now."

Dr. Stevens returned with her X-rays from Ellen's mammogram and placed one of them directly into the lighted view box, so Ellen and Porter could follow her explanation. She pointed to the X-ray of Ellen's left breast, showing them where the tumor was located, and began discussing the biopsy results.

"It's my opinion that we remove this tumor immediately, Ellen. After removing the tumor and checking the surrounding area, we can then determine what type of treatment is necessary. Once I get in there, I may have to decide to do a full mastectomy of that breast. I just cannot tell you right now what else we may be confronted with. But radiation or chemo is a strong possibility. We need to treat this aggressively, and soon."

"Understood," Porter said.

Ellen's head was down and eyes closed. She didn't even want to think of what lay ahead of her right now. She could only think the worst.

"Ellen, you're a strong woman. Overall, you're in very good health. You can beat this. I've known you a long time. You have the willpower to overcome this. But we need to get on it right away."

"Thank you, Dr. Stevens," Ellen said. "We better get this scheduled."

"Yes, let's get it done, soon," Porter babbled.

Ellen knew Porter was stunned. He was in more shock than she was. It looked like he just took a punch to the gut. Ellen wasn't used to seeing her husband look this out of sorts. She reached out to him and they held hands. He was at a loss for comforting words.

"I'm going to have my nurse set things up and I will send her back in here and discuss everything with you."

"I can't believe this is happening," said Ellen. "I felt something was wrong."

"We'll get through this together. You have to get this surgery as quickly as possible."

"I hate to dump all this on Kristine right now," Ellen worried. "She has been so down in the dumps. I don't know if she's concerned about her grades or the job search, but she hasn't been acting like herself at all lately."

"We'll talk to her together," Porter said. "Let's get everything set up first, so we can tell her the entire plan of attacking this thing. I don't want to leave anything vague with her."

"She'll just brood over it, forever."

"I know, but she needs to know what's going to be done about it, right?"

"You're right," Ellen replied. "Thanks for coming here with me today. I wondered if you'd be able to leave that meeting you were in."

"My boss knew I had to go."

"Is there something serious going on at work?"

"Just a new little tweak in an undercover case we are expanding."

"Does this mean more hours for you?"

"I'm sure it will. I'll fill you in on it when we get home. I don't want you to worry about my work."

Ellen laughed. "You mean, you'll tell me what you can tell me?"

"Same ole song and dance."

"Nothing changes, does it?"

"No, not really, but that isn't anything you should be concerned about. Let's worry about you right now. All I care about is you. The police department can take care of itself."

"And Kristine, of course."

"That goes without saying," Porter answered. "I can't believe this is happening to you. It's so surreal."

"I know, things like this always happen to other people."

"How true. You go along with life and then, boom, you get hit with a ton of bricks."

"The next several weeks are going to be rough, Porter."

"I can't stand to think about it. I can't stand to think of you in any pain."

"I'm a pretty tough broad, if you haven't noticed, Lieutenant," Ellen smiled, as she squeezed Porter's hand. "I'm still married to a cop after twenty-two years. That takes a lot of strength."

"I hear you...I don't know how you do it, quite frankly."

"It has its benefits." Ellen leaned over and wrapped her arms around her husband. They kissed, and then both sighed. They knew their future was about to get challenging.

"You're my girl, Ellen. That's something that will never change. I am here for you. Always."

Just then, the nurse walked in with Dr. Stevens' orders. Ellen's surgery was scheduled for the following week. They both looked at each other as if to recognize the seriousness. Surgery this soon was a sign that Dr. Stevens needed to get on this immediately. Rachel Stevens was a very busy doctor. Just getting an appointment to see her was a feat in and of itself. She was a renowned surgeon at Sundown Surgical Center, so both Ellen and Porter felt they were in good hands. Hopefully, Kristine would be strong enough to handle the tragic news.

SEVEN

DANNY TRASK RAN WHAT he thought was a successful business, insulated from the outside world. But there was always competition from other clubs, and the mob. It may have seemed that the mob was only interested in the casino business, but they loved to get their greedy hands on the drug market as well. Trask needed to stay ahead of his competition, protect his turf, and come up with smarter ways to acquire ingredients, cook, and market his product. He was also wise enough to know that running an illegal enterprise was risky. And even though Trask was not risk averse, he knew that criminals generally are not a very smart bunch. This increased that risk. Some of his men fit that bill perfectly.

What his men lacked in intelligence was hopefully replaced by their allegiance to him. Stump and Hammer were loyal, no matter what. Trask knew that and respected them for it. They enjoyed the lifestyle of being in a biker club. The money from selling meth was frosting on the cake. Bear was another story though. He was no dummy. He was loyal, yes, but Trask needed Bear to feel like he was a valuable part of the organization. Bear was a natural born leader, even though demented, and wanted more power to wield.

It was obvious to everyone beneath him that Trask ruled the Hell Riders, alone. This bothered Bear. Trask saw to it that Bear was often in on big decisions and was viewed not only as the enforcer, but also the criminal operations manager. These were two positions that Bear felt went hand in hand. The one thing that Danny Trask knew for sure, he had to keep one eye on the business and the other eye on Bear's ambition. If there was one thing that was more important to Bear than money, it was power. And there was only a certain amount of power to go around in the Hell Riders. Danny Trask knew it. But he wasn't sure if Bear agreed with him.

There were things going on in the meth business that were of concern to Trask. He had one worry that was completely unrelated, which began to keep him up at night. Trask never thought of himself as paranoid, but some of the other Riders began to question his short temper and sudden outbursts. Something was eating at him. It was time to discuss business. He called for a secret meeting at the Hard Times Tap. Seven members from the club arrived and the doors were locked. All of the men Trask wanted for this meeting were there: Mike Carlin, Jake Severs, Nick Emerson, Willie Morrison, Nate Thomas, Sam Wiggins, and Joe Sterns. Trask led the meeting.

"Fellow Riders, thanks for showing up on such short notice," Trask began. "It's been a while since we talked about business. We need to shore up some loose ends."

"What do you need, boss?" Bear quickly responded. It was obvious he wanted to step up and represent the group, as a whole. He figured if he could answer Trask's questions it would go a long way in solidifying his higher position within the gang. He wasn't about to let any of the others speak before him.

"Give me some numbers from our sales."

Bear took charge. "Willie, you go first. What do you have?"

"I've got four runners under me. They're bringing in about five hundred a week, each."

"How about you, Nate?"

"I got three. Probably doing four hundred."

Bear went right down the line. "Sammy?"

"Five guys...five to six yard a week."

"Joe?"

"Four guys...four-fifty."

"I'm getting a good feel for where we're at with the money. Keep an eye on your runners. We're talking about sixteen guys running our shit, roughly seven to eight thousand a week. Is that right Bear?"

"That's right."

"That's just about four-hundred-thou a year. That's with one cook," Trask said. "We can do better though."

"The pseudoephedrine we've been getting from the Mexicans is drying up," Bear said. "The feds have been hitting the southern cartels harder than hell."

"I have some ideas for dealing with that," said Trask.

"I also have an idea that I've wanted to talk to you about, for a while now," Bear replied, seemingly taking the challenge. He wanted Trask to know that he was well-educated on the meth trade and that he could run the operation if Trask allowed him.

"We'll talk about it," Trask nodded. "Moving on with some other business. Hammer, what's going on with stolen bike parts?"

"We are sitting on about five Harleys right now. They're over at Reggie's shop. He's getting them stripped down, ready to sell the parts. We stole a couple of those Jap bikes, too."

"What are we making off those parts?"

"Couple hundred dollars a week, after Reggie takes his cut."

"What's the problem with that business?"

Bear jumped in, cutting off Hammer. "The risk versus reward is bad."

"Why's that?"

"There's too much risk in stealing other guy's bikes. If these bikers do report them stolen to the cop shop, you not only have the owners out looking everywhere for them, but you also have the pigs out looking for them, too."

"So, we have to chop them up faster, wouldn't you say?"

"That's only part of it, D.T." Bear replied. "Those parts we are trying to sell on the black market, we're selling them right back to some of the same people we stole them from. These guys are looking for their own stolen shit."

"I get it...too risky," Trask agreed. "From now on, the only bikes I want stolen are from the suburbs. Look where the money is, where the alarms aren't. You know the type. The weekend wannabe bikers. The ones who make sure there is never a single bit of dust on their thirty-thousand-dollar custom baggers."

Hammer laughed. "You mean the guys with the brand-new black leather chaps and the fifty-dollar haircuts under those new shiny helmets?"

"Yeah, those wannabes, Hammer," Bear laughed. "They won't ever come out here looking for their bikes. At least not without the cops behind them."

"Any other old business before we move on to some new business?" asked Trask.

"I'm staying on top of some loans we've been making," said Stump, "and we've made some decent money on most of them, but some of our customers aren't reliable when it comes to paying us back."

"How much time are you giving these pricks?" Trask asked.

"No more than two weeks."

"Percent?"

"Charging them seventy-five percent."

"And when they don't pay?"

"I have some fun cracking heads," Stump said.

"Crack them even harder. You like to crack heads, right? Anything else for now?"

"That's it," Bear answered.

"Let's talk some new ideas," Trask said. "I'd like to get one big shipment of ephedrine before the Mexicans stop selling to us."

"We could do that, boss, but I think we ought to try to head north," Bear suggested.

"What do you mean by north?"

Bear grinned. "Far north."

"Canada?"

"That's where it's gonna happen for a while, until the Canadian Mounties catch on."

"You have a contact in Canada?"

"Yeah," Bear answered. "A guy in a club up there wants to do some business with us. We've been talking for a while now."

"Why haven't you told me about him?"

"Why haven't you asked?"

Trask didn't push any further. Bear was starting to show his teeth more and more lately, so Trask decided to let him prove himself. "So, what's your plan?"

"We'll send two guys up there for a pickup," Bear began. "The pseudo will be hidden in four custom Harleys this guy will have for us. They have false bottoms in their tanks. The same in their hard bags and fairings. You'd be surprised how much shit can be hauled in those bikes. The enclosed bike trailer will also have a false wall at the front. When you drop down that rear door you won't even be able to tell. He said they build the wall very narrow. It's only about four inches deep, but at about six feet in height, there's a lot of storage space for the pseudo. And other shit."

"What do we do with those motorcycles?"

"Good question," Bear said. "We could restore them back to their original form and sell them as customs."

"The Canadians want their cut of that, right?"

"All depends," Bear explained. "If they front us the bikes, we will sell them and they will get an agreed upon cut."

"But, if we front them the money for the bikes and trailer, we do the after modifications and sell the shit, keeping all of the profit," Trask said. "I get it."

"This guy says Canada is getting away with this for now, but when the cops and border security catch on, every trailer, boat, motorcycle and guy that looks like me is going to be searched."

"Now's the time to try and score big."

"Who do you want to make the first trip, Bear?"

"Me for sure...this guy won't deal with anyone else," he said. "Hammer should make the first run with me. He knows bikes better than any of us. We need someone that knows what they're looking at and talking about."

"What club is this guy with?"

"He rides with Satans Crew," Bear replied. "They call him *the Frenchman*. He says that the Satans Crew members are getting closer and closer with the Fallen Angels."

"Does he see them merging?"

"No doubt."

"I suppose that could be good for us."

"Yes, but right now he considers himself pureblood Satans Crew, which means he plans on profiting as long as he can off the crystal trade. Until he can't make any more green."

"Does he think the Angels will take over and eventually wipe out their business?"

"He knows it's just a matter of time."

"How do you know this guy?"

"I met him at Sturgis last year. He rode down from Toronto."

"Would it be worth having him bring the shipment across the border, meeting you somewhere on the U.S. side? Would that lessen our risk?"

"That's something I can run past him," said Bear, "but that just increases the risk on his end. He'd ask for more money, that's for sure."

"How much more?" Trask wondered. "He may want more money, but he may also know of places to cross the border that would be much safer, maybe even risk-free altogether. That's better for us."

"I'll see if he's willing."

"Depends on how much more money and how hungry he is for it."

"True," Bear grinned. "Hammer, are you up for a trip to Canada?"

"If he's not, I am!" Stump shouted.

"Back off, Stump," Hammer said. "You're not going anywhere."

"When you can tell the difference between a Harley and a moped, you can make the trip," Bear said as he grabbed Stump around the neck and began to choke him out. Bear pushed him away and laughed.

"Good point," Hammer jabbed.

"Fuck you two," Stump said as he rubbed the back of his neck. "I'll stay here in the good ole U.S. of A. I can't speak Canadian anyway."

Hammer grinned and shook his head. "What a dumbass. And this guy runs our loan operation? Jesus Christ!"

Trask interrupted. "The official meeting is over. I need to talk to Bear in private. We'll see all you guys later."

"We're outta here."

Stump and Hammer headed for the door. "See ya all later." Willie, Nate, Sam, and Joe followed without saying a word.

Hammer unlocked the front door of the tavern and swung it wide open to the bright Las Vegas sunlight. The rest followed behind. Within seconds the roaring engines of six Harleys could be heard being revved. And then they were gone. There was always a need for crime to be perpetrated, in order to further the club's mission.

Bear grabbed two beers from the refrigerator and handed one to Trask as he pulled a stool up to the bar. Bear stood behind the bar and took a long swig. "What's up D.T.?"

"I want to talk about Ray."

"What about Ray?"

"I'm worried he is starting to know too much."

"He's our only cook," Bear stated. "He's bound to know a lot about how much we're selling. For Christ's sake, he's cooking the shit."

"I'm more worried about Ray when it comes to those four college girls."

"What do you mean? You're worried about those four college tramps?"

"And what Ray knows."

"Why do you think Ray gives a shit about them?"

"You told me he was acting nervous about the whole incident. He was trying to get them out of the bar before something bad happened to them. Sounded like he grew a heart or something."

"That's just Ray," said Bear. "He would never rat us out. Especially you, boss."

"Have you had any cops come around asking any questions?"

"About that night?"

"About us fuckin' those girls."

"I think if those girls told the cops, we would've had a visit already from some detectives, don't you?" Bear pointed out. "I'm sure they thought better of it. They don't remember anything. There's no way."

"I guess it would be useless to report to the cops that you came into a bar during spring break and got really drunk and passed out."

"Why are you so worried about that night?" Bear wondered, noticing Trask's ever-increasing paranoia. This was not like him.

"I found out something about the girl I banged."

"What's that?"

"When I threw her stuff on the chair next to the bed, her purse fell to the floor and her driver's license came out."

"And...?"

"Her last name was Steele. Kristine Steele."

"Who in the hell is Kristine Steele?"

"I can't say for sure, but it could be the daughter of an asshole cop I know. Porter Steele."

"Congrats D.T.! You just got to fuck a cop's daughter. That makes it extra special."

"Steele isn't any ordinary cop. He's a fucking pit bull," Trask warned. "He finds out I raped his daughter, he'll never quit coming after me."

"Why's this guy got a hard-on for you, boss?"

"He tried to put me away. I got out of one felony beef after scaring the living shit out of one of the jurors...got a hung jury out of the deal."

"Intimidation works. You won."

"The prosecutor tried me twice, but wouldn't try the case a third time," he bragged. "Wasn't worth wasting the county's tax dollars."

"Porter Steele can go fuck himself."

"I just wonder if daddy were to ever find out, would he put some pressure on Ray before he gets to one of us?"

"Ray won't give us up. Ever. He knows what would happen," Bear promised. "We can't get rid of Ray. Not now. He's our one and only cook. If we do drug runs to Canada, we're going to need him."

"We've gotta keep our eye on him though," Trask said. "If I get any more nervous about this guy, I'm going to have to take care of the problem myself."

"You do anything to Ray right now, and you'll have a harder time with the cops than just screwing some college pussy. Besides, those girls will never talk in a million years. They probably don't remember a goddamn thing about that night. The dose we gave them would drop a horse."

"I'll ignore Ray. At least for now. Put a plan together for the Canadian trip and get back to me."

"No problem."

"You can go ahead and take off. I'll get this place locked up."

Trask sipped on his beer, as he scanned the inside of the tavern. Bear chugged his beer and headed for the door. After he exited the tavern, Trask locked the door behind him. Bear fired up his Harley and was gone. Trask wanted to take a closer look around the bar. He hadn't checked out the Hard Times in a while. He began to get anxious about audio bugs and hidden cameras. They could be concealed anywhere, at any time. Time was never on a criminal's side and Danny Trask was well aware of that. Getting sent to the penitentiary, or maybe even to the grave, was probably just a matter of time. It seemed the older Trask got, the more suspicious he became of everyone around him. He had the personality of a loner. He didn't like being accountable to anyone or depending on the loyalty of others. True loyalty was a myth, and he knew it. He was not as enamored with the brotherhood that flowed through the bloodstream of the other Hell Riders. Trask was loyal to one person. Himself.

Danny Trask was beginning to question his own paranoia. Was the methamphetamine business getting too dangerous? Was the thought of raping Porter Steele's daughter starting to eat at his psyche? Normally, a guy like him would welcome any type of revenge against Porter Steele, or any other law enforcement official for that matter. Vengeance could come in many forms and causing pain to a cop's family member was definitely one of them. The problem with getting on Porter Steele's bad side was the certainty he would stop at nothing, no matter how long it took, seeking his own revenge. Payback would be hell and a guy like Porter Steele wouldn't hesitate to follow him straight down into Hades' burning pit.

Trask did his walk-around inside the tavern, looking behind shelves, windows, the bar, and bottles of liquor. Nothing seemed out of place or unusual to him. As a businessman, in his line of work, he felt it was smart to make sure there was nothing that could hurt his business. He thought it was time to do these types of security checks regularly. There was one place that he had not checked in a long time. He usually left this job to Mike Carlin. Trask knew that he could not completely trust Ray with managing the Hard Times Tap, so leaving it up to him was not wise.

Trask walked behind the bar and knelt down to the floor. There was a long black rubber mat that ran the length of the bar, approximately fifteen feet, and was three feet wide. He rolled the mat up about halfway and reached down to a well-hidden trap door. It was just big enough to crawl down into. As soon as he opened the trap door, he leaned over and stuck his head down inside to take a brief look around. There was no one down there. Just inside the trap door was a rope ladder, which was about eight feet long and reached the concrete basement floor below. He safely climbed down the ladder, knowing if he fell and got injured it would be difficult to crawl out. He got close to the bottom of the ladder and dropped down to the floor.

Surrounding him was the Hell Riders' meth kitchen. The room was thirty feet by twenty feet, concrete walls, and floor, with no windows. The lab was vented out through a commercial grade venting system that was sent out of the back wall of the tavern. There was a system of three steel racks, with four shelves each. The shelves held the necessary laboratory glassware, burners, and cooking instruments. There was also a water source, and metal sink, for cleaning glassware. In the corner, stood a special shower for chemical decontamination.

This was the perfect set up for a meth lab and Ray had complete access. After all, he was the head chef and in charge of the kitchen. He had to have a safe place to do his operation. It was obvious that Ray took care of the lab. The dangerous chemicals alone could kill. Fire was a severe risk. Spills were a risk. Inhalation sickness was a risk. Long term contamination of the Hard Times Tap, above the lab, was also a risk. The business of selling meth was a major risk. And even though Ray knew that selling the meth was someone else's job, the product itself was his baby. And like a good daddy, Ray wanted to take good care of his baby. He didn't want to ruin his only sure thing and method of income.

Ray wasn't good at holding down real jobs. He didn't get paid for his bartending skills. Cooking meth was a hazardous job, but he chose that risk. In one way, Danny Trask respected Ray's primary incentive; he really needed the money. There was nothing more important than the almighty dollar when it came to keeping a man's mouth shut. Trask was smart enough to know that keeping Ray in line simply meant keeping the money flowing his way. Ray didn't ask for much of the profits. He was careful not to complain. He just wanted a satisfactory share of the taking, equal to the risk. But was the money alone enough to keep Ray loyal? That was the question that seemed to be keeping Danny Trask up at night. Very, very late.

EIGHT

SEVERAL WEEKS HAD PASSED. Kristine was about to graduate from college. Porter and Ellen both noticed her mental state was declining. They couldn't figure out what was going on with their only child. Porter decided it was time to get her home for a visit. The fact of the matter was, Ellen had made Porter promise not to burden Kristine with the news of Ellen's cancer surgery. She felt that her daughter would not be able to handle the added stress of bad news. Ellen went through with her surgery with the sole support of her husband. Porter felt it was important to tell Kristine, eventually. Although, he respected Ellen's strong wish that he remained silent until a time they felt it was necessary to tell her. Finally, after many weeks of Ellen's recovery, Porter felt that the time had come. Ellen reluctantly agreed. Porter made the call.

"Hello."

"Kristine?"

"Dad?"

"Hi honey. Calling to see how you're doing."

"Just so-so. What's up? Is everything okay?"

"I was calling to ask you the same thing," he said. "How are you doing? What does so-so mean? You don't sound very upbeat."

"So-so means I'm getting by."

"You don't sound like a girl that is days away from graduation and ready to take on the world."

"I'm far from ready for that."

"You sound really down, sweetie. I think you need some of your mom's home cooking, don't you?"

"That just makes me feel like I can't do anything on my own."

"Don't be silly."

"Dad, you know I have to get out there on my own and find a job."

"You will, Kristine. Why don't you think that's going to happen?"

"Because I'm scared of my own shadow. That's why."

"What's that supposed to mean?"

"I feel scared to death to face big changes," she said, "and I don't know what in the heck is going on with me. I'm a nervous wreck all the time."

"Do you feel sick?"

"I get anxious about some of the littlest things. Things I never even used to give a second thought."

"I'm starting to worry about you," said Porter. "Are you eating? Getting any exercise? A good workout can help with anxiety. You have to get your body moving."

"Oh my God, Dad. Don't bug me about exercise. Not everything can be fixed by working out. And I am eating, but this food on campus tastes like crap."

"You don't have to eat on campus, Kristie. I've told you that a thousand times. I'll cover the cost of eating off campus. You know that."

"I think I do need to come home for a few days. You're right. I'm not sure if I even want to go through with the graduation ceremony."

"You are kidding me. I've never heard you talk this way. What's really going on? Tell me what's bothering you. Your mother is going to want to talk to you about it. You know that. She can read you like a book."

"I know she can, but I don't want to disappoint you two."

"Disappoint? Why talk that way. Hey, I have a plan for the weekend," Porter said. "On Friday, I'm flying over and getting you. You haven't flown with me for months. It'll be an adventure. Maybe it will help you relax. I'll call you later with the directions to the airpark. It's just on the southwest side of Chandler. You can get one of your friends to drive you there, like maybe Angie. We'll fly back home here, and we'll have a relaxing family weekend. We'll talk things out. If you want somebody to come with you, that's fine by us. Maybe Angie would want to come and visit. I'll leave that up to you, Kristie, but she's always welcome. You know that. We need to get you back on track. Mom and I are worried about you. Besides that, we have some stuff we need to discuss with you anyway, so you're up to date on some other issues, okay? You and mom can talk more about graduation."

"Sounds good."

"When I call you again, I'll give you the exact time I'll be landing. In the meantime, you can check with Angie and decide if she's coming with you."

"I'll wait to hear from you, Dad."

"It's a plan then. Bye for now. Love you, Kristine."

"Love you, too. Say hi to mom for me."

"Will do."

IT WAS NINE O'CLOCK in the morning and Porter was at the aviation center, just south of Las Vegas, preparing his Cessna for a flight to the airpark in Chandler, Arizona. It was only a little over three hundred miles, so the flight would be about two hours, or so. He wanted to get going by nine-thirty, because of the time change, hoping to land in Chandler by twelve-thirty. Porter had told Kristine to be at the airport by twelve-fifteen, her time, but he figured she'd be late. He was in no hurry to get there. Porter hadn't flown for a while. He had been too busy at work, so he was anxious to get in the sky.

The weather was gorgeous. Sunny skies, low winds, and the thought of seeing his daughter had Porter eager for the flight. The last several weeks had been very trying for Ellen. He had put on a strong front the last month and a half, to appear steadfast in their battle against her brutal disease. He hoped getting up into the clouds would give him a chance to take a deep breath. A chance to unwind. This was a chance to change direction and focus on his daughter.

Whatever was going on with Kristine was confusing him. He could not imagine what was bringing her down. Or was he doing what many loving fathers do, which was to slip into denial? Hoping for the best became the easy way out. If he pretended there was nothing serious going on in Kristine's life and allow her to find her own way, he assumed she would somehow get through it. After all, what could a young, bright, beautiful girl have to fear in life? The whole world was in front of her. It was right there, waiting to be explored.

Porter revved up the engine of his Cessna and began moving down the runway. He climbed upwards through a wall of fluffy white, low hanging clouds, when all of a sudden it opened up to intense blue skies and bright sunshine. Was this a good omen? Porter had been hoping for better days ahead for the two people he loved most. Ellen and Kristine were the only people he had in his life.

He rang Kristine on his cell phone.

"Hi, honey. Just letting you know that I'm in the air. If we get cut off, it's just bad reception. I will call you back."

"Okay, Dad. I wanted to tell you that Angie has made a last-minute decision to come with me, if that's alright?"

"That's great," Porter said. "We have plenty of room in the plane and at home. Mom will be glad to see her. It's been a while."

"Why didn't mom fly with you?"

"Say that again. You cut out a little bit."

"Mom…I said why isn't mom with you?"

"She just didn't feel like taking the trip. She was going to go to the store and get things ready for a good dinner tonight."

"We'll be hungry."

"I hope you will. Please, do me a favor and call your mother and let her know Angie will be coming with you. That way she'll get enough food for all of us."

"I'll call her. We'll be there by twelve-fifteen."

"That's perfect. I'll be there by twelve-thirty. I'll need to take some time to get some fuel and check out the plane to make sure it's ready for the trip back home. We should be back to our place before three o'clock, for sure. Mom will be there waiting."

"It'll be nice to see you both."

"We can't wait to see you, and Angie."

ANGIE AND KRISTINE drove to the airpark and began to have a serious conversation. Facing Kristine's father would be a challenge, considering the amount of guilt both girls held deep within. The memory of the assaults would never relent. The four girls were unable to talk about the attacks between themselves, let alone consider speaking to Kristine's dad about it. Angie knew how much Kristine was suffering since the incident. She, too, was dealing with her own issues since the rapes. Angie didn't know if she had the strength to speak about it to anyone. Keeping her secret seemed easier. How would they handle an entire weekend with Porter and Ellen?

"Angie...just a warning, my dad is going to be all pumped up when he sees us," Kristine said. "He'll love flying us home to see my mom."

"I love your mom and dad," Angie replied. "They're so nice."

"I know we've never talked about the thing at the Hard Times, but you don't know what it's like having a father for a cop. It weighs on my mind every single day. I can hardly speak to him knowing what I've been hiding from them. Sometimes I feel like he knows what happened to us and he is waiting for me to open up and tell him."

"I can only imagine."

"What do we do when they bring up our spring break trip?"

"I don't know. Maybe it won't come up."

"You're kidding, right? They can't wait to ask us about the casinos, Céline Dion, and if we won any big money. Blah, blah, blah."

"I don't think you can keep it in. Eventually, you'll have to tell your dad. Or maybe tell your mom first, and then she can tell your dad. I don't know what to do. But I know we can't live with this secret forever."

"Maybe we should both open up about it," Kristine suggested. "I think between the two of us, we might be able to get through it."

"What about Jen and Lynn?"

"I don't know what they would want us to do. I do think Lynn would support us, but I think Jen wants this whole fricking thing to just fade away. Ignore it, I guess. She thinks she can block it out of her mind."

"I guess my biggest worry when your dad finds out, is what he will go and do about it," Angie said.

"Good point. I don't know if he would try and investigate the case or, even worse, go take care of things on his own. You know, the whole Green Beret thing."

"That's what worries me. You know your dad. He'll be furious at these men, and may go and track them down, and do who knows what."

"He could find himself in big trouble."

"I think we've screwed up any criminal case they could build against these guys anyway, Kristine."

"You think?"

"Any evidence that was once there is long gone. There won't be anything left at the bar and at that abandoned motel. Or on us, that's for sure. When we went back to school, we had to have washed away any evidence."

"We may have hurt ourselves even more by hiding what happened to us."

"Your dad would be so damn mad at us."

"No, he won't, Angie. He would never be mad at us. He loves us no matter what. But he will be furious at any biker he sees on the road. Could you imagine what he knows about the biker gangs in Las Vegas?"

Angie raised her hand to cover her mouth. "My God, Krissie, your dad probably knows every single one of those assholes. If we had to ever describe them, he could probably name them all."

"There's no doubt about it," said Kristine, "because he's been supervising the gang unit for a long time. He probably knows everything about the Hard Times and those jerks. I guarantee you, if he doesn't know them his detectives sure would."

"I'm sure he knows about crimes we don't even want to think about."

"That's why I don't know if we should tell him anything at all. Maybe we should just forget about it."

"Krissie, you won't be able to live with this forever. You can't keep it a secret. It will eat you up."

"What about you, Angie? Truthfully."

"Honestly, I don't know if I'll be able to, either. I just haven't been strong enough to even ask myself what I'm going to do. I just ignore my feelings."

"Maybe the two of us together will have the strength to tell him. I know that I can't do it alone. There's no way in hell."

"Let's just see where the weekend takes us."

They arrived at the parking lot and found a space to park for the next few days. Angie leaned over and gave Kristine a strong hug. She was worried about her best friend. Kristine didn't look well. She was losing weight. She had a disheveled look about her. Angie thought Kristine's hair was even thinning. Stress was an evil byproduct of such a hateful crime.

The sexual assault was wearing Kristine down, day by day, hour by hour. She had to free herself from all this guilt, somehow, some time. Perhaps now was the time to open up to her parents. The girls got out of the car and opened the trunk to retrieve their bags for the flight. Angie closed the trunk lid, and they walked toward the small terminal, where Kristine caught a glimpse of her father waving. Both girls looked at each other and hoped a higher power would intervene. They simply did not want to face the truth. They did not want to face a new kind of pain. They did not want to face Porter and Ellen. These were two people that only wanted the best for the girls.

Because of that fateful night, Kristine and Angie could have never comprehended the disgusting chain of events that occurred to them. The night they pulled into the Hard Times Tap, on nothing more than a childish whim. All they wanted was to create one silly memory from their last spring break together.

Down the long concrete runway Porter accelerated, building enough speed for the takeoff, leaving the Arizona desert behind. Flying to Las Vegas was giving Kristine and Angie weird sensations. They were hoping to spend a relaxing weekend with Kristine's parents, but just being in close proximity to south Vegas was churning Kristine's stomach. Angie had feelings of apprehension as well but was excited to be flying with her surrogate father, as she jokingly referred to him. She trusted Mr. Steele with every fiber in her body and couldn't wait to see Ellen. Kristine sat in the passenger seat, up front beside her father, and Angie sat directly behind Kristine.

Porter noticed right away that Kristine was quiet and distant. She was visibly anxious about the weekend ahead and struggling to decide whether or not to reveal to her parents what had happened to her and her friends just weeks earlier. Angie tried to fill the emptiness by talking as much as possible, hoping to reduce the awkwardness inside the cabin.

"Have you been flying much lately, Mr. Steele?"

"No, not really. I've been so busy at work I haven't had a chance to get up in the air."

"How's Mrs. Steele doing these days?"

"Much better," Porter said, realizing the way he just answered her question was going to draw suspicion from Kristine. Sure enough, it did.

"What's that supposed to mean, Dad?"

"I mean she is doing fine right now."

"Dad, what's going on?" Kristine asked. "What do you mean by, doing much better?"

Angie could tell that she had, unintentionally, opened a can of worms. She remained quiet until Kristine was done talking to her father. One thing was for certain, Angie's attempt at small talk with Mr. Steele brought Kristine out of her state of silence.

"Listen, your mother is going to kick my butt for this, but I should tell you that mom has been sick for the last several weeks."

"What in the hell, Dad? Sick? Sick, with what? What's the matter?"

"Calm down. She's doing much better. We were going to talk to you about it when you got home. Mom and I had agreed that we wouldn't stress you out while you were busy with school, so we decided to bring you home to discuss it with you."

"So, it's not that bad, whatever it is?"

"Mom wants to talk to you about it."

"You're scaring the shit out of me. You are acting weird, Dad. Tell me what's going on, please."

"Mom had to have some surgery."

"Surgery? What's the matter? Why didn't you tell me sooner?"

Angie leaned forward and placed her hand on Kristine's shoulder, gently squeezing, calming her down. Angie whispered in her ear. "Kristine, let your dad talk. Obviously, your mom didn't want to stress you out over this."

"Dad. Talk to me."

"Mom had some surgery, weeks ago, and has been recovering nicely. She didn't want you to panic over it. She knew you'd respond like this."

"You haven't even told me what she had surgery for," Kristine confronted. "I respond like this because you two treat me like a child and keep secrets from me. Stop with the secrets. What happened?"

"She had a lump removed from her breast."

"What? Cancer?"

"Yes, but Dr. Stevens believes she got it all."

Porter felt terrible for Angie, but he even felt worse for Kristine. He knew he was overprotective. He knew that his only daughter was like a gift from God. To say that Kristine was still daddy's little girl, in his eyes, was an understatement. Maybe he had sheltered her way too much as a child. Maybe, as the protector of his family, he didn't understand the social dynamics of letting his only daughter find her way in life. Of course, he had no clue about the secret Kristine and Angie were keeping from him. He was ignorant of the psychological undercurrents playing a detrimental role in her life.

Kristine became more withdrawn. She stopped speaking. Angie knew exactly what was going on. All Kristine could think about, at this very moment, was the fact that her mother had been having to deal with the thought of surgery around the same time she thought about partying with her friends in Las Vegas. If Kristine would have known about her mother's cancer surgery, she would have stayed home for spring break, to be with her.

There was a convoluted mixture of guilt and anger, regret and blame, and remorse and rage. All of these emotions were swirling around in Kristine's brain. All of these psychological triggers elicited anger, not only toward herself, but also at her parents. Angie now realized Kristine would reject even the slightest mention of what occurred to her and her friends in Las Vegas.

Kristine never felt more alone. She hastily turned to her right, facing the Cessna's passenger window, tucked her feet up underneath her, positioning her legs into a fetal position. She began to stare indignantly toward the blue sky, wondering how in God's name she could have ever gotten herself into this mess. The blue skies and sunshine should have made her smile. Instead, the beauty of the day only reminded her that she had done something ugly. She had caused her own demise when she decided to walk into that tavern.

Kristine now wholly blamed herself for all the agony that was haunting her. The tunnel she was falling into quickly narrowed, twisting tighter and tighter, spiraling faster and faster, pulling her deeply into a crevasse of depression. She could no longer see enough light above to find her way back out. Angie had been witnessing Kristine's decline for weeks now but didn't know what to do. She was fighting her own demons but kept them secret from Kristine. Angie refused to add to her best friend's psychological pain.

Porter landed at the aviation center, and he and the two girls began their short drive home to meet with Ellen. Kristine was still despondent. Porter hoped that seeing her mother face to face would give Kristine some solace and help bring her out of this sullen state of hopelessness. He didn't know the true depths of his daughter's aching. He didn't know the grip this depression had on her soul. He couldn't know that there would come a time that he would weep for her battered innocence. Would Angie come forth? Could Angie save her friend? If Angie told Porter what had happened to them, would Kristine finally face the evil wrath of her despair? Or would it cause her to descend even deeper into the darkness?

"Mom, we're home!" Kristine yelled as she entered the front door of her house.

"I'm in here, honey. In the kitchen."

Angie walked into the kitchen with Kristine and they both went straight up to Ellen and gave her a big hug. "Hi, Mrs. Steele."

"Hello, Angie. Hi, Kristine," Ellen smiled. Porter walked into the kitchen behind the girls and looked straight toward Ellen. He shrugged his shoulders and slowly mouthed the words, *she knows*. He was trying to get Ellen to understand that Kristine and Angie knew that she had been sick, but this was the only warning he could give her. Ellen was able to interpret what Porter was trying to express. His body language, and well-formed mime-like communication, helped to prepare her for what was about to come.

"Mom, what have you been hiding from me?"

"Well, that didn't take you long," Ellen responded. "Could I at least offer you both something to drink? I have some freshly made lemonade."

"Sure, I'll have some," Kristine answered. She looked over at Angie and quickly followed up. "Angie will have some, too."

Ellen poured two glasses. "Porter, do you want a glass?"

"No thanks. I'm good. I'll have some with dinner later."

"Dad told me you've been sick. What in the heck is going on?"

"I'll tell you if you want, but Angie may not want to hear about my medical problems, now, would she?" Ellen smiled at Angie.

"Stop it mom. Angie is like family. She's worried about you too, right Ange?" Kristine looked over at Angie as she sipped her lemonade.

"I don't want to interfere with your discussion," Angie said. "I can wait in the other room if you'd like, Mrs. Steele."

"That's okay, Angie. I really don't mind you hearing about it."

"What happened, Mom?"

"Well, several weeks ago I had to have some tests. Dr. Stevens thought she saw something on my mammogram."

"Oh my God."

"Kristine, it's been removed. Dr. Stevens found a lump, and it turned out to be cancerous, but she believes that she got it all. I will go back and see her next week."

"She doesn't know for sure, does she?"

"What do you mean?"

"If she got it all?" Kristine was shaking. "Are you going to need chemo or radiation?"

"That's what we'll find out very soon."

"Why didn't you tell me, Mother?"

Kristine's face was flushed. Tense. She paced. She was angry and sad for her mother at the same time.

"How could you just let me go off on spring break without telling me this was going on?"

"That was a decision I made with your father."

"Dad told me," Kristine said, "but I don't get it."

"I didn't want you in a constant state of worry while you were studying at school. That's all there is to it. Telling you was not going to change anything."

"So, I guess you were planning on telling me, eventually?"

"Of course, honey, but I was going to plan a weekend just like this one and tell you all about it," Ellen explained. "Now, here we are and now you know. Let's have a good weekend before you girls graduate and have to set out and confront the real world."

"I love when adults call it the real world," Kristine huffed. "My God, it sounds so dreadfully frightening."

Angie laughed, hoping to get even a tiny grin out of her friend, but it never happened. "My parents tell me that it's time for all the fun to end and for the work to begin."

"Sounds so goddamn depressing, Angie. Pardon my French. It zaps the motivation out of any young person."

"C'mon you two, stop with all this nonsense," Porter lectured as he entered the kitchen. "I'd give anything to be in my twenties again. You two are starting to bring me way down."

"Sorry, Dad. I guess we're just two big downers," Kristine replied.

"What are we having for dinner?" Porter wondered, trying to change the subject.

"It's a good chicken recipe I found, baked sweet potatoes and broccoli."

"I'm starving now," Angie said.

Porter looked at Angie and thought to himself, *that isn't far from the truth*. Angie had been working out so hard and so often, she was the skinniest Porter and Ellen had ever seen her. He could tell she was burning far more calories than she was taking in. Ellen was also worried about Angie's thin frame, even though she was always quite muscular.

"Both you girls are looking a little too thin to me. Aren't you two eating enough at school?"

"Too busy with classes to eat," Kristine joked. "Angie works out all the time. She's gotten ripped. Or is that shredded? Whatever bodybuilders call it."

"That's right," Angie smiled. "Don't worry about me, I've just been in the gym a little too much the last month or so. I promise to put on a couple of pounds while I'm here," she laughed. "Dinner sounds great, Mrs. Steele."

"What do you girls want to do tonight?"

"Totally relax, Mom."

"Maybe rent some movies?" Angie asked.

"Movies it is then," said Porter. "Tell me what you girls want to watch, and I'll go to the movie store and get them before dinner. I have to run a few errands anyway."

"Ice cream, too?" Ellen asked as she looked over at the girls. "Might as well take advantage of Dad's generosity while you two are here."

"I'll really put on the pounds this weekend," Angie answered. "But what the heck."

"Sounds good to me," said Kristine. "Angie, let's run up to my room for a minute."

Porter and Ellen were now alone in the kitchen. "Am I overreacting to their weight? Both girls look thinner than the last time we saw them. Don't you think?" Porter cringed.

"I was just thinking the same thing."

"I don't think Kristine looks good at all," he stated. "I'm worried about her."

"Me too," Ellen agreed. "I hope telling her about the cancer won't make her get worse."

"She's taking it pretty hard."

"I think you were right, Porter."

"What do you mean?"

"Remember when we first discussed Dr. Stevens' findings? You said we'd be better off telling Kristine right away."

"I remember."

"I was the one that told you to slow down and that I didn't think we should tell her?"

"But I hadn't thought it through, Ellen. I was on board with waiting."

"I know, but maybe we were both wrong to wait," Ellen worried.

"I hope we can fix whatever's going on."

NINE

THE UNDERCOVER OPERATION was about to begin. The strategy was agreed upon by the supervisors assigned to the mission. Captain Ryan, Lieutenant Steele, Detective Rockwell, and S.A. William Jennings sat in a room without a view and met for the afternoon. They were putting the final touches on the official launch of Operation Iguana.

"John will give you a brief on the phases of the operation he's put in place," S.A. Jennings began.

Detective Rockwell spoke. "Gentlemen. We've put an initial plan in place, we'll call Phase One, for your final approval of course. We will utilize some built-in flexibility as we go along with the operation. Our belief is this beginning phase will run smooth and safe for a couple of reasons. We plan on utilizing a strategy that should do two important things: First, it will draw one of the gang members, Nick Emerson, or Hammer as he's called, toward us. This will take place for a couple of months. Second, it will provide us good cover and a safe place to operate until we move into phase two of the operation."

"Give us some details regarding phase one, John," Captain Ryan said.

"First, you need to know my new identity."

"This should be interesting," Porter smiled. Over the years, law enforcement's nickname process was curious to say the least. Monikers for undercover agents, operations, secret missions, were often humorous.

John smiled in return. "My undercover name is Rocky Danner."

"Where'd that come from?" Ryan smiled.

"Well, frankly, they were my two favorite tactical boots that I wore during my SWAT assignment. Two great companies."

"Should be simple to remember," said Porter.

"The easier, the better." Detective Rockwell went on. "We have a prime location for our motorcycle shop. My partner at the shop is on board and is anxious to start building some bikes."

"He knows the dangers, correct?" Ryan questioned.

"He does, but he will not be in the picture too much," Rockwell added. "It'll be obvious that he's just a businessman and not a bit interested in participating in the biker life."

"What's your strategy for connecting with Hammer?" Porter asked.

"I know that he's going to come around when he learns of a new bike business in the neighborhood," Rockwell said, "but I will make sure he notices us. Hammer can't resist a custom motorcycle builder. It's his passion, although he isn't a great builder himself. He does know a lot about bikes. He can tear old motorcycles apart and put them back together, but that's about it. Nothing custom. He's too busy trying to make money for the Hell Riders."

"Then?"

"It will be within several weeks or maybe a couple of months and I'll be too essential to Hammer to be ignored. I should get an introduction to their top dog, Danny Trask."

"What's your plan for reporting?" asked Ryan.

S.A. Jennings stepped in. "That's been worked out between Lieutenant Steele and me."

"Porter?"

"Yes, the plan is to have my undercover unit supervisor as Rockwell's direct connection to our agency."

"Who did you assign?"

"It'll be a Sergeant on our end and that will be Martina Savala. She likes to be called Marti," replied Porter. "Savala was a highly successful undercover officer and is one of our top investigative supervisors."

"How long has she been on the department?" Rockwell wondered.

"Seventeen years."

"And in an undercover capacity?"

"Seven of those," Porter answered, "and supervised in our undercover unit another four years. She is highly reliable. Solid as a rock. Very bright."

"I can't ask for anything better than that, sir," Rockwell replied. "When can I meet her?"

"I hope today. That's the plan."

"I've checked out her resume, and I am more than satisfied," Jennings agreed.

"I'll be planning on meeting with her weekly, but sometimes it will be longer. There will be times I go dark, for safety reasons. I'm sure there will be phone calls between us frequently. It all depends on how things are progressing," Rockwell said. "Depends on what I need."

"I'll be meeting with Sergeant Savala regularly," Porter assured everyone.

"John will be turning in his original notes and his reports every two weeks, or so, to Sergeant Savala," Jennings advised. "He'll need some leeway on that depending on his initial progress."

"When she receives his reports, Marti will be reviewing them, turning them over to me for final approval and signing. Then, I'll return them to Marti for filing. They will be filed in a special computerized system by Marti's staff. This software will compile all reports chronologically.

We will have the ability to run reports by date, name, moniker, and offenses," Porter said. "At any moment, we will have the capability to print out a detailed timeline chart for review."

"This will help us build a solid RICO case on all our core players in the Hell Riders and beyond," Jennings added. "Keeping on top of our documentation will make our prosecutor, Ms. Sanchez, happy. She will get very grumpy if we don't stay on top of our reports. She told me she hates spending several weeks playing catch up on the status of her cases."

"I can't blame her," said Captain Ryan. "Been there. Done that. It's not efficient if we get too far behind on paperwork."

"Gentlemen...let's move on," Porter suggested.

WHILE THE SUPERVISORS of the Gang Task Force were meeting to discuss Operation Iguana, there was another meeting going on. This one was taking place at the Hell Riders' clubhouse. The players were much different though, and they were as committed to perpetrating crimes, as much as Porter and his team were committed to fighting them. The core group met. Bear, Hammer, Stump and D.T. sat around the bar in the clubhouse. The boss, Trask, led the meeting and was interested in one thing. He needed an update on Bear's plans for the Hell Rider's new ephedrine connection in Canada. This had become a priority in Trask's mind. He projected making more money, expanding markets, and international exposure within the biker world. If he was able to be successful, he might be able to start moving toward the top of the food chain within the entire Hell Riders' organization. And not just the local Vegas chapter.

"Bear, give me an update on your Canada connection," Trask said. "When do we move on this thing?"

"When you say we go, we will go," said Bear. "*The Frenchman* says they're ready to move some large amounts of ephedrine. We'll start with an order of four custom bikes, carried in a sixteen-foot trailer."

"Connection point?"

"He said their hauler will use the Ambassador Bridge, crossing the border near Detroit. He's crossed there many times doing legitimate business, so he knows he can get across with no problem."

"Where will you guys pick up the trailer?"

"The drop-off point will be at a designated motel parking lot on the southwest side of Detroit. Closer to Ann Arbor. There are several to choose from. It's isolated and the traffic will be limited around the motel."

"So, the pedestrian traffic is very low there?"

"The transfer of the trailer won't even be noticed. My connection will drop it and disappear. We'll latch on and go."

"Then what?"

"We'll drive about three or four hundred miles the first leg and get far enough away from the connection point to safely stop and get some sleep."

"How long's the trip?"

"We're talking just under two thousand miles, so thirty hours or better."

"What truck are you taking? You'll need something reliable."

"Hammer said we can drive his, right Hammer?" Bear confirmed.

"That's right. No problem."

"Unless you don't think that's smart?" Bear asked.

"I'll decide on what we'll do," Trask replied. "Hammer is seen around in his truck quite a bit. I may have you take that Ford F250 that belongs to Wiggins. It looks rough, but the thing runs great, and he hardly drives it. Good towing power. He's always on his Road King. The less we are noticed by the cops the better."

"That works for me, too."

"All cash deal, right?" Trask confirmed.

"All cash," Bear replied. "What did you decide about fronting the entire amount for all four bikes and trailer?"

"I like that. Let's front all the money," said Trask, "and then, we'll get rid of the bikes ourselves and keep all the profit."

"I agree," Bear replied. "Once we take the trailer and bikes off their hands, I don't want any other drug related debts owed to Satans Crew, or *the Frenchman*. It's not good business."

"That way we'll just be doing one deal at a time with this guy," Trask explained. "We can keep the trailer and use it when needed. It'll come in handy for other runs. We may even just keep the bikes and use them for future runs. They're already rigged for hiding our shit. Might as well use them for what they were designed and built for."

"This will be a huge load of effies," said Hammer. "This stuff will be hidden in the seats, tanks, saddle bags, and the front wall of the trailer. That's a lot of shit we're hauling. Ray will be able to cook for months."

"That's a ton," Stump said. "We may never have to buy from the Mexicans again."

"We'll make a lot of cash, too," said Hammer. "That's what I like."

"How much will this cost us, Bear?" asked Trask.

"I'd say this first haul will be seventy stacks or better. Maybe seventy-five."

"And that's counting the trailer and four Harleys?" Stump asked.

"Yeah, Stump," Bear answered. "What the fuck do you know about it?"

"Just asking," Stump said as he took a big chug of his beer.

"That's about what I expected, so I'm good with that price," said Trask. "I'm sure five thousand of that is the cost of doing personal business with *the Frenchman.* He's going to test our partnership at first."

Bear noticed that Trask seemed nervous. He ran both hands through his hair, pulling it back into a tight ponytail, perhaps trying to relieve the pressure. Bear could see that artery in Trasks' forehead pulsating again. Seventy-five thousand was a lot of cash to lose if something went wrong. He was not sure who *the Frenchman* was. But he did know that some of the Satans Crew club members wouldn't be interested in working with the Hell Riders. Bear wondered if Trask had the guts to go through with this deal.

"Trust me D.T.," Bear said as he got up and opened a couple of beers. He slid one over. "*The Frenchman* is tight. He won't screw us over."

"This is your deal, my man," Trask reminded. "Just remember, you're the one that vouched for this guy."

That was the first time in a long time that Danny Trask sounded the least bit threatening to his right-hand man. Drug deals were dangerous and tremendous amounts of money were at stake. Trask was not in the mood to lose a lot of cold hard cash. Business partners often became ruthless enemies when money and drugs were involved. Bear knew that his boss had some other ideas after buying all of this ephedrine. Stump and Hammer quietly drank their beers and listened as the two top dogs began to challenge each other. Was the thin line of loyalty beginning to fray between these two?

"What are you planning if this connection pans out in Toronto?"

"I have a guy in Riverside that's interested in getting his crank straight from us," Trask replied.

"Who's your connection down there?"

"A guy called Diablo. He rides with the Vipers," said Trask. "He's spreading his meth business south of Riverside, down toward Oceanside."

"So, he wants to test our product? He heard Ray was a good cook, is that it?"

"I told him that we were about to work on cooking some better crystal," said Trask. "He's tired of dealing with the Mexicans from Ensenada."

"They're getting too expensive and the ephedrine is harder to get their hands on for their cooks," Bear assumed.

"People are looking for cheaper ways to move their product," Trask replied. "I wanted to prepare us for the southern market if *the Frenchman* becomes a trusted supplier."

"And if he doesn't?"

"We have another option."

"What's that?"

"Diablo told me that the Vipers have a chapter in Ontario...in Peterborough."

"Where's that?" Bear questioned, worried it might infringe on *the Frenchman's* territory.

"That's just northeast of Toronto."

"We've got to be very careful, boss," Bear warned. "We don't want to fuck ourselves before we test this business deal with *the Frenchman*. If he finds out you're considering a deal with the Vipers' chapter in Peterborough, he may cut us off quicker than shit. The last thing we want to do is cause any local tension between the Vipers and Satans Crew in the Toronto area."

Bear was now getting suspicious of his own boss's motives. Perhaps the pulsating artery in his forehead was due to his reluctance to reveal his information to Bear about Oceanside. And also, this unknown connection named Diablo. He could see that Trask was already prepared to sabotage the deal that Bear had set up in Canada. It was this type of backstabbing that Bear despised in Trask. He acted as though he was giving Bear free reign to set up a drug deal. Only to use Bear's intelligence to set up his own drug deal if Bear's were to fail. It was one thing to screw with the enemy, but another thing to screw with a brother in the same club. Trask could tell that Bear was starting to get pissed off. He was a partner, but he could be a dangerous man and Trask knew it.

"Listen to what I'm saying. It's only a backup plan if our deal with *the Frenchman* ever falls through."

"I know, but you can't guarantee us that Diablo won't start talking to his Vipers' connection in Peterborough about the potential of a deal with us. You may have started something you can't control."

"Hey, brother...calm down," Trask said as he grinned and took a drink of his beer. "I trust Diablo as much as you trust *the Frenchman*, so he's not going to open his mouth until I give him the green light. Don't worry so much about it. I'm just hedging our bets. It's good business to have a backup plan."

BACK AT POLICE HEADQUARTERS, the plan for Operation Iguana continued on schedule. Like all high-level administrators, Captain Ryan was concerned about the operation's timeframe. His constant worry was that serious crimes will be committed during the undercover operation, while they build a RICO case on the Hell Riders. A year and a half, or even two years, can be a very long treacherous road to prosecution. A lot of misery could be brought upon a community, while an undercover officer witnesses and documents the destruction.

Ryan realized the fact that these investigations were tedious, long-term commitments, but were necessary for success.

Captain Ryan forged ahead with opening up communications. Porter knew that he was pushing the limits of sharing intelligence, but if it was ever needed, now was the time. It was known that law enforcement agencies had spent years holding important information close to their vests. Sharing detailed Intel, with other police agencies, was sometimes viewed as crossing the line. Independent, beneath the radar, types of secret investigations were always going on.

Porter was aware that building your own casefiles, gaining your own ground on the criminal element, and making your own big cases, was paramount for the success of an individual department. But he also knew it created barriers with other agencies. This caused a serious dilemma when it came to true teamwork and intelligence sharing. There was a lack of trust, not only between municipal and county agencies, but also between local departments and the feds. Captain Ryan recognized that collaboration was going to be central to changing the mindset among the agencies involved. It was critical to the strategy of battling criminal biker gangs in the Southwest.

"What's some of the current Intel you can share, Porter?" Ryan asked.

"I have a confidential source inside the Hell Riders. Kind of a fringe player, but he feeds me some good information."

"Who is he?" Rockwell asked. "I'll have to know him when I see him. This guy could create havoc for me if I don't know everything about him."

"His name is Ray. Ray Caruso."

"Is he a member, or a prospect? Just a hanger-on, or wannabe?" Rockwell pressed. "Fringe player?"

"He's their bartender and meth cook."

"Holy Christ," Jennings stated. "Their cook? Jesus, Lieutenant, you were going to tell us about this, right?"

"That's what I'm doing. That's what this meeting is for," Porter stated. "We're laying everything out on the table now, before we start to roll on this operation."

"We don't want this guy to know who I am," Rockwell advised. "As far as he's concerned, I'm just another new Hell Rider."

"He probably isn't in deep enough to ever know strict details, but he does feed us good information on the amounts he cooks. He knows the main players by name. He hears a lot. If we can corroborate his Intel, it's good for us in the long run."

Rockwell shook his head. He wasn't happy. "I will have to know everything he gives us from here on out."

"Absolutely. We hope his information makes your investigation that much more successful," Porter agreed.

"Having the cook in our back pocket can be a godsend, unless Trask gets tired of him. The leadership of the Hell Riders will view a meth cook as a double-edged sword," Jennings explained. "On one hand, they feel like they can't get rid of him. They need him at their beck and call to get their product on the street. On the other hand, who knows more about the amount of meth a gang is dealing than the guy that is in the lab making the batch?"

"If Trask ever gets suspicious about this Ray guy, he's a dead man," said Rockwell. "No question about it."

"Ray gave us some very thin information about a deal Trask wants to set up in Canada. It's something he's having Carlin work on."

"Did he say when?"

"Could be very soon."

"Probably an ephedrine run," said Jennings.

"I'd say so," Rockwell agreed. "We're getting more and more Intel on Canada lately. It may be the future for these bikers."

"What else do you know?" Ryan pressed.

"Ray said that Trask is restless and tense, lately," Porter stated. "He said it could be from a couple of new things going on."

"Like what?"

"He thinks Trask wants to expand his business to the south. But Ray has no details about where, with what club, or how far south. Or anything like that."

"You said a couple of things were going on?"

"Ray also said that something else happened at the club recently with some women," Porter explained. "He said Trask is unusually hyper, nervous...most of the time women come and go out of the Hard Times, but these were very young ladies. Ray says Trask is worried about what happened that night."

"Did Ray see anything?" Rockwell asked.

"He says he was sent home early. Trask said he'd lock up. Ray actually tried to get these women out of the bar, but Carlin made sure he kept his nose out of it."

"Drugged? Raped? What did Ray see?"

"He didn't speculate, but that could be because Ray actually knows more about what happened and he also knows the dangers of him knowing."

"That's what I mean by Ray being expendable to Trask," Rockwell said. "Is Ray worried? Maybe Trask thinks he knows too much about whatever occurred."

"He says that he's just focusing on doing his job, you know, bartending and cooking. Ray says he's trying to stay invisible. He's staying on Trask's good side for now, but he feels some tension between them over this thing. I can tell that he hopes just cooking his meth and keeping the batches going will keep Trask off his back."

"Ray Caruso wouldn't be the first snitch that ever disappeared," said Rockwell. "These guys usually don't get to just up and quit that job. There's no retirement party."

"I'd say the quicker we get Detective Rockwell in there, the better off we'll be," Jennings added.

"I would agree, gentlemen," Captain Ryan said as he stood. "I have to leave this meeting and head to another. The mayor wants my full attention for a few political matters. Porter, you can wrap up the meeting when you see fit. I'll meet with you later."

"Will do, Cap."

"This seems like a good time to take a break," Porter said. "If you guys want to get some coffee or take a bathroom break, I'm going to go find Sergeant Savala. She wanted to introduce herself and she asked me to let her know when she could crash this meeting. Is that alright, Bill?"

"Yes, sir. This would be a good time to meet her."

Rockwell agreed. "Once she and I are on the same page, we can get this operation rolling."

"I'll be right back," Porter replied. "Looks like Operation Iguana is about to begin."

Porter went and found Sergeant Savala. He brought her back to the conference room, and they waited for S.A. Jennings and Detective Rockwell to return. Both of them entered the room and Lieutenant Steele made the introductions.

"Gentlemen, I'm going to allow you to get to know Martina. I apologize, but I have another pressing appointment that I must attend."

"Not a problem, Lieutenant. We'll get to know each other and start talking strategy," Jennings replied.

Detective Rockwell shook Porter's hand. "Thanks again. I do appreciate the coordination on your part. Sergeant Savala and I should be able to come up with an exact date to start Phase One."

"Thank you both, and thank you Marti for being available today," said Porter. "When I get back, you and I will sit down and clarify our next step in this operation."

Porter darted out of the conference room, ran to his car, and drove straight to Dr. Stevens' office. He knew Ellen would be there expecting his arrival.

TEN

PORTER AND ELLEN ANXIOUSLY waited. It was a nerve-wracking time for both of them, but especially hard on Ellen. Post-operative checkups were brutal. They both knew that Ellen had not been feeling right. She knew her body. She felt different, although hard to describe. She told God in the dark hours of the night. Ellen kept most of her deepest fears to herself. No matter how many times Porter asked her to please talk to him; to reveal her emotions and to use his shoulder to cry on, Ellen had her own way of dealing with all of her apprehension. She tried hard to pretend that there was no cancer in her body. Ignore it, she thought. Dr. Stevens walked into the exam room. Porter and Ellen sat upright in their chairs, straightened their shoulders, and looked into her eyes. Ellen saw doubt. Porter saw regret. Dr. Stevens saw two people that waited in agony to hear the words roll off her tongue.

"Ellen. Porter."

"Dr. Stevens," they both replied.

Dr. Stevens sat down on her exam chair, rolled toward them, laid her folder down on the examination table and reached out, offering one firm hand to Ellen and one to Porter. "Okay, you two. I have some news about your tests."

"I'm ready," Ellen replied.

"I see a spot on your lung, Ellen, and we'll need to do a biopsy right away."

"You think the cancer spread to her lung?"

"Porter, we just can't say for sure, but we'll know as soon as we get this test done."

"I knew this cough I've had wasn't just a cold," Ellen said, shaking her head side to side. "I just haven't felt right."

"I notice her wheezing at night more when she sleeps," Porter said. "She's acted like she's had an upper respiratory problem."

"Any chest pains?"

"Some. But I thought maybe it was just from all the coughing."

"You do have a low-grade fever as well," said Dr. Stevens, "so how long have you felt this way?"

"The last few weeks."

"She assumed it was all just part of her recovery," Porter added.

"I thought feeling crappy was expected during the healing process."

"You're right, feeling crappy is part of the process, so don't blame yourself for not knowing what's going on," Dr. Stevens stated. "It's not easy to know what's brewing inside your body, especially after major surgery."

"I want to do a CT scan, so I have that scheduled for the day after tomorrow."

"Then when do you do the biopsy?" Porter asked.

"My plan is to do it right there and have the CT scan guide us to the area I will be looking at," answered the doctor. "My colleague, Dr. Baker, has told me that he will meet with me and assist in the procedure. We'll know so much more after we get that done."

"Dr. Baker?"

"You'll love Dr. Baker, both of you," she said. "He's a wonderful surgeon with an expertise in this area. I also want a second set of eyes that I can trust to look at your tests with me."

"Okay, we'll be here right at...what time did you say again?" asked

Porter, visibly flustered. He appeared to be in a state of shock.

Dr. Stevens smiled. "Let me take a look at my notes again."

"The sooner the better," Ellen whispered to Porter as she squeezed his hand.

"The day after tomorrow, at nine a.m. I need you to report to the X-ray department. They will direct you to your scan."

"We'll be there by eight forty-five sharp."

Porter was concerned and Ellen felt it. She could see he was more than worried about her. His face was pale. He was trying to stay strong by showing his support, but he had a look on his face like that of a scared child. Dr. Stevens left the exam room and gave Ellen and Porter time to hold each other, catch their breaths, gather their strength. They wanted to walk with each other, hand in hand, past the other cancer patients sitting in the waiting room. The others with shaved heads and thinning hair. Women with scarves covering their bald heads. Men with a certain struggle deep within their eyes. All the others fighting battles they never asked to wage.

SHORTLY AFTER GRADUATION from ASU, Kristine decided that she was not prepared to go out into the world and start her career. She decided to stay on campus and pursue her master's degree in the field of social work. She became interested in mental health counseling, which was somewhat confusing to her parents. Kristine took a part time job inside the counseling department and was relating more and more to the mission of the therapists. She saw a tremendous number of students receive counseling where she worked. Ironically, she resisted the temptation to seek help for her own personal issues, which stemmed from the sexual assault.

Prior to graduation, Kristine was planning a career in marketing. Porter knew that college students often changed their pursuits in life. He and Ellen decided this was not the time to pressure Kristine to get away from the campus life. Looking for work out in the job market would have to wait. They both knew that she was still searching, and struggling, although for the life of them they could not understand why. She was still battling the blues, as Porter perceived it.

Questions haunted their waking hours. Were Ellen and Porter enablers to Kristine's current state of mental health? Were they perpetuating an ongoing problem, which they couldn't put their fingers on? Were they so overprotective of their only child, they didn't allow themselves to believe there could be something serious brewing deep within?

Perhaps it was one of these things, or all of these things. One major issue stood in the way of seeking real answers. That was Ellen's battle against her cancer. The focus had to be on Porter's wife. Even though it was not his intent to ignore his daughter, he felt Kristine was safe and secure as long as she was working and attending ASU. Porter believed that she was familiar with her surroundings and accustomed to her life there. Perhaps, still searching for some unknown path that would lead to her future. He accepted her decision, because he didn't think there was a better choice. He simply didn't have the energy to oppose it at this time in his life.

Ellen was in a struggle she could not fight alone. If Porter was ever Ellen's knight in shining armor, now was the time to prove it. He had to carry her when she was too weak to walk. He knew those days were coming and he feared her cancer was about to crush them like an avalanche. Ellen convinced her husband that telling Kristine about her latest bad news from Dr. Stevens would overwhelm her.

The secrets Kristine begged her parents to never hide from her, continued. How ironic that Porter and Ellen's silence was equally matched by Kristine's silence about her own rape. Secrets held captive, reluctantly, but persistently, concealed for noble reasons. Secrets intentionally obscured from view, locked deeply within their souls. Secrets that burned like acid through the lining of their stomachs, leaving behind only the charred remains of the truth.

ANOTHER BATTLE WAS BREWING within the Hell Riders, and it was also a well-kept secret. There was a lot happening lately within the organization and Danny Trask was getting antsy. He was growing even more suspicious of Ray Caruso. He was beginning to let his paranoia overwhelm him regarding what Ray may have witnessed the night of the rapes. Trask knew there was no way Ray could have actually witnessed any of the rapes, but he surely witnessed everything that led up to those crimes. Trask was also concerned about the fact that Ray tried very hard to persuade those girls to get up and leave the bar. Why so protective of four girls he didn't know? Why was he sticking his nose in where it didn't belong? He had witnessed many crimes inside the Hard Times Tap. Sexual assaults, meth, cocaine, weed, and violence perpetrated on drunken men who simply wandered in off the street for a little more alcohol. Not only did he witness crimes, but Ray also regularly committed crimes down inside the secret basement. Down inside the Hell Rider's kitchen, where he cooked his crystal meth for the addicted. So, what was it that jabbed at Trask's gut now? And why was Ray getting so deep under his skin?

There was one thing that Trask couldn't get out of his mind. There was one kind of criminal that Trask knew could get away with committing crimes on a regular basis and never fear being caught. That criminal was the one that worked both sides of the fence. The one that fed information to the police but continued to get a pass on the crimes he committed himself.

Trask had no real evidence of this, but did he really need any evidence? After all, this was not a court of law. Trask never needed a legitimate reason to deal with guys like Ray. Suspicion alone was more than enough. A man like Trask would do whatever he saw fit to protect himself and the Hell Riders from police suspicion. He would never admit it, but most of his worries stemmed from the fact that he was the one that raped the daughter of a very determined and tenacious cop.

The inability to make a final decision about what to do with Ray was starting to aggravate him. There was no good answer to this dilemma. If Ray truly was a snitch, and Trask decided to take care of the problem his way, the cops would be all over him. The Hell Riders would feel tremendous pressure. If Ray was not a snitch, then all of this paranoia was for naught. And the recently planned business moves would go off without a hitch. Ray was unaware of Trask's deep suspicion about him being a confidential source.

For now, Trask decided he would ignore his own instincts. Perhaps that would be a mistake, but his new Canadian connection and his pact with his new partner down near Riverside were about to get even stronger. Trask kept one thing in the back of his mind. Any problems with Ray could be alleviated in the future, at a moment's notice. He knew if he decided to take care of his, so-called, snitch problem, he would have to follow through with it before Ray was ever called to take the stand and testify.

ALMOST FOUR MONTHS had passed by, and Detective Rockwell was fully submersed into his undercover character, Rocky Danner. He and Lonnie Stickler opened a small business they called Iron Horse Builders, on the south side of Vegas. It was several miles from the strip, but easily accessible by the biker community. Operational plans were progressing smoothly. Rockwell's partner, Stickler, already had four bikes that were nearly finished, which he brought over from his old business. That gave them a head start when it came to focusing on developing a clientele within the Hell Riders.

It didn't take long, and they noticed Nick Emerson had been in the shop at least three or four times. He made small talk, never prying into their business. Emerson didn't even introduce himself or ask their names. He only seemed fascinated with Stickler's fabricating skills and soon became friends with the man he thought owned the business. The man he knew as Rocky Danner.

Danner had begun to build a promising rapport with Emerson. Emerson was proud of the Hell Riders and made sure he displayed his colors in front of Danner and Stickler. Emerson wanted something more than just visiting a couple of new bike builders in town, and Danner knew it. He was equipped with the recent Intel on the Hell Riders' ephedrine connection in Canada and believed Emerson wanted to develop a small criminal enterprise, by utilizing the Iron Horse garage.

Nick Emerson walked in one afternoon and began to pry further.

"What's up boys?"

"Just working," Danner replied.

"I'm starting to like this place."

"We like it here."

"What are your names again, fellas?" Emerson asked. "I don't think we've ever introduced ourselves."

"I'm Rocky and this is Lonnie," Danner answered. "And you are?"

"I'm Nick. They call me Hammer. Your boy here is quite the

fabricator."

"If you can think it, he can fabricate it."

"That's good...just think it, huh?"

"I'd say he can fabricate just about anything the customer desires."

"Anything?"

Danner smiled. "Anything."

"I've been thinking of some things I'd like on my bike."

Stickler lifted his head to look over the seat of the bike he was working on. "What sort of things are you talking about?"

"There are some custom additions I'd like put on my bike."

"Such as?"

"I'd like to hide some things once in a while," Hammer replied. "You know...I need to conceal some shit once in a while."

Stickler stood up and leaned up against his workbench. "What'd you have in mind?"

"Seat and tank. Maybe saddle bags built with some concealed compartments."

"You mean to carry a gun, or a little weed or something?" asked Danner.

"Maybe a little dope, sure. Maybe a lot of dope. You never know."

"You want a whole new custom bike or are you talking about customizing an old bike you already have?"

"I'd like to start with my own bike and see how it works out."

Danner pushed for a more serious commitment. "Do you have your bike outside, or do you need to bring it in another time? We can take a look at it."

"I got it outside."

Stickler looked over at Danner and stepped toward the garage door. "I guess it won't hurt to wheel it in here and take a look...see what you have in mind."

"Let's do it," Hammer said. "Your boss here said if I could think it, you could build it. Is that right?"

"Let's see the bike, then I can tell ya."

Emerson went outside, while Stickler opened the garage door to let him in. Emerson rode in on an old black Tour Glide Classic. The paint job was fading and a little rough looking. That, of course, is exactly how guys like Hammer want their bikes to look. A beautiful gleaming shine off a recently waxed motorcycle didn't fly in the Hell Riders, or any other biker club for that matter.

"Here she is, boys."

"1987. Good year," said Stickler.

"What could you do to give this bike some places to hide shit?"

"Does this have a tour pack?" asked Danner.

"At my place, yeah."

"That could hold a lot of weed or whatever you want to carry."

"What changes can you make?"

Stickler said, "First, we can make custom inserts for the tour pack and the saddle bags."

"How do you do it?"

"We would fabricate an insert that is slightly narrower on just one side and also shallower than the full depth of the bag. This makes it less visible to the naked eye when opened."

"What can it hold?"

"I can't give you the exact amount if I don't know what you're carrying."

"Meth. What about meth?"

"I'd say you can carry a lot of meth, because you can drop the bags down the side of the insert, where they'll sit between the inserts and the hard shell of the bags. Also, you can put a lot underneath the insert, where you can hide several bags."

"How many ozees?"

"We can't tell you that, man, gimme a break," said Danner. "But remember you can take those times two. Both saddlebags could be customized. Also, with the size of the tour pack, that should hold twice as much as one saddlebag."

"Can you do anything with the seat?"

"We could, but the main issue we would have to get around is the amount of heat that comes off the motor," Stickler warned.

"But you think you might be able to design something?"

"I guess we could always experiment," Danner said. "Wouldn't hurt to try."

"Another possibility..."

"What's that Mr. Fabricator?" Hammer joked.

"Have you ever pulled a small trailer behind you?"

"If I was a fucking pussy wannabe, going camping with my wife of forty years, yeah."

"I assume, that's a no?" Stickler grinned. "I was only thinking about the amount of room you'd have to carry a load of meth, coke, or whatever."

"The insert we could design for a trailer like that would be pretty wild," Danner explained. "You'd get a couple hundred bags of crystal in that thing."

"I'll think about it."

Hammer was getting tired of the conversation. "Don't get too excited boys, I haven't said I was hiring you to do a fucking thing, yet. Just asking."

"Iron Horse would love to do business with you," Danner offered. "You know where you can find us."

"I do know where I can find you," Hammer smirked, "so just

remember that. I know exactly where you both are, so keep this conversation just between us."

This secret chat was the first time in months that Detective Rockwell knew that it was only a matter of time before he was introduced to Danny Trask. Rockwell, aka Rocky Danner, and the Iron Horse garage, would become a topic of discussion between Trask, Carlin, Emerson and Severs. Their mutual business relationship began that day and Rockwell knew it. Nick Emerson knew he would be able to convince Trask that the two guys at Iron Horse were trustworthy enough to build drug transport bikes for the Hell Riders. Emerson was proud of himself.

The Iron Horse garage soon began customizing some of the Hell Riders' personal motorcycles, so transporting small amounts of contraband became much easier. The first bike they customized was Hammer's. He paid Danner and Stickler in a manner that Sergeant Savala hoped would become a common practice. They were paid three hundred bucks in cash and one bag of crystal meth. That was the first hand to hand drug transfer of Operation Iguana, and the cash and drugs went straight into the evidence lockup for testing. This was just the beginning of a long, mutually beneficial relationship.

As the connections developed inside Ontario, with *the Frenchman,* and now with Danner and Stickler at Iron Horse Builders, Trask believed he could develop and control a meth corridor between the Canadian border and south to Riverside. Perhaps it would even stretch beyond, to Baja California. Only time would tell. Trask definitely needed Mike Carlin on board though. Business relationships with the Vipers, in Riverside and beyond, remained a difficult proposition at best. He knew money talked and whoever had the cash, and the crystal meth, ruled. As of right now, Danny Trask was that ruler.

TRASK MET WITH BEAR at the Hard Times for a private meeting. He knew that Bear was the architect of their ephedrine business dealings with *the Frenchman* in Toronto, so he wanted to get some feedback on how the business relationship was working. They sat in the corner of an empty tavern, with only Ray inside cleaning up the bar area, and stocking up on alcohol for an expected busy weekend.

"So, how's business been?"

"Business has never been better?" Bear proudly answered. "We've been making at least one run a month now."

"Using the motorcycles and trailer for concealment still working?"

"Still working...why do you ask?"

"We need to expand."

"Where?"

"South of Vegas and beyond."

"Mexico?"

"Riverside, first, then Oceanside."

"Then Mexico?"

"Baja."

"Where did this idea come from? Hammer's little connection over at the Iron Horse, I suppose?" Bear was obviously pissed off that Nick Emerson was trying to step up and impress Trask with some business dealings. "What do you expect from me?"

"I expect you to start setting it up," Trask said as he slapped Bear across the top of his shoulder. "Damn, man...you expect me to have Hammer work this out?"

"I'm not going to diss Hammer. He seems to have set something up at the Iron Horse that could benefit us all in the long run."

"Yeah, Yeah, I agree, but he doesn't have the brains to see it through. He doesn't have the clout or the leadership pull I'm going to need to move us south. Hammer can be our connection with those guys at the Iron Horse, but that will be the extent of it. I can't send him down to Riverside. Not alone. You know that."

"What's your plan, boss?"

"We continue our relationship with *the Frenchman*. We buy the ephedrine regularly. Keep those guys swimming in cash up there in Canada. We then transport it here. Ray cooks it up and we haul the shit directly to Riverside. As the Riverside business grows, we are going to move further south. There are some guys in Baja that want in on our crystal."

"And the more we cook and move south, the more ephedrine we'll need from the boys up north. Is that it?"

"That's it. Money is always the key. With a lot of cash changing hands, everybody's happy."

"What's the connection then with the boys over at Iron Horse?"

"For one thing they are damn good bike builders. We may have to spend some of this money on new custom bikes," Trask smiled like a child. "The other thing Hammer is convinced of is that they are really good at fabricating concealed compartments on old bikes. Doesn't make any difference, they can modify anything we have."

"What are they going to cost us?"

Trask leaned over next to Bear and lowered his voice. "That's the other good thing. They don't really charge that much money, because Hammer has thrown in some meth as part of their payment. They seem to want the meth as much as they want the green. They're probably serious tweakers."

"So, some of the shit we skim off the top can go to them as payment?"

"It'll be like getting their labor for free," Trask replied. "Keep them high and they're ours until we don't need them anymore."

"I thought Hammer was interested in introducing one of them to the club as a possible member?"

"That's what he says. We'll see about that later on."

"Which one is it?"

"It's the one named Danner."

"Hammer says he is impressed with the guy," he smirked. "Says he's club material. Can't shut up about him."

"Like I said, we'll have to see where it goes," Trask repeated. "Hammer is going to have to vouch for this guy. After that, Danner will have to prove himself."

"Not just vouch for him. Maybe we need to have Hammer beat this guy into the club."

"Sounds like fun," Trask smiled. "It's been a while since Hammer's thrown down. If Danner can stand up to him, I'll be impressed."

"He may just get his ass beat by this guy."

"I'd have to see that to believe it."

"Well then, there's only one way to find out."

"Get Hammer and Stump over here. I'll get ahold of Danner and get his ass over here," Trask said. "And to make this interesting, I got a hundred bucks on Hammer."

"That leaves me hanging, boss. I don't know this Danner guy at all, but it wouldn't be much of a wager if I didn't bet against Hammer," Bear laughed. "I'll put a hundred bucks on Danner. What the hell. We'll see what he's made of."

An unplanned special meeting was now called. Danny Trask grabbed some beers for himself and Carlin and then pulled his chair up to the table in the corner of the room. They sat, talked, and drank, waiting for Hammer and Stump to arrive. Just like always, it didn't take long. Hammer and Stump walked in and saw Trask and Bear sitting at a table, smiling.

"I've called you guys here for a short meeting."

"What's up, boss?" Stump asked.

"Let's wait a few minutes, I've got one more coming."

"Who's that?" Emerson asked. He had a hunch who Trask was referring to but wasn't sure.

"I invited your boy here."

"My boy?"

"Your boy, you know."

"Danner?"

"Yeah, Danner," he answered. "Is that okay with you?"

"No problem. He's not my boy, though," he clarified, "but I was hoping you'd take a closer look at him."

"You think he'd make a good Hell Rider, is that right?" Bear mocked.

"Why not consider it? He's right for us."

"Why not?" Trask yelled. "That's your question for me, Hammer? Well, maybe Danner doesn't deserve to be a goddamn Hell Rider. That's why not."

"Maybe he isn't tough enough to be one of us," Bear growled.

Hammer caught on quickly. He knew where this conversation was going. Danner was about to be lured into a trap he should've foreseen.

Stump jumped in. "You want me to test this guy, boss?"

"No, no, he's Hammer's boy. Hammer can test him, unless he wants you to do his light work for him."

"I'll fuck this guy up for ya, Hammer," Stump grinned. "Or at least give you a hand."

"Fuck you, Stump."

Within minutes Rocky Danner pushed opened the unlocked front door to the Hard Times Tap. He scanned the bar to gain an awareness of his surroundings. There was no way he could be sure as to what he was walking into. He saw Ray Caruso behind the bar and gave him a nod. Ray tilted his head to the left, directing Danner to a table in the corner of the room. Trask, Carlin, Emerson and Severs were sitting, laughing, and drinking beer. Hammer had taken a couple of shots of whiskey as well, to pump up his desire to brawl. As a rule, this was something he didn't need. The pure impulse to fight was always brewing deep within him.

Danner cautiously walked toward their table. There was one empty chair waiting for his arrival. He looked at the four men staring at him. Trask pointed to the chair, ordering him to sit. Danner sat down. Always prepared for the worst, he didn't want to show any fear or anxiety in the presence of these men. That would be a death sentence. Bear slid him a beer across the tabletop and Danner began to drink. Going along with the program was important. Did he want to be an insider or not? Danner knew what it took. He was also well aware of the tactics the Hell Riders used on prospects. Hammer made it obvious that he wanted Danner in the club and Trask was the only one that could make it happen.

There were questions about to be answered. What was it going to take? Danner told himself to stay calm, alert, and roll with the punches. He was even prepared to take that literally. Was he called there to be tested? Was he called there to be judged? Was he there to take a beating for entry into this club? Was there any way possible that Trask had already made him? After just four months, was he about to embarrass Hammer in front of the others? If so, this would be an unpleasant, and violent, meeting with this group. Danner began to feel that fight or flight sensation.

"Hammer, go get Rocky another beer. And grab some shots for everybody," Trask ordered, winking at Bear.

Treating Hammer like a waitress got his attention, fast. This pissed him off. Trask could have easily had Stump get the drinks.

For that matter, he could have made Danner get them. After all, he was potentially the new boy of the group. He knew what Trask was up to. This was a good way to get Hammer livid. Having him wait on everybody, like he was a low-level player in this club, was a good tactic for getting him ready to fight. Trask was treating Danner like he respected him more than he respected Hammer. This was intentional.

There was only one way to satisfy his boss and that was to make an all-out attack on Danner and end this charade quickly. Hammer would get the credit for beating Danner into the club. He had been there, done that, on several occasions. That was one reason the nickname, Hammer, stuck to him. He had a reputation of being a ruthless brawler. Many new club members faced off with Hammer and even some drunken idiots, just looking for a fight, had chosen him as their combatant. He had proven himself time and time again for Trask. If this was going to get Danner in the club, why not do it one more time?

When Hammer returned to the table, Stump was still laughing at him. He handed everybody their drinks and as he went to his chair he had to walk directly behind Danner. It was his blind spot. He knew this would be his best opportunity for a first strike. And that became a real dilemma for Danner. Hammer may have been known as a fighter, but no one ever accused him of being a fair fighter.

With a quick left hook, out of nowhere, which Danner never saw coming, Hammer caught him on the left side of his jaw. It knocked him completely out of his chair. Bear, Stump and Trask all slid their chairs backwards away from the table and, once again, watched Hammer go to work on a new club prospect. The punch to Danner's face was devastating. Powerful. Hammer was convinced the fight was already over. He went over to Danner just to make sure he was knocked out cold. He was lying face down, eyes closed, blood dripping on the filthy floor, seemingly unconscious. But when Hammer got close enough,

Danner leg swept him to the floor. Now, they were both on the ground. This is when the special forces hand-to-hand combat training kicked in. Danner rolled over onto his back quickly to protect himself. The whole left side of his face was already swelling, and it had begun to close his left eye. Was his jaw broken? An orbital bone?

Now was not the time to worry about it. *Survive this*, he thought. He may be in a world of shit. Danner was lucky it didn't knock him totally unconscious, although just for a brief moment he wasn't sure where he was. Hammer quickly got to his knees and began to throw more punches at Danner's face. Hammer knew he had him seriously injured. He landed a couple more blows, but Danner was able to get ahold of Hammer's right forearm, rolling him over, tucking his arm underneath him, and pulling him down to the wood planks. This gave him a much-needed break from the relentless punches. Danner was now able to get on top of Hammer. The tide of this battle had surely turned.

Bear grinned and scowled at Trask. "Fuck yeah, brother. I'm about to make me some money."

"Hammer's not done with this guy yet," warned Trask.

Within seconds, Danner began to throw vicious elbows to Hammer's face. One elbow caught him above the right eye, laying it wide open like a filleted fish. The blood began to flow freely down the side of his face onto the floor. Danner knew that the blood was going to impair Hammer's vision, so he used his elbows to intentionally wipe the blood into both of his eyes. Hammer was able to find enough power to hip throw Danner off of him. There was just enough separation from Danner to slide off to the side and get enough room to try and get to his feet. Both men were now standing, face to face, toe to toe. Hammer began throwing blind wild roundhouse punches that gave Danner time to sidestep and throw left jabs, landing several times to his nose.

Hammer was blinded by all the blood. His nose was undoubtedly broken and even more blood spilled to the floor.

"Goddammit, boss, this guy can throw down," said Bear. "I thought that first sucker punch Hammer landed was the end of this fight. No fucking way."

"I was about to ask you for my hundred bucks."

"It ain't over yet, brother."

Both men were starting to slow down, but Hammer was getting the worst of the blows. His nose was broken, lips were bleeding, one eye severely lacerated and the side of his face was swollen from ear to chin. Danner realized he was in control of the situation. As a Green Beret, this was time for the kill. But Danner knew he was not at war. Even though he felt like it. He was hoping he hadn't sustained a broken jaw. That kind of injury could be a major setback for Operation Iguana. As Hammer got to the point of staggering and losing complete balance, he charged Danner in a last-ditch attempt to tackle him to the ground. He had completely run out of gas and could barely stay upright. As he rushed in, Danner threw a left uppercut, landing directly under Hammer's jaw, stunning his mandibular nerve. The concussion knocked him stiff. His arms locked in place, rigid. His eyes rolled back. Trask, Bear and Stump could see that Hammer was out on his feet. The only question was how long it would take for his body to hit the floor. When Danner brought his fist back from the blow, he stepped to the side, giving room for his rival to fall. Hammer dropped to the blood-soaked wood planks. The fight was over.

Ray Caruso was standing behind the bar, shaking his head from side to side, thinking to himself, *it's about time Hammer finally got the worst end of a fight he started.* There was no question as to the outcome of the battle. Trask manned up and handed Bear a hundred-dollar bill, still in disbelief as to what he'd just witnessed. Hammer losing a fight was a rare thing. None of the men could actually remember it ever happening. Trask was impressed. So was Bear. Danner had won them over.

Trask leaned over to Bear, looking down at the hundred bucks he was holding.

"As far as I'm concerned, Hammer's boy is in."

"You're the boss. You want me to give him his colors?"

"Give him his colors," Trask ordered. "Hey Stump, make sure Hammer's okay, will ya?"

"What about Danner, boss?"

"He can take care of himself."

ELEVEN

TWENTY MONTHS INTO Operation Iguana, a solid case was being built by the undercover task force. Lieutenant Steele, Sergeant Savala and Detective John Rockwell were in charge of a massive operation. But there was more to be done, of course. There always was a need for more evidence, more witnesses, more drugs to be purchased, more cash to be inventoried into the evidence lockup. These kinds of cases were tough. They were tough on cops. Tough on families. Tough on the community. This case was tough on Porter. The fight never seemed to end. Porter's ambition and drive was waning, for many reasons. He was getting older and the long, drawn-out cases were beginning to take their toll on an aging cop. He knew it. Others knew it. The young blood needed to take over and begin their long push upward, toward the pinnacle of the justice fight.

Time was the one constant. Time never stopped for anyone. Time never ceased to march forward. It harassed Porter like a playground bully. Time never put his arm around Porter, offering him a brief moment of respite. To sit and catch his breath. It was time that taunted fate, like the mountain climber who stops to close his eyes just long enough to become frozen in the moment. Porter never gave in to those feelings of dread, because time was something his precious Ellen no longer even considered. Time for her was just a reminder that her days had gone by and there were few days that lie ahead.

Ellen fought a quiet, graceful battle against her enemy. An enemy that had no regard for race, gender, the young, or the elderly. It was an enemy without a conscience, without empathy, and without respect for its prey. Cancer took and took and took until there was no more to take. In a sad and pathetic way, it was as if the cancer did not know any better. It was not aware of its own evil. It was doing exactly what it was supposed to do. To kill whatever stood in its path.

Ellen softly called his name. "Porter…"

It was nine-thirty in the morning on a Saturday and Porter had been awake for hours. He wondered how Ellen's day would be today. He was standing in the kitchen, just twenty feet from her bedroom, but he still could not hear her gentle voice calling out. Not just because he was aging and so was his hearing, but mainly because Ellen was too weak to force the sound from her body.

"Porter…come in here, please."

He heard her this time. Like always, he ran to her side fearing the worst. Never wanting to leave her alone. "Ellen…what's wrong, honey?"

"Sit down." Ellen patted the bed next to her.

Porter pulled the chair over next to the bed. Ellen reached out her hand, and he obliged, holding it tightly, promising to himself, *I will never let go.*

"I feel very strange today," Ellen said as she managed to form a smile. A smile that had not been showing itself lately.

"Maybe it's the medication."

"I suppose it could be, but there's something else going on," Ellen said. "Something I've been afraid to admit."

Porter squeezed her hand. "Don't say it, Ellen. Please don't."

"You're so sweet, Mr. Steele," she said, "and so afraid, aren't you?"

"You're damn right I'm afraid."

"Why? We've had so many wonderful years together."

"Because it's just not right, that's why. I want to spend the rest of our lives together."

"So, you're still holding onto that picture in your mind of us being so old we have to hold each other up as we walk around the ranch?"

"I cannot handle this changing world without you. There's no way."

Ellen managed a grin. "You're a hopeless romantic, aren't you, Mr. Steele?"

"That compliment will not get you out of taking your morning pills."

"I will. I will. Just give me a few more minutes," she replied. "I'm sort of procrastinating. I don't want to interrupt your loving mood this morning."

They both laughed. Ellen had always kept her sense of humor, no matter how sick she had become. Porter couldn't understand where in God's name she got all of her strength. Not just physical, but mental. Spiritual. How she could not be violently angry at the world was beyond his comprehension. He had enough anger for both of them. He knew it was eating him up inside, but he tried not to show it. That was impossible to do around Ellen though, because he wanted to protect her from the evils of the world. He wanted to step in front of that proverbial bullet for her, but he could not change the path their lives were taking. For once in his life, he felt helpless. He was not able to control destiny.

"Could you get me some water?"

"Yes, I'll be right back. Can I get you something to eat?"

"I'd like some toast, dear."

"Butter? Or jam?"

"I'll live it up today. Make it two slices. Jam on both," Ellen laughed. "I'm such an easy date, aren't I?"

"Speaking of dates, why don't I rent a movie today and we'll kick back and be lazy?"

"Sounds like the kind of date that's impossible for me to resist." Ellen's eyes were narrowing. It was not easy for her to keep them open. "Have I ever told you how handsome you are?"

He smiled, in spite of his hidden regret.

Porter left the house to drive to the movie store, while Ellen gathered enough strength to move from her bedroom out to the living room. Once she was up and moving around, she began to feel some energy. She decided to surprise Porter with a big bowl of popcorn and ice-cold soda for the movie. Ellen sought out her stash of chocolate that the two of them shared once in a while as a movie-watching treat. All that seemed to be left were the small blessings, but wasn't that the true essence of life? Weren't the most precious moments the simplest, the most uncomplicated?

When Porter returned, he found Ellen on the couch. Candles were lit, lights were dimmed, her lap covered with her favorite blanket. She had a big bowl of popcorn on her lap, and two sodas on the coffee table in front of her. Ellen was sound asleep. Porter quietly laughed, so as not to wake her. All that she had done had simply worn her out. A nap was in order, so the movie would have to wait. Porter lifted the blanket higher, so it would cover her shoulders. He grabbed the popcorn from her lap, blew out the candles, and walked across the room to sit in his chair. He sat quietly and watched his loving wife sleep. She was comfortable when she slept. Porter was so alone. A tear gently streamed down his cheek and fell onto his shirt. He often cried when he was alone. He never wanted Ellen to see. His tears were dwindling these days, gradually slowing like the fading trickle of a dying brook.

IT WAS LATE AFTERNOON and Ellen was still sound asleep. Porter received a phone call from Kristine.

"Hi Dad. How's mom doing?"

"She's been better. Today will be a long day."

"What's next?" Kristine asked.

Porter hesitated. "She gets a PET scan on Tuesday. Then, she may start a new treatment program. Something even more aggressive."

"Has it spread?"

"That's what Dr. Stevens is worried about, although she wouldn't say until the PET scan is complete and she gets the results."

"She's very meticulous, huh?"

"Yes, she is. To a fault I suppose but, as a doctor, I'm sure she doesn't want to get our hopes up too high, and at the same time she doesn't want us to feel like there's nothing that can be done."

"What did you two do today?"

"Well, today was going to be a day to just chill. Movies and popcorn. You know mom, cozy up on the couch, and relax."

"That didn't happen, did it?"

"I came back from the movie store and there she was, on the couch, popcorn in a big bowl, and sound asleep."

"She just doesn't have the strength to stay awake."

"She's in bed now. She might be out until morning, unless she wakes up feeling sick."

"It will be a long night, won't it?" Kristine worried. "How does she not get her days and nights confused?"

"It's a vicious cycle."

"How are you holding up, Dad? Truthfully."

"Hanging in there. All I care about is your mom right now," Porter answered, although not too convincingly. Kristine knew that he always worried about her, too. "How are things in Arizona?"

"That's sort of why I called."

"What's up? Everything alright?"

"I want to come home."

"Honey, is this about school or mom?"

"Mom. I can't take being here, worrying about her every day. It's not fair to mom that I'm off at school and you're the only one to take care of her."

"I can do it, Kristine."

"Dad, I know you're capable," she replied, "but you shouldn't have to face this all alone. You are still working your butt off like usual, right?"

"Of course, but you know police work."

"I want to come home and help with mom," sounding more demanding. "I can take care of mom when you're at work and then take some night classes."

"At UNLV?"

"Sure, why not? That's where mom went."

"Do they have the same master's program you are in now?"

"Basically. It's close enough," she replied. "I'm not so far into it that it'll make that much of a difference. They have a master's program in social work, which is much the same. UNLV is so close to home, the drive will be easy, and I can save money on rent living with you guys."

"True, but I feel terrible and so will your mother."

"She'll feel terrible having me as company during the day? Thanks a lot, Dad."

"That's not what I meant, Kristine," he answered. "She knows how much you enjoy ASU."

"Honestly, I could take it or leave it."

Porter could feel that same sense of hopelessness rising up again in Kristine's voice. Some of this conversation was about Ellen, sure, but much of it was also about Kristine and her state of depression. Porter knew whatever was eating at his daughter was not going away anytime soon. He could not focus on her as much as he would like. The RICO case was building and with Ellen being so ill, his focus was limited. Maybe having her come home, and being able to watch her closer, was a smart move.

"Kristine, I want you to be where you want to be," he stated, "and if it means you live here and go to UNLV, that's fine with me."

"Then its settled."

"Not quite. I have one stipulation."

"Stipulation?"

"You're going to be helping out a lot with mom and the house. I will be paying you, just like I would pay someone coming in from an agency."

"You're crazy, Dad."

"No, I'm not crazy. Think about it. You're not only giving up classes at ASU, but you'll be giving up the job you have on campus. That's your money you'll be losing out on."

"We'll talk about that one when I get home."

"Okay, but we will only be talking about how much I'll be paying you," Porter demanded.

"Tell mom I love her and I'll see her soon."

"I will. When you start wrapping up your current classes and talking to your supervisor about your last day at work, we'll talk about when I need to come and get you."

"You'll probably have to bring the truck."

"No problem, Kristine. Talk to you soon," he replied. "Love you."

"Love you more."

THE PET SCAN WAS COMPLETE. Porter and Ellen sat together, again, waiting for Dr. Stevens to arrive. This had become a common occurrence. Waiting, listening, crying, holding, calming, hoping; hoping for miracles, for more sun-filled mornings, more star-filled evenings, more dreams fulfilled, more life with Porter and Kristine. But the news was not good.

Dr. Stevens walked in. "Hello, Ellen...Porter."

"Hello, Doctor," replied Porter. He could see the regret on her face. Porter had learned to read the body language of every suspect he had ever interrogated, and although Dr. Stevens was not a suspect, she was acting suspiciously and Porter could see it in her eyes.

"Ellen, how have you been feeling?"

"Tired. No energy. No drive to get moving," she answered.

"Have you had an appetite of any kind?"

"Somewhat, but most food doesn't sound good to me. I feel like it goes back to the energy thing. I just don't feel like I want to waste my strength eating. I know that sounds weird."

"That's more typical than you may think. You need the food for energy, but you don't have the energy to consume it."

"How was the scan, Doctor?" asked Porter.

"That was my next topic for discussion," she said, "and it may answer some of the questions behind Ellen's issues."

"What is a PET scan, exactly?" asked Ellen.

"Think of it as a very specific way of looking into your body, as a whole," she answered. "PET means Positron Emission Topography. That radioactive stuff we put into your system helps us see exactly where any problems may be arising throughout your body."

"And?" Ellen pushed.

"We have found a couple new spots I'm concerned about."

"Jesus Christ," Porter tried to whisper under his breath, but it came out louder than he expected.

"That's perfectly fine," Dr. Stevens responded. "I don't blame you."

"Where?" Ellen asked.

"We see spots on your brain and your liver."

"What do we do?" asked Porter, clearly stunned by the news. He now knew that Kristine's offer to come home and help take care of Ellen couldn't have come at a better time.

"I'd recommend a series of targeted radiation and chemotherapy treatments," Stevens answered directly. "Let's get aggressive and see what kind of progress we can make."

"I guess the options aren't very appealing," said Ellen. She too could see into her doctor's eyes and hear the sense of urgency in her voice.

"How's this going to make her feel?"

Dr. Stevens looked at Ellen, then back at Porter. "Honestly, she's going to feel worse before she feels better."

"When do I start?"

"I'll give you more information regarding a scheduling of treatments before you leave today but expect the first round to begin within a few days. We want to get moving on this as soon as possible."

Porter and Ellen looked at each other. They knew those looks they shared. The sadness, the pain of her struggle, the guilt he felt witnessing his wife's suffering, wishing it were him. When Dr. Stevens left the exam room, Ellen leaned toward Porter and began to cry. He held her tightly; with all the resolve he could muster. She could not see the tortured expression on Porter's face, but his eyes filled with puddles of despair.

While driving home, Porter opened up about Kristine's offer to come home.

"Ellen, I received a call from Kristine."

"Is she okay?"

"She seemed okay," he hedged, "but she's really worried about you."

"You didn't tell her about my tests."

"We've been over this Ellen. We can't shut her out completely."

"Porter? I hope you didn't ask her to…"

Porter interrupted. "To come home? I didn't ask, no. She surprised me with the news."

"I don't want her to postpone her schooling."

"She wants to come home to help out with you. Keep you company when I'm at work."

"What about school? Her work?"

"She's giving notice to her work, and she's going to finish out the two classes she is currently taking."

"Then what?"

"She's going to start up at UNLV, at night."

"What girl in her twenties wants to stay at home with her sick mother?"

"Ellen, please don't think of it that way. She wants to come home," he said. "I'm going to pay her, since she won't have a job and she will be continuing with her master's degree. She said the UNLV program is similar to the one she's in and should crossover easily."

"I guess it would be nice to have her here, but I'm going to be so sick. I don't want her to see me that way."

"I think you're going to be happy she's home, Ellen. I'm sure it will lift your spirits. Don't you think?"

"Honestly, I do," she answered. "Maybe she's going to need us as much as we need her."

TWELVE

PORTER AND HIS TEAM worked tirelessly building a case against the Hell Riders. At the same time, he tried to do the impossible task of staying focused. Kristine was settled in at home, spending a lot of time with Ellen. She realized for the first time how sick her mother truly was and helped take care of her during the day. Kristine was able to transfer to UNLV and enter two night classes. Taking care of her mom and studying kept her busy. Although, she was never busy enough to wipe away the memory of her rape. Focusing much of her attention on her mother gave her a sense of worth. Would that be enough to help rid her of the psychological throbbing she couldn't shake? The pain became physical, as well. Porter was glad to have Kristine home. He felt as though he would be able to watch over his wife and troubled daughter. He had no clue what was going on with her, but he thought if she was living under his roof, he might get to the bottom of whatever was disturbing her.

For this moment in time, it was imperative that Porter wrap up the RICO case that had been going on now for nearly two years. His meeting with Federal Prosecutor Sanchez gave him hope that his life might just return to some semblance of normal.

Porter entered Sanchez's office for a one-on-one meeting to discuss final plans in the RICO case.

"Lieutenant Steele, please have a seat."

"Thank you, Ms. Sanchez."

"Don't be so damn formal. Call me Gabi."

"Just a habit, Gabi."

He was always known as the guy on the department that was respectful to the women he worked with. Sanchez appreciated his professionalism, because it made her job dealing with aggressive cops just that much easier. She was a tough lawyer but needed full cooperation with Porter and his team to build a RICO case that would stick. There was no room for error.

"I wanted to meet with you and give you an update on where I'm at with the case," said Sanchez.

"I'm interested in knowing what else we need to do. It's been two years now."

"I know that seems like a long time, but we are close."

"How close?"

"Very close."

"I think Detective Rockwell is getting worn down. He needs out."

"I agree. The reality is, I will be ready to bring indictments within the next sixty to ninety days."

"I can live with that. I like the sound of sixty more. Can that happen?" asked Porter.

"Possibly. Considering nothing bad happens within that timeline that will throw a wrench into the case."

"How many Hell Riders will be going down?"

"I have solid, winnable cases on the seven or eight guys you are focused on."

"So, we are looking at a lot of years?"

"If everything goes as planned, these guys will be looking at eight to twelve years. Some less, some more. I'm not promising anything."

"Danny Trask will be getting the most, I hope?"

"For sure...that's a given...if we need some of the lower-level players to testify against him, they may get somewhat of a break."

"But the core group of Trask, Carlin, Severs and Emerson are going down for a long stay behind bars?"

"Absolutely. No exceptions?"

"Keeping Detective Rockwell safe is paramount."

"I am aware that every day that passes for John
will be dangerous."

"What will be done with Ray Caruso?" he asked.

"I think we need to devise a plan to get him out, safely. I know he's a piece of shit, but..."

"...a valuable piece of shit." Porter finished her thought.

"There is no arguing with that, but dealing with this element of society is extremely risky. Ray Caruso is no exception," she reminded. "He will be doing some time. There's no way around that."

Porter shrugged. "Like I said. A piece of shit, but a valuable one."

"Put a plan together. It's going to have to involve Detective Rockwell."

"What's your timeframe for this? When do you want Ray Caruso out of there?"

"You have less than a month to deal with Caruso."

"I'll take care of it and let you know what we come up with."

Porter stood and reached out to shake Prosecutor Sanchez's hand. He turned and walked out, then called home, worried about Ellen. The RICO case was finally winding down. If things went smoothly there were going to be several Hell Rider club members serving an extended stay at a federal penitentiary. A couple of months didn't seem like a long time to wait for indictments, arrests, and prosecutions. But ninety days could seem like a lifetime in the world of undercover work.

Danny Trask was getting very paranoid. It was as if he felt that his world was about to come crashing in and had no control of what was going to happen. The dilemma haunted him. He had no tangible reason for the hyper distrust he was feeling. Or did he have a good reason, but just couldn't fully comprehend where his overwhelming feelings of paranoia were coming from?

First, and foremost, his animosity for Ray Caruso was becoming a barrier to leading his organization. Getting rid of Caruso was now a daily consideration. Finding another meth cook became a secondary issue. He resolved he could remedy that problem in a short period of time. Trask seemed to be the only one in the club who did not trust Ray. His decision? Take care of this Ray problem himself.

There was a time when Danny Trask had no qualms about eliminating the enemy. And even though he was never prosecuted, he had in fact murdered at least four other rival biker gang members. But this time the target was different. Perhaps Trask was simply aging, and his role as the Hell Rider's leader was burning him out. Or could it be his paranoia was causing him to question this decision? Whatever the reason, there was an amusing irony to his madness. Trask was about to order the one person whom he should not trust at all to eliminate Ray Caruso for him. And that was Rocky Danner. Or as Trask would learn soon enough, Detective John Rockwell.

Danner's phone rang. The voice on the other end of the line was familiar. "Meet me down at the Hard Times ASAP."

"What time?" Danner asked.

"Within a half hour. Don't be late. It's important," Trask said.

"I'll be there. Is everyone else going to be there?"

"No, just you and me. This will be private."

"Is Ray working the bar?"

"I just told you that it's going to be you and me. There's no one at the bar right now."

It was obvious that Trask was getting annoyed at all of the questions Danner was asking. After all, he still was not looked upon as one of the core members of the club. That would take a long time or take a special show of dedication to the club. Trask's bizarre behavior was beginning to display itself more and more lately. As a detective, Rockwell was trying to determine if Trask's recent distrust was aimed at him, or someone else. That was the reason Rockwell asked so many questions. He had to survive these final months of the operation, but Trask was becoming unpredictable.

Being alone with Danny Trask could be a major safety issue for anyone, let alone an undercover cop. Just because he says they will be alone, doesn't mean he won't employ secret security measures outside of the Hard Times. Trusting Trask was becoming more and more difficult for all of the club members at this point. Being an undercover cop embedded in this club, for almost two years now, made things just that much riskier. It was not possible, this late in the game, to refuse Trask's orders. Danner headed straight to the tavern for their private meeting.

DANNER WALKED INTO the tavern and scanned the room. He couldn't see Ray Caruso behind the bar. There were no customers, or other Hell Riders, inside. The last time Danner let his guard down, for just a second, he was brutally blindsided with a fist to the jaw. He took a few steps inside, calmed his breathing, and continued scanning the bar.

"Back here!" He heard Trask yell but could not see him.

"Where?"

"In the back room, over here," Trask repeated.

"Okay," Danner said as he approached the table. He was sitting alone in the corner. Trask's back was to the wall. "What's up?"

"Come and sit down and have a beer and I'll tell you what's up."

Danner pulled up a chair, looked around the room again, nervously hoping they were alone. He grabbed his beer and took a long swig. "Why do you need to meet with me, alone? The boys are usually here with you. They're gonna miss the party," he laughed, hoping a little humor would lighten the serious atmosphere. The tension emanating from Trask was palpable.

"This is no party...just a meeting...an important meeting."

"I get it," said Danner. "What can I help you with? You're happy with the products we're building for you down at Iron Horse, I hope."

"This isn't about Iron Horse, and the stuff you guys are building. I have no problem with that."

"That's good. We need the work. We want you to be happy."

"I have another job for you."

"And what job is that?"

"It's about Ray."

"Caruso?"

"Yeah, Ray Caruso."

"What's going on with him?"

"That's a good fucking question. I'm not so sure, but I don't like Ray working for us anymore."

"And why's that?"

"I don't trust him."

"He's a good cook, right?"

"He's a good cook. That has nothing to do with it."

"What don't you like about the guy?"

"Did I fucking stutter? I just said I don't trust him."

"I know what you said. What's going on with him?"

"So, now you're the goddamn boss of the Riders, is that it?"

"Don't get me wrong. I'm just asking."

"You ask too many fucking questions."

"That's just the bike builder in me. I want the customer to be satisfied."

"This isn't about bike building. I need Ray removed. For good. Gone."

"Why me?" asked Danner. "What about Bear? Or Hammer? Even Stump could take care of your Caruso problem. He'd enjoy it."

Detective Rockwell was hoping that it was not obvious to Trask that he was nervously breaking away from his undercover character, but he was trying to bide some time. He needed to think about his next response. Maybe this was a test to see if he truly was a cop. Rockwell had no clue at this point what Trask knew about him. What has he found out? Maybe he was intentionally putting him into a corner to see how he reacted.

It was clear that Trask wanted Ray Caruso killed, even though he was never about to use those exact words. Detective Rockwell was prudently walking a very fine line. This was no time to panic. After more than two years, even he was beginning to question his own identity. He had to be precise with his reaction to Trask's demand. *Keep playing the role of Rocky Danner.* Refusing a hit order from the boss and trying to push it off onto Bear, or one of the underlings, might get Caruso murdered. He was going to have to accept the hit job, police officer or not.

"I think Caruso might be a cop. Or at least a fucking snitch," said Trask.

"Why do you think that?" asked Danner, feeling his blood pressure rise. Trask was staring directly into the eyes of a cop and didn't even know it. At least he hoped he didn't know it. What kind of game was this guy playing?

"Ray bothers me. And when people bother me, it's because something is fucked up. He needs to go."

"It's just a gut feeling?"

"A strong gut feeling, and I need you to take care of the problem."

"What are you going to do for a cook?"

"What do you care? You don't run this chapter, do you Danner?"

"I want to keep building bikes and help you move your product. Aren't you going to need a cook if you're going to keep selling crystal?"

"I'll deal with getting a new cook. Do you want to move up in this club or not?"

"If I take out Caruso, I move up? Above Bear?"

"Who the fuck do you think you are?" Trask scowled. A vein in his forehead pulsated. "This isn't a goddamn job interview."

"Just seeing what I can get out of this deal. Killing somebody is damn serious business."

"You'll move up. Over Hammer and Stump for sure, and you'll also be respected. Even feared. That's more important in this game."

"I'll take care of Ray for you, but it's gonna be my way, or I won't do the job."

"What do you mean...your way?"

"No Bear, no Hammer and no Stump getting in my fucking way, screwing things up. It'll be me taking care of Ray my way, with no interference. Clean. Quick. And nontraceable. They can't interfere."

"I'll agree to that. I like it better that way. I don't want them involved. They all like Ray. They'll be pissed. I want this to be done quietly. I want this done soon. I don't want my name connected to Ray's disappearance. The less I know about this hit, the better."

"Then I'll take care of it."

Trask raised his beer and gave Danner a nod. There were no more words to be spoken. There were only expectations left hanging in the air. Expectations that would test Detective Rockwell's imagination. He had an idea that came to him as he sat there in silence, finishing his beer, staring back at a troubled man who had lost his way many years ago. This was a man with no excuse for the life he lived. There was no explanation. There was no rationalization. There could be no justification, other than whatever it was that soiled his soul.

In a world where there is always a long list of excuses for bad behavior, Detective Rockwell could not think of a single one that would explain a man like Danny Trask. Rockwell remembered being told, as a special forces soldier, in this world there are men who are evil for evil's sake. And although he believed in evil, witnessing pure evil sitting across the table from him was an eye-opening experience. Trask was one of those men. All Detective Rockwell could think about was how he counted the days until Trask was placed into handcuffs, standing alone in silence, listening to the sound of a steel prison door slamming.

Both men stood to leave the bar. Trask spoke one last time.

"I will need to know exactly when the job is done?"

Danner replied, "You'll know. I'll make sure you know."

THIRTEEN

PORTER AND KRISTINE ENTERED the building. The walls were made of red brick, rough stones adorning the corners, with an entrance of wide double doors. Glass windows on each side running the height of the doors, and an expansive entry way, obviously to accommodate large numbers of people. It was eerily quiet. They were greeted by a partially bald elderly gentleman with wire rim glasses. He wore a black single-breasted suit over a stark white, stiff, dress shirt, without button down collars. His necktie was black, revealing faint gray pinstripes designed at a slight angle. The man wore gleaming black wingtip dress shoes, which were seldom worn by the younger generation. Noticeable, was his empathetic three-quarter smile.

"Good afternoon, folks. You are here for the Ellen Steele service?"

"We are. I'm Porter Steele and this is my daughter, Kristine."

The somber man pointed them to the correct room. "I'm sorry for your loss," he said, as they passed by.

Porter and Kristine were an hour early to meet with the funeral home manager to make sure everything was in order. Family members were asked to arrive thirty minutes early. This would allow for private time with Ellen, before friends and acquaintances arrived to pay their respects.

Ellen was the love of Porter's life. He seemed so strong to those who watched from the outside but looks can be deceiving. He was a broken man. There was nowhere to turn and no one to turn to. Just emptiness filled this day. Kristine was fragile. He felt an obligation to hold her up during this time. After all, his only child, in her twenties, lost the mother that raised her, loved her, and supported her in everything she did. He did his best to greet those who came. The funeral home was as they always are; clean, solemn, sacred, eerily quiet, and pensive. The religious music played unobtrusively in the background. It was as if it was hardly noticed, yet if it were not playing the silence would be unbearable.

The visitation line of people was long. The suits were black and the shirts were bright white. Dresses were dark and conventional. Their faces were reverential and their gaits were measured and deliberate as they approached Porter and Kristine. Those familiar words, *please accept my condolences*, rolled off the tongues of many who knew Ellen as a wonderful, gentle, loving person.

Porter was in a fog. He was doing his duty, but his mind would not allow him to take in the full impact of the finality of Ellen's death. Everything was surreal. Was this truly happening? Had their lives reached this distant moment of inevitability? Operation Iguana had escaped his thoughts entirely. It was amazing how trivial important duties become in one's life, when the only things that truly matter are lost. When the only loving partner in your life is taken. Would Porter survive this ordeal? Maybe the brain works in mysterious ways. Perhaps his mind and body were creating an impenetrable defensive shield, which allowed his physical being to stand tall and face the onslaught of those who communicated their sympathies. Those that would soon walk out that set of heavy doors and begin again to focus on their own lives and their own fragilities. To consider their own uncertain demise. It was always just a matter of time.

Time was the friend of the young, yet the enemy of the old. At least that is how it was perceived. But even the young sometimes viewed time as just a long sentence of a life filled with pain. Kristine showed signs of this. Porter could see it but could not understand why. Now that Ellen was gone, how would this affect his only daughter? How would she handle the void? How would she perceive her own given time? This worried him to the core, and as he stared down at Ellen's still and motionless body, and cursed her unforgiving killer, he felt an overwhelming loss of control.

Mourners came and went, one by one, some quickly without many words, and some as slow as molasses, sharing stories that never seemed to have an ending. He had to keep telling himself that this was a time for people to grieve her loss as well. For Porter, it seemed as though there was this delicate balance. The pure sharing of emotion with everyone that passed through the line, and a certain funeral service protocol. One which reminded him to keep the line moving. A protocol that he had witnessed over the years but had never contemplated its impact on those left behind. He was always one of those standing in the line, just passing by, speaking those familiar words. *Please accept my condolences.*

Porter was only a child when his parents died. Remembering their funeral was not so much about pain, but a sense of guilt for barely recalling the pain. It was there. He knew he felt it. He remembered his grandfather taking control. Porter never once imagined that Papa was hurting deep down inside. He had just lost his son and daughter-in-law in a horrific plane crash and was faced with raising an eleven-year-old boy. Perhaps, he didn't have the time to grieve. When Papa passed away, he was in his nineties, had lived a full, vigorous life, and would have never wanted anyone to grieve his passing. Papa was all about the celebration of life.

Porter knew his grandfather wanted him to be happy, to take over the ranch someday, to fly his cherished plane, and always keep looking ahead. Looking forward toward the next sunrise. That's how Papa Steele walked through life. That's how Porter was raised as well. At this moment though, he did not feel as strong as his grandfather. Even though Porter could never be certain, perhaps Papa felt the sting of death in the exact same manner as he did. Lost, lonely, and as fragile as a newborn colt fighting to get up onto his feet. Struggling in that single moment to simply stay upright.

The service was as peaceful as a funeral service can be. Sadness surrounded Porter and Kristine. There were some smiles, brought on by those who reminisced. There were tears of joy, tears of pain and hurt, and tears that fell without reason. But life went on. People began to leave. There were places to go, lives to be led. There would be no long line of unhurried cars to a nearby cemetery. That was not in their plans. Porter and Ellen had planned on a long and wonderful retirement, back at the ranch in northwest Arizona. They had their burial plots at a small cemetery just six miles down a long, secluded road from their ranch house. Ellen would be taken there. It was peaceful in this place. A small piece of land, under an old oak tree, awaited her arrival, yearning to protect her. She would rest there, not knowing that her soulmate would visit her every Sunday until there were no more Sundays. It was a long way from Las Vegas. It was a long way from the streets Porter worked for so many years. It was a long way from the hectic pace of a gambler's town. Porter knew she would be happier there, not far from the ranch.

Shortly after the service, a small luncheon was held at one of Ellen's favorite restaurants. Friends and family met for a couple of hours, reminiscing, mourning, remembering, and wondering what may have been. Porter arranged with the funeral home to transport Ellen three days later to her final resting place. The drive was over a hundred miles to the Oak Hill Cemetery, just six miles from the ranch in Arizona. Porter planned to meet with them and complete the final burial. He felt he needed the solace of his ranch, as quickly as possible, to unwind. He suggested to Kristine that they drive there as soon as they could pack a couple of bags of clothes.

"Let's go to the ranch now, Kristine."

"What about the relatives, Dad?"

"I don't mind if they come with us, if they want, but chances are they will have to get back home soon. You know how it is. Grandma is not in the best of health. I'm sure Uncle Bill wants to get on the road and make sure she gets home safely. Katie and Steve have to catch a flight tonight to get back to the east coast and Aunt Laura will be leaving in the morning, back to Texas."

"So, it'll just be you and me?"

"Just you and me, that's how it is now." Porter forced a half grin. His eyes welled up with tears, quietly regretting the harsh reality that Ellen would never be at the ranch with him again.

Ellen's mother attended the funeral, but she was already in her eighties and not in the best of health. She was able to come to the funeral because of Ellen's older brother, William. He was kind enough to drive his mother from Scottsdale to be at Ellen's service. William had decided that it was best to get on the road, while there was still daylight, and drive his mother back home. She resided there in an assisted living facility. Ellen's sister, Katie, and her husband, flew in from Durham, North Carolina for the service. But they had to catch a flight that evening to make it back home, so they could go to work the next day.

Porter's only living blood relative, his older sister Laura, attended the service as well. This was a special gift for him, because he was not sure if his only sibling would be able to make it. Laura lived in Houston and over the years she had become estranged from her younger brother. It was not because they didn't love each other, but it was because Laura was almost ten years older than Porter. She was only a junior at the University of Houston, when their parents died. After their parents' funeral, Laura found the strength to finish school, find a job, get married and reside in Texas. She has lived there ever since. Laura has a good husband, a great career, and a wonderful life.

When it came to Porter, Laura simply let Grandpa Steele raise him. She was not able, at her age, and he knew it. Laura dealt with their parents' death in the only way she knew how as a twenty-one-year-old girl. She grieved, went back to school, fell in love with her boyfriend and tried very, very hard to forget. And although Porter never believed it was intentional, or with one ounce of malice, Laura also found a way to forget about him and Grandpa Steele. They became invisible.

When Laura walked through the door at the funeral home and hugged Porter, it would have been difficult to separate them. The memory of their own parents' funeral came back to them both and they were overwhelmed with emotion. They loved each other. They understood each other. They wished each other well. They just happened to live totally separate lives. They both knew, as brother and sister, there was no animosity for how their lives took different paths. Porter always wondered how close they would have become had their parents lived on into their later years. Living in the past wasn't Papa's way and because of him, it wasn't Porter's way either. He could only look forward, toward the future. It was all he knew.

For now, it had become how Porter knew it would be. Just him and his daughter, heading out on a somber hundred-mile trek toward the ranch. Only a few more days and he would have to bury his beloved wife and return to work. Operation Iguana would soon be coming to an end.

THE NEXT COUPLE of days at the ranch would be difficult. Porter and Kristine were alone. For the first time, he realized how much Ellen was the glue that kept the conversation going. She was the communicator. The consoler. She made sure the days and nights were enjoyable. She was the connection, and sometimes buffer, within the relationship between Porter and his daughter.

He didn't know how to approach Kristine about her state of depression. He didn't know the right words to say. There was no way for him to understand what was happening. His assumption was that much of what was going on had to do with Ellen's illness and death. Porter assumed that when problems with Kristine arose, they were issues surrounding her graduation from college. Or perhaps the fear of tackling a new career. She didn't know what she wanted to do with her life. Wasn't this normal? Don't all young people her age go through a rough time when their lives change so significantly? Facing the inevitability of the real world is difficult for everyone.

The questions he asked himself always justified what was going on in her life. He never imagined that there could have been any one thing that was overwhelming her. The real reason. Porter would have never thought to ask questions that were personal: Has someone hurt you? Have you been assaulted? Has someone done something bad to you? These questions never crossed his mind. Why would they? What he saw at work, he couldn't imagine happening to his family.

Porter looked at the world through a completely different lens. His life was made stronger from adversity. He came from a generation of people who were convinced it was the hard times that made a person stronger. But this was different. Porter didn't know the right questions that would elicit the right answers. Never once had he thought that Kristine needed counseling, or medication. His brain was not allowing him to go there. Porter always rationalized her state of mind. *She's going through a rough patch*, was a familiar justification. He never once thought that he was only protecting himself from pain. He didn't have the strength to tackle anything more serious. He didn't have the courage to face what could be a graver problem with his daughter. After burying his wife, he didn't have the emotional capacity to face any serious issues that would be difficult for him to conquer.

Kristine's mental health issues from the rape festered inside her stomach, like a pot of boiling stew. She didn't have the wherewithal to understand how to shut off the heat; to stop the churning; to calm the raging storm that was building inside. Porter told himself, *when Operation Iguana is over and everything at work has calmed down, I'm going to completely focus on Kristine and see what I can do to help her.*

IT WAS THE FINAL DAY at the ranch and Porter and Kristine decided to get dressed up for their final goodbye to Ellen. He put on his one black suit, white dress shirt, and solid black tie. In his right hand, he held onto his black Stetson cowboy hat. Kristine put on a bright, yellow dress. Ellen's favorite color. A local funeral home had gone out to Oak Hill that morning and prepared the burial site. There would be no fanfare. There would be no sermons. There would only be Porter, Kristine, and Ellen.

He drove the six miles, in the truck, to the cemetery. The drive was quiet. The morning sun had broken through the clouds. There was light dew on the ground. This would be worse than the memorial service, where so many people surrounded them. They were supported by coworkers, friends, and family. There was no time to pause and think about how much they loved their sweet Ellen. Kristine noticed her father starting to tear up, but he never made a sound. She reached over with her left hand and placed it in his right. He squeezed her hand, as if to thank her for being by his side. They drove up the long dirt road, quiet sniffles coming now and again from them both. Silence filled the cab, until they reached the peaceful lot that Porter had reserved at Oak Hill.

There were two men, ordinary men, waiting for them. They were in work clothes but stood respectful. These men knew their job. They knew the sadness that always waited for them to complete their work. The hole had been dug the day before. Ellen's casket hung motionless, above the hole. It rested upon three straps, attached to the casket-lowering device, which was used to lower it downward into the vault. Her final resting place. It seemed so utilitarian, but Porter knew how things were done. He didn't expect anything different.

Porter and Kristine got out of the truck and walked together, holding hands, toward Ellen. One of the men had placed two chairs on the ground, facing Ellen's casket. They knew Porter would want some private time. One of the men approached him. It was obvious that he told him to take as much time as needed and that the two men would return after a while and finish their job. Porter shook his hand and sat down in the chair next to his daughter. Their final thoughts, prayers and special memories began to well up inside. This was it. This somber moment had arrived. Time, again, showed its persistence.

Porter stood first and laid a dozen roses on top of the casket. He kissed his fingertips and gently touched them to the glossy surface. He whispered, but Kristine still heard his gentle words. *Goodbye my love. I will always miss you. Thank you for our wonderful life.* Kristine stood and walked up next to her dad. She placed one hand on his lower back, comforting him. She had picked one beautiful desert lily, Ellen's favorite wildflower, and placed it on top of the roses. One petite, cream-colored flower expressed Kristine's love for her mother. Abundant, rich, and although childlike, lasting. It was as though she were telling her mother for the last time, *you were my rock. Thank you for your love and always being there for me. No one understood me like you.*

Porter and Kristine sat for only ten minutes. Perhaps the pain was too much. He stood and hugged his daughter, telling her to take as much time as she needed. He began to walk toward his truck. Kristine stood once again and began to cry as she placed both hands on her mother's casket, kneeling, mourning the loss of the woman that gave her life. She whispered one last message to her mother. One message that Porter was unable to hear. *I will see you again.* She turned and ran to catch up to her dad, so they could leave the cemetery together. Porter nodded toward the two workers, who had patiently waited nearby. Ambivalent, and afraid to leave Ellen alone, they began their solemn journey back to Las Vegas. Back to school. Back to Operation Iguana. Back to a certain loneliness that would haunt each of them in different ways. Yet haunt them no doubt.

FOURTEEN

LIEUTENANT STEELE WAS BACK on the job. He wasn't healed, by no means, but he was focused on the operation. Within a week of his return, the most important meeting of his career was about to take place. When Friday arrived, his nervous energy was intense. Law Enforcement personnel at the federal, county and state level and the Las Vegas Metropolitan Police Department were chomping at the bit.

It was two p.m. and the much-anticipated meeting, which was being led by Federal Prosecutor Sanchez, was being held for one reason. To discuss a very important legal statute. The Racketeer Influenced and Corrupt Organizations Act, or RICO. The time had finally come. Ms. Sanchez was prepared to release the specifics of the indictments on each of the members of the Hell Riders to the assigned arrest teams. The indictments were based on a wide range of predicate offenses, which were committed by several core members of the Hell Riders. Porter was especially interested in the fates of the top four players in this two year plus grind: Danny Trask (Double Tap), Mike Carlin (Bear), Nick Emerson (Hammer), and Jake Severs (Stump).

Their criminal acts under this statute were many, and the necessary evidence was also well-documented. Prosecuting motorcycle club members under the RICO statute wasn't a leisurely walk in the park, but Prosecutor Sanchez was well aware of the legal challenges she would face. There were hurdles to clear, but she was confident that once certain players from the Hell Riders began to jump ship, most of the others would fall like proverbial dominoes.

The conference room at the LVMPD was full. A group of dedicated officers watched as Gabriela Sanchez entered the room. She was a formidable presence, due to her courtroom skills. Straightforward and professional, she was well-respected and made it clear that she appreciated the people sitting in front of her. These were the risk-takers.

"I want to thank all of you for being here today. Operation Iguana has been a major undertaking and there is a long list of people that I must thank. I want to start out by thanking the man in charge of this operation...Lieutenant Porter Steele. Porter, on behalf of my staff and everyone in this room, I want to again express our condolences for the passing of your wife, Ellen. We are glad to have you back with us, but we know this is an extremely difficult time for you and your family."

Porter lowered his head and then raised it appreciatively, looking around the room, as if to thank everyone for their support since the death of Ellen.

"I also want to thank two of Lieutenant Steele's supervisors for allowing us to, basically, kidnap and hold Porter hostage for the last couple of years," Ms. Sanchez joked. Everyone in the room laughed, fully aware of the amount of time dedicated to this operation.

"Captain Ryan. Deputy Sheriff Johnston. Thank you very much for your cooperation and leadership. I want to thank Special Agent William Jennings for his analytical guidance and supervision of our undercover officer, who was embedded in the Hell Riders during this operation. This was a dangerous and life-changing assignment, and our officer went above and beyond the call of duty. There will be a special thank you at a later date for this undercover officer, but for now he will remain nameless for this meeting. His safe removal from this undercover assignment within the Hell Riders organization is underway as we speak. My final thank you today is to Sergeant Martina Savala, who was the direct contact and go-to person for our undercover officer. Martina has proven that she has the supervisory skills to be an effective operations manager during tremendously sensitive and time-consuming cases. I know you're out there Martina, so thank you very much."

Sanchez was scanning the room for Sergeant Savala. She waved from the back of the room, graciously accepting the praise being placed upon her.

"Now, let's get to why we are all here today," Sanchez announced. "I have indictments on the following people: Daniel Trask, Michael Carlin, Nicholas Emerson, Jacob Severs, William Morrison, Nathan Thomas, Raymond Caruso, Samuel Wiggins, and Joseph Sterns. I also have warrants out of California drawn up for the arrest of one Vipers' member, Diego García, from Riverside. We are also giving assistance to the Toronto Police Service and the Ontario Provincial Police, in Canada, in regard to a major case they have built against biker clubs up north. There is one particular player in our RICO case they are interested in, and that is a man named Phillippe "the Frenchman" Gaudet. The following predicate offenses have been taken into consideration against the first nine men listed: drug trafficking, fraud, gambling, embezzlement, money laundering, and theft. Also, in Danny Trask's case, one count of conspiracy to commit murder. Lieutenant Steele is going to discuss Operation Iguana's strategic arrest plan. Porter, the floor is yours."

"Thank you, Ms. Sanchez," he replied. "Here's the run down on the arrest teams: We will have eight teams of seven officers. Three SWAT members will be utilized for the initial takedown. Then, two detectives for any initial interviewing that takes place at the arrest sites. Searches, seizures if called for. We will have two patrol officers for transport and scene security. You all should have the arrest team packets, with all assignments. We will be hitting the street and heading to each arrest site at the exact same time. This will take place at zero four hundred hours on Sunday morning. We will need everyone here by zero three hundred. Ready to go. We want to hit each target arrest site simultaneously. At least as close as possible. This renders it impossible for any of them to contact and warn each other. The element of surprise, precision and controlled necessary force, will benefit us. If all goes as planned, each suspect should be taken into custody in a swift and safe manner. We want their state of mind, during this stage of the operation, to be one of confusion. Also, reactionless, if that's even a word. That is exactly what we want. Quite frankly, any anticipation of excitement that you may have regarding these arrests should be considerably dampened. We want to overwhelm our targets with expertise and proficiency. This assignment should be boring if we are completely successful. I will take boredom any day of the week, people, over any of you getting injured or, God forbid, killed. These are violent men. We want to make these suspects feel like they never stood a chance."

Prosecutor Sanchez stepped forward and added her final words of encouragement. "The number one concern of mine in any operation is officer safety. Do not take any undo risks. I want everyone in this room to feel proud of the arrests you are all about to make and then I want you to get back here all in one piece, so you can continue a long successful career. Thank you again for your dedication."

Porter wrapped up: "Okay, let's all return here Sunday at zero three hundred hours, dressed and ready to go. It's time we all bring Operation Iguana to a safe and successful conclusion."

IT WAS SATURDAY AFTERNOON, just hours before the takedown of the Hell Riders, and Danny Trask was meeting with Mike Carlin at the Hard Times Tap. He needed to get an update on their Canada to Baja corridor methamphetamine operation. Both men were in a good mood. Carlin felt, to a certain degree, in charge of his own destiny when it came to the organization. He felt as though he was the one that made this growing operation a success. After all, it was Carlin that set up the deal with *the Frenchman* in Canada. Trask saw it a different way, although he was about to give Carlin his due. It was Trask that had the Vipers' connection in Riverside, and it was his connections in Baja that stretched their meth business to the far southwest.

Trask walked into the bar and sat down at a table with Carlin. He noticed a large leather bag sitting on the floor right next to Carlin's chair. They were the only ones at the tavern for the moment, but Trask took a quick walk around the bar anyway. His paranoia was on display. He was still overly cautious these days. Perhaps it was the rapid growth of their drug business, or the amount of cash flowing through his organization. Either way, it was eating away at his psyche.

One person noticeably absent these days from the bar was Ray Caruso. He was nowhere to be found. He hadn't been seen for at least a week now. Carlin had no knowledge of his whereabouts. Did Danny Trask know? Perhaps there was a good reason for his absence. Perhaps there was a violent reason for his absence. Trask knew, or at least thought he knew, the reason for Caruso's disappearance. Mike Carlin was not privy to Trask's recent meeting with Danner, so he had become confused about Ray Caruso's current role as meth cook and bartender for the club.

Trask sat down. "Update me, Bear."

"Things are rolling fast. Full bore."

"How's Canada doing?"

"Hot. Very hot," Bear smiled as he reached down and picked up the heavy, leather bag. "You'll see how hot."

"What do we have?"

"Hundred-K."

"We need to get it downstairs and into the safe."

"Are we going to take a little bonus from this haul?" Bear grinned. "We deserve it."

"Let's deal with that downstairs," Trask answered. "How are the Riverside deals working? Is my guy down there keeping his end of the bargain?"

"García is on top of things," Bear replied. "He always has the cash."

"Is Hammer working out?"

"Hammer and Danner have both been making runs down to Riverside. A lot of meth is being hauled down there and the money is rolling in."

"Baja?"

"That's beginning to take hold, but I can't say I totally trust your connections down there."

"What happened?"

"I've sent Stump down there for at least two initial meetings. I gave him a small amount of Caruso's crystal to take with him. You know, free of charge, to test our product."

"Trying to build some trust?"

"Yeah, you got to find ways to get these guys on board. Some free shit always helps."

"It does, but I'm not sure Stump can handle the Baja connection on his own."

"You want me to send Hammer with him next time?"

"No, send Danner with him instead."

"Danner? What are you talking about?"

"Let's face it. Danner is ten times smarter than Stump. We'll see what Danner is made of and let him negotiate the deal."

"I'll set it up, but you can deal with Hammer and Stump over this one. They're going to be really pissed off."

"Fuck those guys. They'll do what I tell them to do."

Trask and Carlin heard someone trying to get into the front door of the Hard Times. No one else was supposed to be coming to this meeting. Carlin used his foot to gently slide the leather bag under the table, keeping it out of plain view. Someone began pounding on the door, louder and louder, so Carlin went to see who it was. He yelled through the door.

"We're closed!"

"It's me. Rocky."

Carlin turned to Trask. "It's your boy."

"Let him in."

Carlin unlocked the door and let him inside. They both stared at each other. It was obvious that Danner would not be staying long. He had a look of determination on his face. He walked right past Bear.

"Where's Trask?"

"He's in the back." Carlin made it clear he was not a big fan of Danner. "What do you want?"

"I want Trask."

Danner walked straight back to the table where Trask was sitting. When he reached the table, he didn't say a word. He threw a photograph down on the table in front of him. "Just in case you're wondering."

Trask picked up the photo to see what Danner had brought him. "What's this?"

"It's your proof."

Carlin returned to the table as well. "What the fuck is going on?"

"Some business with the boss."

"What's up?" asked Bear, staring at Trask.

"A job I needed done," Trask said as he stared long and hard at the photo.

Carlin looked over Trask's shoulder. "What the hell is this?"

"It's Ray."

"Caruso?"

"Yeah, he no longer works for us."

"Goddammit D.T."

They both stared at the photo, not exactly sure what to think. Danner remained calm. Determined. Silent.

"I'm outta here," Danner stated as he turned around and headed straight for the front door. "I'd burn that if I were you. I'd burn it fast."

The photo was of Ray Caruso on his back, in a shallow grave, somewhere in the desert. His face was badly beaten, almost unrecognizable. There was bright red blood all over his head, face, chest, and clothing. There was still a lot of oxygen in the blood. The wounds were fresh. Both eyes were completely swollen shut. His body was half-covered with weeds and dirt. There appeared to be a gaping wound to his chest, which may have been intentional or an accidental strike of the shovel during the burial. It appeared as though Caruso was in the process of being buried, when Danner decided to take one last photo of his body. Proof of the murder. Trask and Carlin recognized Caruso's face, even though badly beaten, his clothing, and a gold chain he wore around his neck. But what they especially noticed was his prized watch. It was a Bvlgari Diagono Chronograph that he had purchased for sixteen thousand dollars the first time he got paid for the largest batch of meth he had cooked for the club. Ray always wore that watch on his left wrist when he worked. It was his outward sign that he had made the big time.

"Jesus Christ, Danner," Trask laughed. "You could have brought me that goddamn watch. It's worth a shitload of money. What fucking idiot buries a Bvlgari?"

Carlin glared at Trask, as Danner quietly walked toward the front door. He didn't know what to think. He was perplexed about the hit job.

"You better fucking explain yourself. Now."

Danner ignored the men and kept walking away. He didn't want to look back.

Trask shouted at him, "Get your ass back here!"

Danner froze just as he reached for the front door. Before he opened it, he turned to face Carlin and Trask. He was calm and collected. John Rockwell realized, in this very moment, he had finally mastered his role as Rocky Danner. All he needed now was to play the role to the very end.

"I said, get back here," Trask demanded.

Danner walked back toward the table. Carlin was standing and Trask was still sitting down, focusing on the photograph. Trask reached into his pants pocket with his right hand and removed a chrome lighter. With his left hand, he pulled an ashtray from across the table, so it was directly in front of him. He held the photograph over the ashtray and flicked his lighter. Trask ignited the bottom corner on fire and watched as it slowly began to burn. He held it up as long as he could, above the ashtray, until the entire photo was engulfed in flames. It went up quickly in a flash of orange heat. The edges of the photo burnt inward, black, crispy, and flaking as the fire crept toward his fingertips. He dropped the remaining burning embers into the ashtray, smiling at Danner. Questions began to swirl in Danner's brain. *Are these guys going to kill me now? I'm the only one that knows. I'm the one that produced the photo. Do I need to tell them I have another photo, just in case? Are they pissed? What's Bear going to do to me? Was this what Trask really wanted, or was this just a test?*

Danner took a step backwards, ready to defend himself. There was no way of knowing with these guys what was about to happen. Carlin was not even sure what his boss was going to do, if anything. Trask deliberately bent over, reached for the leather bag on the floor, under the table. He lifted it up onto his lap and unsnapped the buckles. Grabbing each side of the opening with both hands, he forcibly jerked it wide open. Danner could see the pile of cash inside, filled to the top. Trask reached in and pulled out a handful of bills and began to count. He reached out toward Danner. "Take this. You deserve it."

Mike Carlin watched in shock. His face was bright red. He was seething. Bear liked Ray Caruso, so he was not sure why in the hell he had to die. Why would Trask have Danner kill him? Carlin was furious. He just witnessed his boss hand Danner five thousand bucks and there was nothing he could do about it. It was the first time that it was perfectly clear to him that Danny Trask was helping Rocky Danner move up the ladder within the organization. Carlin sat in silence, envious of Danner's instant gain in status. Danner stuffed the cash down into his shirt and gradually backed away, turned toward the door, and walked out.

"What did you do to Ray, boss?"

"What needed to be done. That's all," Trask said. "I told you a while ago I didn't trust Ray anymore."

"So, you had Danner take him out?"

"Hey brother, there's no blood on your hands, or mine," he replied, "and that's exactly how I wanted it. Anyone goes down for Caruso's murder; it will be Danner. Not you. Not me."

"We need to find a new cook fast," Carlin pointed out.

"I've got somebody in mind."

"Who?"

"Danner's partner over at the Iron Horse."

"Stickler?"

"Yeah, why not? Hammer likes the guy. Says Stickler's smart as hell. He's very technically oriented when it comes to bike building. Hammer sees those sorts of things. Give him a break, Bear. I think Stickler could learn to cook meth quickly."

"What about Stump?"

Trask broke out laughing. "Stump? Are you kidding me. Our Stump. Cooking crystal meth? That guy could screw up a bowl of cereal. Goddamn, Bear. Would you really put Stump in a room full of chemicals? Jesus Christ man, he'd burn the Hard Times to the fucking ground."

"You're going to listen to Hammer now all of a sudden?" Carlin stood, walking in a full circle, his blood pressure rising. "What's the similarity between building motorcycles and cooking meth?"

"More than you think," said Trask. "Think about it for a minute. He goes step by step. Part by part. Following directions, even if it's just from memory. Details, details, details, my man. There's a recipe to follow when you cook meth, just like there's a recipe for building a beautiful bike."

"We're going to need him soon," Bear demanded. "I've heard this guy wants nothing to do with our club."

"I'll meet with him next week, when Danner isn't around," Trask smiled. "I'll change his mind."

Danny Trask was riding high. He felt more in control. Mike Carlin was his right-hand man and felt he was accepting his role in the organization, since the money was flowing in at record pace. Trask and Carlin went over behind the bar and Carlin removed the floor mat, lifting the trap door that led down to the basement, and the meth lab. They needed to hide their bag of cash. Trask started to reach down for the ladder but suddenly stopped. Instead, he opened the bag with the cash and removed ten thousand dollars, handing it to Carlin. "Here, take this. You worked hard for it. Don't mention it to Stump and Hammer though. This is between you and me. Think of it as a bonus for your work with *the Frenchman*. That's five for Danner and that's ten for you. That leaves eighty-five grand in this bag. It's going in the safe right now."

"What about you, boss?"

"I'll get mine, don't worry about it."

Trask climbed down into the meth lab and placed the leather bag of cash into the safe, locking it up. He was the only one who had access to all their money; a cool eight hundred and fifty thousand. As he looked around the lab, he thought about the murder of Ray Caruso. He thought about the drug operation he had developed. He thought about the organization he was building and for the first time in his life he felt as though he was more successful than his old man. He climbed up the ladder and Carlin helped him out. They both headed for the front door, locked up the tavern, and went on their way. Trask thought this was just the beginning of bigger and better things to come. He could not have been so wrong.

SUNDAY MORNING ARRIVED QUICKLY. It was zero three hundred hours, and a somewhat cool morning breeze was blowing through town. The moon hung like a painting and the stars dominated the sky. Every officer was on time, tension filled the conference room, and all were ready to move into the final phase of Operation Iguana. It had been a long time coming. Porter gathered the eight assigned arrest teams, so he could make sure everyone was with their specific group. Each team was numbered one through eight to make it simple for communication purposes. Each team leader had written arrest plans in hand. Each team was equipped with the proper tools for breaching doors or windows, and paperwork for effecting the necessary arrests. Evidence bags and tags for search and seizures, along with medical kits, were available for emergencies. There would be two ambulances on call, strategically placed in central locations to the arrest sites, prepared to respond to any serious medical issues that could arise during the arrests. Whether it was for police personnel involved or the suspects themselves. The officers loaded into eight separate unmarked, black police vans, prepared to head to their assigned arrest locations. Once their watches struck four o'clock in the morning, they would go.

At three fifty-eight a.m. Porter got on a secure portable radio channel and ordered the arrest phase of the operation to begin.

"Team leaders respond at my direction. Are all arrest teams in place and prepared to go? Team 1...are you ready?"

"Team 1...10-4...ready to go."

"Team 2?"

"Team 2...10-4...we're ready."

"Team 3?"

"Team 3...we are 10-4."

"Team 4?"

"Team 4...10-4, sir."

Right down the line, all eight teams acknowledged they were ready to roll. Porter gave the final order to move. "All teams are ready to go. Hit the streets and remember, your safety is a priority."

It was four a.m. and the arrest teams were on the move. The goal was to complete eight felony arrests, swiftly and effectively, of those indicted Hell Rider members. Riverside Police Department had their own plans to do a simultaneous early morning arrest of Vipers' member, Diego García. Expectations were high, so were the anxiety and nerves of many high-ranking police executives. Any major operation was dangerous. Porter felt the tension coming down from Deputy Chief Johnston and Captain Ryan. Although Ryan trusted Porter's instincts and his planning and tactical skills, he knew he needed to bring Operation Iguana to a safe, and successful conclusion.

The prosecution phase of Operation Iguana would be left to Gabriela Sanchez, but it was Porter's responsibility to make sure every last defendant made it to court in one piece. There would be no room for any legal issues, which could give an edge to any of the indicted Hell Riders when it was their time to face a judge or jury. Fingers were crossed and hopes were high that no one would be injured, or killed, during the arrests. The plan called for swift, aggressive, but professional, arrest tactics. Reducing the risk of injury to any person involved was a priority. Even the ones that lived their lives on the wrong side of the thin blue line.

If all went smoothly, nine angry defendants would be whisked away from the warmth of their secure homes and introduced to an eight-by-eight cell of steel and concrete at the LVMPD lockup. Then, and only then, would Porter's interrogators get their shot at breaking these guys down. Taking one last chance at securing confessions, codefendant statements, or even one slight accidental mumble of implicating words. Anytime an offender speaks, it could help prove their guilt beyond a reasonable doubt. On the interrogators' menu, were proffer agreements for those that would give up the goods. Those willing to cooperate in order to help take down higher ranking members of the Hell Riders, and other felons as well.

WHEN THE ARRESTS went down, the defendants were taken by surprise, stunned by the early morning raids. There were no chances to fight back. As the days and weeks passed, many confessions were had. Many Hell Riders tried to save their own skins. Proffers were structured, and plea agreements accepted. In the end, Prosecutor Sanchez was pleased with the outcome. The Riverside prosecutor contacted Ms. Sanchez with the news of a confession from Diego García. He was offered a reduced sentence for damaging testimony against the four primary defendants: Trask, Carlin, Emerson and Severs. That was to be expected, and even though it was a dangerous game to play, it didn't stop Trask and Carlin from offering to testify against Phillippe Gaudet, in the Toronto case. They were willing to give up valuable information on their Baja connection.

They both knew how to play the game. It was a badge of honor to go to prison, but Carlin and Trask didn't want to spend the next twenty years behind bars. They both would testify against each other if they had to. Minimizing the damage to the club, and to themselves, was crucial, but Trask's theory was basic business. Take the best deal you can cut and get on with doing your time.

Word got out quickly that both Rocky Danner and Lonnie Stickler were never located and taken into custody. They were nowhere to be found. Perhaps, they went back to wherever it was they came from. Nick Emerson learned that Danner and Stickler had closed up the Iron Horse Garage just days before the arrests. As suspicious as that may have seemed, Trask couldn't bring himself to believe Danner was a confidential source, let alone an undercover cop. That would offend his keen sense of street smarts. What kind of undercover cop could get away with killing someone? Trask knew for a fact that Danner had killed Ray Caruso. No undercover cop could ever get away with murder. He saw the photograph with his own eyes. Just as his right-hand man Carlin did.

Questions such as these began to keep Trask up at night, lying in a damp concrete cell, while awaiting sentencing. He settled it in his own mind. Trask convinced himself that Rocky Danner killed Ray Caruso. He brought him the photograph of his body, took the five thousand in cash, and shut down the Iron Horse garage so he could get out of town. Trask and Carlin both saw the impact Caruso's murder had on Danner. They could see it in his eyes that afternoon at the Hard Times Tap, when he interrupted their meeting. They could both tell that he was anxious to get out of Vegas and leave Ray's murder behind him.

Trask's self-serving theory at least allowed him to rationalize the ongoing chain of events. It also minimized what he feared was culpability in his own demise. Would Trask decide to testify that Danner actually killed Ray Caruso to save his own hide? Danner had to have ratted out Trask, regarding Caruso's murder. Where is the warrant for the murder of Caruso? And where is his body? To a certain degree, Trask hoped Danner and Stickler got away. After all, they were two guys with intimate knowledge of Trask's operation. If they escaped prosecution, they would not be around town to testify against him.

PROSECUTOR SANCHEZ called a press conference in front of the Lloyd D. George Federal Courthouse on Las Vegas Boulevard. The courthouse building was still relatively new, so a RICO case brought upon a violent biker gang was like a christening. Ms. Sanchez stood tall and proud, visually intimidating, and powerful. She was prepared to share with the community limited information regarding Operation Iguana. There was a distinguished group of high-ranking officials stoically standing in a row behind her, representing law enforcement. Captain James Ryan, Lieutenant Porter Steele, S.A. William Jennings, Sergeant Martina Savala, and one unrecognizable detective, named John Rockwell. It was a proud day for law enforcement, but operations such as Operation Iguana took a toll on those involved. Although not always visually obvious, the stress, the anxiety, and the never-ending state of life on the edge from adrenaline dumps, were the direct cause of an invisible form of torture. Post-traumatic stress disorder, PTSD, was merciless. Even so, it was the public story of conquering the enemy that always came first. The headlines told that story:

SUNDAY EDITION *Las Vegas* **Review-Journal**

The Hell Riders Gamble and Lose

Operation Iguana officially began in the year 1999 with high hopes, intense strategic planning, and the relentless pursuit of justice. A multi-jurisdictional team of dedicated law enforcement officers from the Federal, Municipal and County levels worked in lockstep. The multi-year investigation has led to several federal indictments under the Racketeer Influenced and Corrupt Organizations Act (RICO). At this time, all defendants have negotiated plea agreements, so there are no scheduled trial dates on the court dockets. The following is a list of defendants indicted, the criminal charges listed in the RICO indictments, and the sentences they are facing:

Daniel C. Trask: *Conspiracy to Commit Murder, Bribery, Drug Trafficking, Fraud, Money Laundering, Gambling and Theft*

Sentence: 168 months

Michael D. Carlin: *Drug Trafficking, Bribery, Fraud, Money Laundering, Gambling, Obstruction of Justice, and Theft*
Sentence: 156 months

Nicholas P. Emerson: *Drug Trafficking, Fraud, Gambling, and Theft*
Sentence: 132 months

Jacob J. Severs: *Drug Trafficking, Fraud, Gambling and Theft*
Sentence: 120 months

William P. Morrison: *Drug Trafficking, Gambling and Theft* Sentence: 96 months

Nathan F. Thomas: *Drug Trafficking, Gambling and Theft*
Sentence: 96 months

Samuel Wiggins: *Drug Trafficking, Gambling and Theft*
Sentence: 84 months

Joseph M. Sterns: *Drug Trafficking, Gambling and Theft*
Sentence: 84 months

Raymond P. Caruso: *Drug Trafficking, Possession and Manufacturing*
Sentence: 72 months

Operation Iguana does not stop at the borders of Nevada, and takes some interesting twists and turns internationally, to the south and north. Prosecutor Sanchez released limited information regarding an ongoing investigation in Toronto, Canada involving a motorcycle club called Satans Crew. When discussing the Ontario case, Ms. Sanchez referred to one bad actor in that investigation simply as *the Frenchman*. Our investigation found that this moniker is used by a high-level member of that organization named Phillippe Gaudet. The investigation also stretches to the south, through Riverside, California and on down to Baja California, MX. A Vipers' motorcycle club member, by the name of Diego García, was arrested on the same date as the Hell Riders, charged with Drug Trafficking. It is only speculation at this time, but when reading between the lines Prosecutor Sanchez made the insinuation that some of the higher members indicted from Operation Iguana are cooperating with authorities from Canada and Mexico.

Evidence recovered in the operation includes motorcycles, trailers and trucks used for drug transport, and drug proceeds exceeding a million dollars. There is documentation showing illegal loan sharking activity, stolen firearms, evidence of money laundering and drug offenses, through a custom motorcycle manufacturing business called the Iron Horse Garage. The most significant piece of evidence secured during a search warrant was of the entire Hard Times Tap building and contents. This was a tavern owned by Daniel Trask and used as a meeting place. It was not only a party house, but most importantly, a drug laboratory. Law enforcement officials located, through a secret entrance to the basement, a sophisticated methamphetamine laboratory, which contained a wide array of necessary chemicals for production. Also located within the lab was a secure fire and waterproof safe, which contained an estimated eight hundred seventy-five thousand in cash, and one fifty-gallon drum containing bags of crystal meth prepared to hit the streets.

Sanchez indicated that the crime lab will test all seized cash and property for fingerprints and traces of drugs. One of the defendants was willing to cooperate, regarding the seized evidence within the Hard Times Tap. The entire building, which holds the tavern, and lab, has been seized, sealed, fenced off, and secured for any future evidential, and forfeiture hearings. Ms. Sanchez confirmed that a future demolition will occur. This would only happen following the conclusion of all court proceedings.

The Hell Riders gambled and lost. Even though they strived hard to promote the sin in Sin City, in the end it was the community of Las Vegas that rebuked their ilk. The City of Lights decided it was time to shine those bright lights on the opportunists that flood the streets with a drug that debilitates the users, causing them to gamble away every minute of their lives.

FIFTEEN

WHEN THE DUST SETTLED, the Hell Riders began their prison sentences, and the police department rewarded those that gave so much to Operation Iguana. Captain Ryan decided it was time to retire. Porter was promoted to the rank of captain, which was an emotional double-edged sword. He knew this now meant that most of his time would be spent behind a desk and in a way, he felt he was being put out to pasture. He was near the end of his career, he knew that, but there was still more work to be done, and he was not completely finished with law enforcement. Porter was happy to see that Martina Savala was promoted to Lieutenant. He felt that she worked hard to keep Rockwell safe and she was effective at keeping all police reports up to date. For Porter, it was John Rockwell that was the star of this operation. The amount of risk he took to embed himself deeply within the Hell Riders was tremendous. This was a man that not only risked death, but he risked the chance that coming out of the operation would scar him for life. Post-traumatic stress was a given. The ability to return to society the same man he was when the operation began, was doubtful. John Rockwell would never be the man he once was and Porter knew that. He was awarded several citations from his agency and also special awards from the LVMPD. He returned to his home agency in New Mexico. S.A. William Jennings advised Porter that there would be a promotion in Rockwell's near future. That gave Porter some solace.

AS TIME WENT ON, Porter was getting acclimated to his new rank of captain. As he sat in his new administrative office, he received an interesting, but unexpected phone call.

"This is Captain Steele."

"Hello, I wanted to speak with Lieutenant Steele?"

"You are speaking with Captain Steele."

"You are a captain now? Goddamn!"

"May I ask who's calling?"

"This is Ray."

"Ray?"

"Ray Caruso."

"Ray Caruso? I never thought I'd be hearing from you again."

"I called to thank you."

"You called to thank me, for putting you in prison for seventy-two months?"

"Yeah, that's right. I'm grateful. Six years is nothing, Lieutenant. Excuse me...Captain."

"You did get a major break for your cooperation, Ray."

"I wanted to thank you for saving my life. I was as good as dead."

"What Federal Correctional Institution did they send you to?"

"I'm a long, long way from the bright lights of Vegas, that's for sure. F.C.I. Oxford. Up here in good ole Wisconsin, if you can believe that one. I'm an official cheesehead now."

"That's a good safe place for you. You're a long way from Danny Trask."

"If it wasn't for you and your man inside, Danner, or whatever his real name is, I would be dead for sure and buried somewhere out in the desert. Somewhere that only Trask would know about."

"You were so close to getting whacked, you'll never know."

"Oh, I sure know now. I can still remember when Danner and his two guys snatched me right in the middle of the driveway of my apartment, about two a.m., after I just got home from the Hard Times. They tossed me in the back of a black van and got me the hell out of there. I didn't know what in the hell was going on."

"What'd you think of those guys?"

"After Danner tried explaining to me that he had to fake my murder, I still had no clue what was going on. He told me that Trask ordered him to kill me and get rid of my body. One of the guys in the van was like an expert in using stage makeup and shit like that to create fake wounds and making it all look so damn real."

"I'll just say that guy is good. One of the best. Good enough at what he does to work on a movie set," Porter replied.

"Then they drove me out to the desert. Dug a three-foot-deep hole and put me in it. They covered me in some dirt and after all of that I'm wondering if these guys have changed their minds and are really going to kill me. I have fake blood all over my head, face, and upper body. My clothes are torn and I have these huge bogus wounds all over me."

Porter laughed. "So, they had you shitting your pants, huh Ray?"

"They did, for sure. Then they asked me to lie still, like I'm dead."

"You deserved it though, wouldn't you say? You got yourself into that mess."

"I know that. It was my fault. But after everything that was done to me, your ole boy pulled out a camera and snapped some photos of me lying in that filthy grave."

"You must have thought you had died and went to heaven after you saw the camera come out."

"Your man explained everything to me."

"You knew you weren't getting off scot-free? You can't cook meth for the Hell Riders and get away with it."

"I knew the law would catch up to me. The money was too damn good. I assumed I was going to prison eventually. There was going to be a price to pay. I just didn't want to be anywhere near Trask or Carlin or even Hammer for that matter. One of those guys would have killed me for sure. Or had me killed."

"You're good with the six-year sentence?"

"I can do six years standing on my head, Captain. Less, if I'm a good boy. Especially up here in the great state of Wisconsin."

"Thanks for your cooperation in the case. Take care of yourself while inside. Don't stop looking over your shoulder."

"I'll never stop that. I have to go now. They want me off the phone."

"Alright."

"One last thing, Captain. I wanted to tell you that I'm really sorry about your wife."

"Thanks, Ray. Now hang up and go do your time. When you get out, stay out."

"I think I'll take you up on that piece of advice," Caruso laughed. "By the way, I like the sound of Captain. It fits you."

PORTER'S CAREER CHANGED dramatically after Operation Iguana. His days seemed to be filled with nothing more than monotonous paperwork, useless staff meetings, and administrative gobbledygook. It caused him to spend most of his time trying to solve the ongoing dilemma of the seemingly endless challenge to keep his inbox free of spam. He no longer felt connected to his investigators. His office became like a prison cell. Was his day any different than Ray Caruso's?

There were no important cases lingering on the horizon and his days and nights became a blur, running together like a bad dream. For the first time in his life, he felt alone at work and at home. There was nowhere to hide, no refuge from the desolation. Porter was not able to fight the emptiness that was left in his soul after Ellen died. He made trips to the ranch but felt just as lonely there. It was simply a different place to be alone. Porter could not mend his wounds with busy work and staff meetings. All of his tomorrows became a repeat of yesterday's problems.

As the years passed, Kristine left UNLV and decided to take an offer to return to work for ASU. Back to Tempe. Something drew her back to her old school. There was something Porter didn't understand. He couldn't understand. He was unaware of her secret. Kristine was lucky to receive her old job back in the counseling department and, although it paid little, Porter hoped returning to her old stomping grounds would somehow bring a spark back to her life. Maybe lift her out of her deep depression. Unfortunately, whatever strength Kristine had left to fight her disease had deteriorated further after returning to ASU. Porter was too far away to save her. And now, as he looked back, perhaps that was exactly how she planned it.

It was in the fall, at the young age of twenty-eight, Kristine was found dead in her apartment. After not reporting to work for two consecutive days, employees went to her apartment to check to see if she was ill. When the apartment manager allowed them access, they found that she had committed suicide. Another funeral and another reminder of Ellen's death; another reminder of how Porter failed his daughter.

There was only one place to lay Kristine to rest and that was in the burial plot that had been reserved for him, right next to Ellen, in the Oak Hill Cemetery near the ranch. After the funeral service, Porter returned to the police department to try and finish out his career. Work only became a place to go. A place to hide out from life. A place to forget. But it wasn't enough. His heart was being pulled toward the ranch, to be closer to Ellen and Kristine.

After struggling through three more years in police work, Porter retired. He sold his home in Las Vegas, and decided it was time to move to his Arizona ranch, permanently. This was the only place he belonged. It was here, and only here, where he could be close enough to capture the spirit and presence of Ellen and Kristine. The ranch became Porter's refuge, although it could be a lonely place. Friends he had in Las Vegas went on with their lives.

He spent the next several years building upon his Arizona ranch house. Porter created more work for himself by purchasing two more horses, goats, and even some alpacas. The animals, in a way, were more for companionship than anything else. They were alive. They gave him something to take care of. The ranch, the animals, and the daily grind went on and on. Time waited for no one. Loneliness became his unwanted friend. Porter was not lost on the irony of his life. He loved the solitude but hated the isolation. Things were not the same without Ellen and Kristine. What was there to look forward to? Porter began to fly again, causing him to reach out to his old friend, Sean Wallace.

As time went by, Porter had become fully settled into his retirement. Las Vegas and his law enforcement career were left far behind. Although he felt that he had moved into a new phase of his life, he also knew that he could never shake the agony of the deaths of his wife and daughter. These were open wounds, festering, and infecting every fiber of his being. Never healing. Always asking why. Wounds with which he knew, deep down, he must learn to live.

ONCE HE FOUND the mental strength, Porter decided it was time to face the challenge of going through Kristine's personal belongings.

There were bags of clothing, personal items, and boxes and boxes of books from her days at college. He knew there was no reason to keep them but had no idea what to do with them. As he quickly rifled through the pages of all her books, he stacked them off to one side. When he reached the last book, in the last box, he was puzzled. It was a psychological therapy textbook, but he could not remember Kristine ever taking this particular class. The book seemed brand new. Perhaps it was just a book she was reading on her own. As he thumbed through the pages, he came across a handwritten letter, or at least the start of one. Porter began to read:

May 8, 1999

Dear Mom and Dad,

I am writing this letter, because I have been sick with guilt. I can't get focused here at school. I'm just days away from graduation and I am so afraid of facing the world. I'm having anxiety attacks almost every day. Most of the time I can get through them, but lately it's become more difficult. I probably need some strong meds. I didn't have the courage to talk to you in person about something that happened to me and Lynn, Jen, and Angie while we were on spring break. With dad working at the police department, I was afraid he would be angry with us, and I couldn't find the nerve to talk to you guys. I hope I can get through it in this letter, so I will try. When the four of us went to Vegas over spring break, we decided to go into this bar called the Hard Times Tap. It was the last stupid thing to do before we were to drive home that night. We said we would have just one drink and leave quickly, but when we got inside things changed. I guess this was a bar only used by a motorcycle gang called the Hell Riders. I remember seeing that on their jackets. All four of us now know that our drinks had to have been drugged, probably with downers, or something. We were raped by the four guys that kept talking to us and making us drink more and more alcohol. They wouldn't let us leave unless we had just one more. We know for sure we were drugged with the last drink we had. We all knew we were slipping into unconsciousness but couldn't stop it. It was a terrible feeling. The next morning, we all were just barely capable of walking. All four of us were definitely raped. There was no doubt about it. I will probably never have the courage to send you this letter, but I have at least started to write it, so that helps me release some of my anxiety. If you ever receive this letter, you'll know I overcame the guilt. Being a detective's daughter, I know the first thing you would want to know was who did this to us. All I can tell you are the nicknames of some of them. I remember because of how they talked to each other. There was a bartender they called Ray, but he never tried to hurt us. He actually was trying to get us out of there before anything happened. A fourth guy came in later, but I'm not sure if he had a nickname. Maybe. I remember that they called each other Hammer, Bear, and something like Stump. I'm not sure if that one was right. The guy that came in late was called Danny, or a nickname like Deety. I know that sounds weird, but it sounded like

Dee Tee. All I remember before I passed out was this guy, Danny, acted like he was everyone's boss. Sorry, but I need to take a break from writing. I feel a panic attack coming on. I have to go calm myself down. I'll try finishing this later. I hope I can find the strength to send it to you, but honestly, I'm not sure if I can.

And just like that the letter ended. Never to be finished. Never to be sent. Porter now realized for the first time that the chances he would have ever found this letter, inside this book, after all these years, were a million to one. Who intervened? Who led him to Kristine's innermost thoughts, her pain, her words of regret? Was it Ellen? Was it Kristine? They were now gone for many years. Finally, Porter now had the answer to what caused Kristine's deep and never-ending depression. Who guided his hand to open that one book? One book, out of boxes and boxes of books. It was clearly a higher power. The question now was what to do about it.

Kristine's letter not only made Porter ache for his own daughter, but his guilt over the thought of Kristine's best friends suffering, for almost sixteen years, was a devastating blow to his sense of compassion. How could he have missed this? He was a highly trained detective, for God's sake. How blind was he to the pain suffered by the people he loved most in his life? Was he so absorbed in compartmentalizing every facet of his own existence, he could not see what was taking place right in front of his own eyes?

SIXTEEN

WITH PORTER'S INVESTIGATIVE SKILLS, it didn't take him long to locate the contact information for all three of Kristine's best friends from school. Angie was living in Lawrence, Kansas. Jen was living outside of Milwaukee and Lynn was still residing in the Denver area. Porter knew they would be shocked to receive an actual handwritten letter from him, but he wanted his first form of communication to be compassionate and thorough, but most of all nontraceable. If he were to receive a response from any one of them, he knew that further communication would be acceptable. He was nervous to reach out. He wasn't exactly sure what he would write, except that he wanted to invite them for a weekend to his ranch. Porter believed that if he could have a few days with these young women, he could determine how they were coping in their lives. This would hopefully be the beginning of understanding whether or not plans he had been considering were even the least bit plausible.

He sat down one evening in front of the fireplace and began to write. He chose to write three separate letters. They would all be worded in exactly the same manner. He wrote to Angie first.

Dear Angie,

I hope this letter finds you well and that you are not shocked that I am writing. The years have passed slowly for me and because of the loss I have suffered over the last several years I have neglected to reach out to you. I am truly sorry. Since losing my wife Ellen and daughter Kristine, my life has never been the same. The days pass without a single minute of happiness. The hours linger until the darkness takes over and allows me sleep. Unfortunately, I welcome the sleep, so I can close my eyes and try to forget. Ignoring you, Lynn and Jen, all Kristine's best friends, has created a barrier from the pain of my loss. I was so wrong to put up obstacles to the three of you, but it was the only way for me to forget. So, I thought. I need you to know that I found a letter from Kristine, which she never sent her mother or me. It was hidden inside one of her college textbooks. Inside the letter she writes in detail about the sexual assaults that occurred to all of you on that spring break in Las Vegas, back in 1999. Now my guilt about what happened to you is consuming my days and nights. You suffered the loss of Kristine just like me. It is sad to recall those dark times, but I was blind to the reasons that Kristine became so sick. She could not handle the psychological damage it did to her. I was not there to protect her, and I live with that guilt every day. Now, as I look back, I also was not there to protect you three. For this, I am ashamed. Quite frankly, trying to keep your memory alive has been agonizing. Some days I want to remember you, but other days I try so hard to forget. As you may know, I am retired now and living alone at my ranch in Arizona. The family that once lived here on the ranch moved away, back to New Mexico. Everyone that I ever loved is gone. I have one friend in Utah that helps me get through hard days. We fly together once in a while, but even flying no longer gives me pleasure like it once did.

I hope this letter finds you healthy, but I cannot help but feel that you have lingering memories of that terrible night, which may stand in the way of true happiness. I know when Kristine died you also lost a part of your heart, just like I did. She loved you so much and always hoped that you would do well with your career and life. She would talk about how she wanted you to find love, have kids and raise a family. Kristine never talked about her own life in that way. Perhaps she knew that those things would never be. I wasn't smart enough to read between the lines. I guess I wanted to simply forget. After Ellen died, I couldn't even allow my heart to sink low again with Kristine. I pretended that what I was seeing would somehow mend itself. That God would step in for me and fix the problem. But I was wrong. I was so very wrong. I have three things in my life that eat away at me like a cancer. My dear wife left this world at such a young age, we never got to enjoy the life she deserved. My daughter escaped from a pain in the only way she knew how, because her mind was telling her there was no other way out. Her mind turned on her, fooled by the destructive combination of hopelessness and regret. And, finally, I have the unrelenting guilt that I have done absolutely nothing to avenge your pain, caused by the ruthless criminals that committed violence on you, Jen, and Lynn. And those crimes killed Kristine.

The start of our healing must begin. I believe that it can only begin with our reunion. This letter is being sent to each of you three. I would like you to take the time to read my letter and then if you so desire, reach out to each other and discuss my offer. I am inviting you all to my ranch for a long weekend of healing. In November of this year is your Homecoming reunion at ASU. If you all were to agree, I will gladly pay for your trip there and then I would like to personally fly you from Tempe to my ranch for three days. Please think of my invitation as a chance for renewal. I know I need it and perhaps you are ready as well. If I never hear from any of you, I will understand. If you would respond back to me regarding my invitation, I would greatly appreciate it. Please return your thoughts in a handwritten letter addressed to my ranch. I anticipate hearing from you.

Sincerely,

Porter Steele

AFTER A WEEK WENT by Angie had not heard anything from either Jen or Lynn. She wanted to get their initial reaction to Porter's letter with the invitation to his ranch. She called Jen first to find out if she had received it too.

"Hello."

"Jen, it's Angie."

"Angie, I had a feeling you might call."

"You got the letter?"

"I did. Oh my God, when I opened the envelope, my heart began to race."

"I know, this is all so surreal. I don't know what to make of it."

"It made me think about Kristine so much. I couldn't stop crying while I was reading."

"Me too. I felt so bad for Mr. Steele."

"He sounds so lonely."

"I thought the same thing, but this opens so many wounds. How are you doing?" Angie asked.

"Honestly, not so good."

"Have you spoken to Lynn lately?"

"Not for about a month or so," said Jen, "just Facebook stuff. I don't think she has been doing so well, either."

"Can you get ahold of her and see what she thinks about the letter?"

"I have an idea. I'll get ahold of Lynn and talk to her about it. I'll see if she wants to do a group call. All three of us, tonight."

"That sounds perfect. What time should I expect you to call?"

"Let's shoot for seven o'clock. Tell Lynn Central Time. Will that work?"

"Seven it is. I'll be by my laptop waiting," Angie answered. "It's been so long since I talked to Lynn. I'm nervous."

"Be prepared, Angie," Jen said. "I don't think life has been so great for Lynn. It hasn't been too wonderful for me, either."

"I'm anxious to talk to you both about this letter. I have some very difficult things I'd like to talk to you two about."

IT WAS SEVEN O'CLOCK in the evening and Angie patiently waited for the group call with Jen and Lynn. The anticipation was intense. Angie knew that their rapes back in 1999 seemed like a lifetime ago, but her heart pounded like it just happened yesterday. Porter's letter stirred emotions in all three women that they thought had been suppressed, buried, and hidden from the outside world. All three of them lived with a constant ache from that night. In one way or another, the felonies perpetrated on those four college girls, sixteen years ago, lacerated their sense of security. Ripping away at their innocence. Scars formed upon scars, creating a thick layer of impervious flesh, seemingly protecting them from the excruciating agony of a relentless shame. Maybe talking about the rapes would free them. Maybe opening those old wounds would be a new start. Maybe, just maybe, Porter's letter would be the beginning of their new lives. There was nothing left but hope.

"Angie, are you there?" Jen asked.

"I'm here," she answered. Her image came up on the monitor.

"Hi Angie, its Lynn."

"How are you? It's so good to hear your voice."

"Hi you guys," Jen said.

"Hello, Jen. Thanks for setting this up," Angie replied.

"Hello, Jen," Lynn responded.

"I can't believe we're all talking like this," said Angie.

"It took a letter from Mr. Steele," Lynn replied. "How ironic?"

"What did you guys think about the letter?" Angie asked.

"After crying my eyes out and taking some time to calm myself down, I appreciated it," Jen said. "How about you guys?"

"I'm still crying about it," said Lynn.

"I am too," Jen replied. "Mr. Steele sounds so depressed."

"I felt terrible for him," said Angie. "We have an invitation to think about. It sounds to me like Mr. Steele would like all of us to come out to his ranch. All of us or none of us? Is that the way you two read it?"

"I would say so."

"Me too."

"What are your initial thoughts?" Angie probed.

"Well, first things first," Lynn answered. "We need to talk seriously about what we have been going through."

Jen sighed. "I don't know if I can. Those memories are still so raw for me."

"I agree," said Angie. "I don't know if I can force myself to talk about what happened that night."

"I don't see how any of us can agree to go out to Mr. Steele's ranch without facing this head on."

"I think you're right, Lynn," said Jen. "We need to help each other through this."

Angie risked stirring strong emotions. "So, Lynn, how do you get through the day? Honestly."

"Sounds like it's time to face the truth," said Lynn. "I'm still at the hospital. Same job. Same old grind. All I do is work, then come home and drive myself crazy all night. I can't remember the last time I enjoyed life at all. I can't get over my husband's death. My kids are at my parent's house more than my own. They would rather be with them. This has to stay between the three of us, but my pill problem has gotten bad. I can't get myself to even talk about that, or I might start confessing to crimes. I'm not ready to do that."

"So...things are really, really bad?"

"Angie, they're beyond bad," Lynn answered. "What about you guys?"

Angie hesitated. "I can't exactly put my finger on when it all began, but I've suffered with anxiety, depression, eating disorders. You name it. If it wasn't for a good staff, my businesses would probably go down the drain. I still sink every last minute of my day into my business, but I can hardly concentrate when I'm there. It's just become a place for me to go. When it comes to relationships, they're a joke. I haven't been on an actual serious date for over five years. I know I need therapy of some kind, but I can't find the courage to speak to anyone about what happened."

"I can relate to that," Jen began. "I'm still at the same bank branch where my dad got me the job. He's since moved to Florida full time. I don't think he wanted to deal with my problems anymore. Probably ashamed. I work. I come home. I drink a bottle of wine and watch television, then go to bed to face another day. During the week, I don't get so drunk that I miss work, but that's because it takes a lot of wine to get me drunk nowadays."

"How much are you drinking?" Angie asked.

"Well, that first bottle goes down pretty quickly," Jen admitted. "A bottle is nothing. I'm so cheap I buy my weekend party wine in the box. That's pathetic. Miss Wall Street. Big stock picking tycoon, getting drunk every weekend with a box of wine, partying in my own apartment, all by myself. I started smoking again a couple years ago. That's to try and calm my nerves. I'm quite the catch. I can't even get any old men to look at me."

"Do either of you two believe for a minute that we would have sunk this damn low if we had never stepped into that tavern on that miserable night clear back in 1999?" Angie asked.

Jen shouted, "No fricking way! There is no way I would have. That night destroyed me."

"I totally agree," said Lynn. "That night screwed up my self-worth. Sorry for venting."

"Don't worry about it, Lynn. You deserve to let it out," Jen said. "Fuck, fuck, fuck! That's exactly how I feel, too. God, I'm so sorry you guys."

"Sixteen shitty years. Goddamn it, I'm mad. I'm as mad as hell that I let myself be a victim for so damn long."

Lynn lowered her head. Angie and Jen could tell she was starting to cry. It was part anger and part regret.

"Let me ask the two of you one question," Angie said. "If we're able to get some of this crap off our chest, and out in the open, are you two willing to at least consider Mr. Steele's invitation?"

"I'm more than willing," Jen reacted.

"I will definitely consider it," Lynn answered, "but, I have to know in my heart that I'm not revealing all this crap in my life and then in the end it's going to hurt me even more. I'll be frank with you both. My life has been turned upside down since that night. What could a visit to Mr. Steele's ranch hurt?"

"I know what you mean," Angie agreed. She began to cry. Jen began to cry.

"Jen, are you okay?"

"No...I'm not okay," she answered, "and I'm done telling people I'm okay. My life has been a fricking disaster. Sixteen years of hiding. I've wondered why I couldn't get my shit together. Failed marriages, failed jobs. I cannot focus. I cannot organize a single thought, or emotion. I'm still a miserable wreck after all these years."

"I feel so terrible we haven't reached out to each other sooner," said Angie. "I've put up an amazing front for everyone. I could have won an Oscar for a sixteen-year performance. I'm still struggling daily with depression. More than I'll even admit. I'm still battling eating disorders. For all these years, for God's sake. What in the hell is wrong with me?"

Lynn was clearly shaken to the core. "My kids don't even know who the true Lynn is. I'm a stranger in my own house. Since their father died...who am I kidding...even before I met their father, I was a total mess. I cannot get off these damn pills. I know they're killing me. I don't have the courage to do what Kristine did, so I just keep popping them, hoping I will accidentally overdose or something. Just so the secret of that fucking night dies with me. This was not part of my life plan. You know, my wonderfully planned out life. No one would've planned this kind of mess."

Angie tried to calm the moment. "Lynn, please don't be so hard on yourself. We're all struggling. Maybe now is the time we unite and help each other, once and for all."

"I want to do this you guys. I need to do this," Lynn cried. "We have to understand that we were all victims that night. And now, after all these years, we need to pull ourselves together and start being survivors."

"Isn't this what Kristine would have wanted if she had the chance to be on this call with us, right now?" Angie asked.

"We can't let Mr. Steele down. We can't let Mrs. Steele down. Most of all, we cannot let Kristine down anymore," Jen stated. "This has gone on too long."

Lynn was abrupt. "I want to go to the ranch, for sure. I need to go and face Mr. Steele. There, I've decided."

"I want to go, too," said Jen.

"Then let's effin go. Let's do this. I'm all in!" Angie shouted.

The more they talked, the more they opened up. They felt relieved, and even though they were repeating the stories of their pain, finding the power to talk about it was a beginning. All three ladies wept through their reluctant smiles. It reminded them of the day of their graduation from ASU, when they were saying their sad goodbyes to each other. Their emotions could not be contained. Now, a thousand pounds was lifted off their shoulders, and there was a true merging of so many sentiments. There was grief for Porter, Ellen, and Kristine. There was sadness at the realization that they had never reached out to each other to talk about the rapes. There was a fear of the unknown. There was the hope of a new start, but a reluctance to let go of their misery. After all, they had learned to exist with that misery. Within all of their hurting and despair, there was also one emotion that they could not explain.

Angie, Lynn, and Jen were unable to pinpoint what was happening to them at this very moment but would soon realize it existed. They would eventually grasp this emerging resolve and hold it tightly, like the secret they held for so many years. This mounting emotion was one created by the thought of vengeance. The thought of revenge was a scary sensation to behold in others, but even more frightening to realize in oneself. Would thoughts of revenge become more than just an emotion? Would it become an action? Would it dominate their daily thoughts?

This hadn't seriously crossed the minds of any of these young women, although anger and hatred had surely simmered deep within for years. They could not know that their reunion with Porter Steele would expose many of these questions. Questions that still lingered, buried deep. Perhaps now, after sixteen years, the answers to all those nagging questions would break free. Escape, through the fog of shame, and offer them a much-needed respite from their self-imposed prison.

IT WAS FOUR O'CLOCK in the afternoon and Porter was returning from a trip into town after an early dinner. As he was driving his truck up the lane toward the ranch house, he pulled over to his mailbox. He noticed there were a few bills on top and the typical daily advertisements, before he noticed an envelope with a Kansas return address in the corner. A rare smile came to his face. Porter couldn't remember his last one. He knew that it had to be a letter from Angie. Even though he couldn't be certain Angie was writing to accept his invitation, at least he knew that she took the time to write him back.

Porter drove the rest of the way up the lane and pulled into the driveway. He sat in his truck, too anxious to walk inside, and threw the junk mail up on top of the dashboard. He took a deep breath and opened the letter. As he began to read, he felt as though he was in the same room with her, listening to her quivering voice, talking directly to him, feeling his guilt. Feeling his pain.

Dear Mr. Steele,

Thank you so much for reaching out to us. Receiving your letter brought back many memories but also reminded us of the hurt you have suffered over the years. I will admit that after speaking to Lynn and Jen, your letter also reminded us that our lives have not gone exactly how we wished either. We all have dealt with problems we cannot explain and, often times, wish we never had to give it a second thought. We miss Kristine and we also miss the loving friendship offered by you and Ellen. We cannot begin to express the sorrow we all felt at the loss of Kristine and also Ellen, who was always like a second mother to Lynn, Jen, and me. Those years seem so long ago, but we want you to know that your letter opened up feelings that the three of us have not had the courage to face. It breaks our hearts to hear about your loneliness, and we regret the fact that we have not reached out to you in all the years that have passed. After a lengthy discussion between the three of us, we have decided to accept the invitation to your ranch. It was so kind of you, and I must say, brave of you to write to us. I know that it must have been extremely difficult to find the words to express your feelings. You were always a man the three of us looked up to, like a father figure really. I now realize that your strength, persistence, and character are the attributes that sustain you in this struggle to understand what happened to the four of us on that terrible night back in 1999. And even though you didn't express this directly in your letter, we all understand that it is one of the main reasons you want to meet with us. So, we will be attending this year's homecoming reunion in November, then spend a few days with you at your ranch. I'll wait for your response with the exact place and time you will pick us up and then relay the information on to Lynn and Jen.

Thanks again for reaching out,

Angie

Porter was taken aback for a moment, because deep down inside he wasn't confident they would accept his offer. He thought, *what do I do now?*

He knew he had to write to Angie one more time to relay his instructions. There would be an exact date and time to meet him at the airpark, which was located on the southwest side of Chandler. All they would need to do was arrive in Tempe for the Homecoming and find a ride to meet him. Porter could make sure he flew them safely to his ranch. His home was a short flight, so the trip would be quick and easy. But what would happen once they were all at the ranch? What would he say? What would he do? How would he explain why he invited them for this reunion? How would they react to the serious, yet mind-boggling, proposal he was about to offer? Porter had time to prepare for their visit, but the most significant question he had for them was not going to be an easy one. He was beginning to believe that even he would not have the courage to explain himself. The risks were tremendously high.

For the next several weeks, Porter contemplated his scheme. He devised his strategic plans, tactics, and formulated his communication strategies. Ultimately, Porter believed, he had created a failproof mission. This would be his one and only attempt at achieving complete restorative justice for these young women. In a strange, but loving, way there would be justice for Ellen and Kristine as well. Yet there was one potentially hazardous outcome of this meeting that had to be considered. Would these three adult women think that Porter Steele, a wonderful father, loving husband, retired police captain and highly respected man, is one hundred percent, certifiably, out of his mind?

SEVENTEEN

DURING THE FIRST WEEK of November, the three women flew into Arizona for the ASU annual homecoming events, but their focus was on meeting with Porter. On Friday afternoon they made their way to the airpark where they waited patiently for him to find them. He had been there for an hour watching and waiting. He was nervous. He wasn't sure if he would recognize any of them. It had been several years since Porter had seen the girls and he didn't have the emotional strength to reach out to any of them since Kristine's death. He had a much younger image of all of them in his mind, but somehow his brain allowed him to adjust to the years that had slipped by.

He saw three women, who appeared in their late thirties, sitting at a table outside near the private gate he had instructed them to locate. As he walked toward them it was obvious that these were Kristine's best friends. To Porter, they still looked the same as they did so many years earlier. College students trying to find their way. His mind had a coping mechanism for dealing with the aging process. His brain told him they would always be young, innocent girls to him. Perhaps Porter had forgotten that he had been aging this whole time as well. He hadn't stopped to think that maybe the women would not recognize him. The closer he got to them, the more all of their memories began to click.

"There's Mr. Steele," said Angie. She waved. He waved back as he approached.

Porter reached out and hugged Angie, then Lynn, and Jen. "Hello ladies. I wasn't sure if I'd recognize you."

"It's so nice to see you," Angie said.

"It's great to see all of you, too. Are you ready to fly home with me?"

Angie looked at the other two. "I think we're ready."

"I'll be the first to admit I'm a little nervous," Lynn confessed. "I can't remember ever flying in such a small plane."

"I flew with Mr. Steele several years ago," Angie replied. "He's a great pilot. No worries."

"Okay, Mr. Steele, I'm putting all my faith in you."

"Have you ever flown in a private plane like this, Jen?"

"I have on a few occasions," she answered. "My second husband was a pilot, so I flew with him once in a while. Oh my God, listen to me. That sounds so tacky talking about my ex-husband."

They all laughed at Jen's sense of humor. Porter reached for some of the luggage the women had with them and headed toward the gate. They grabbed their remaining bags and followed. Porter lifted the bags into his plane and got the three of them situated into their seats. He had already done his walk-around of the plane before the flight, so he was ready to go.

Porter lightened the mood before take-off. "Okay, ladies, this is your last chance to disembark if you don't want to take this flight. There are no flotation devices, so I won't go through that safety spiel. We won't be flying over water anyway. The only exits are pretty obvious. You're all sitting right next to them. So, sit back, buckle up, and enjoy the flight. Sorry, but I have no peanuts. We only have a little over two hundred miles to go, and we'll be at my ranch. The wind is calm, the sun is shining and there's plenty of daylight left, for those of you who don't like flying at night. It's a beautiful day to be up in the sky."

"Now I'm ready," Lynn smiled.

"Me too," Jen said.

Angie was sitting in the front passenger seat across from Porter. She smiled at him, checked her seatbelt for snugness, and gave Porter a thumb up, as if to say she was ready for takeoff. Angie felt she and Porter shared an important moment when they looked at each other. They shared the exact same memory, at the exact same time. She saw it in his eyes. She felt it in her heart. It was a memory of that day, almost sixteen years ago, when Porter flew to Chandler and picked her and Kristine up for a weekend at the Steele's residence in Las Vegas. That was the weekend she and Kristine learned about Ellen's cancer. It was also the weekend that Kristine decided she couldn't tell her parents about the rapes at the Hard Times Tap. Angie felt a deep sense of sorrow for Porter as she watched him power the plane down the runway. She saw a man who did not deserve the pain he had to endure. Within minutes they were in the air and, once again, just like she remembered years earlier, she felt like a feather floating in the wind.

Angie's heart was torn in two directions. She wanted to be right where she was at this moment, but she also felt as though she wanted to turn back and run for home, where she could continue to hide from the past. As they flew toward Porter's ranch, the plane's cabin was filled with an awkward anticipation of things to come, brought on by lingering questions, which had no answers, and reoccurring memories that could not be erased. All three of these women accepted whatever was about to come. They trusted Porter to lead the way and take them to a place in their lives, which they hadn't been brave enough to travel to on their own.

After less than two hours of flying, they approached Porter's property and private runway, preparing to land. All three women heard of Grandpa Steele's ranch from Kristine when they were in college but had never been there. When Porter retired from the Las Vegas

Metropolitan Police Department, he moved full time to the ranch. On one hand, his home was a source of tremendous peace and tranquility. On the other hand, it was also a constant reminder of all the loved ones he had lost over the years. His memories as a small boy of his loving parents, his mentor and caring grandfather, the love of his life, Ellen, and his sweet daughter, Kristine, were all there with him at the ranch. He felt their presence, he missed their smiling faces, and he often shed tears for the loss of their companionship. There were times he heard them speak to him as he walked the quiet wood planks of his rustic ranch home. His parents gave him life. Papa encouraged him to live that life. Ellen comforted him with memories of their marriage.

Kristine, though, was a complicated and enduring agony. Her memory reminded him that he had failed her. Although, he knew that this sentiment derived from deep within his own mind and not from her tender heart. She would have never wanted her father to feel guilty for her death. Kristine was too gentle, too kind, and too empathetic toward those around her. Porter's guilt haunted him like the persistent shriek of a bullhorn, penetrating his brain, reminding him that he had never defended his daughter's honor. He had never brought retribution to bear upon her attacker. Those strong feelings were gripping him like the death roll of an angry crocodile. He could feel the unrelenting force of guilt dragging him down into the deep waters of despair. It robbed him of the ability to catch his breath, forcing him to gasp for one ounce of freedom from his culpability.

Porter knew he had to release himself from this spiral of emotional torture, which spun faster and faster with each passing day. Would Angie, Lynn and Jen understand? Were they suffering the same plight? *They had to be*, he thought. Were all of them in dire need of the same remedy? Their visit to his ranch would, hopefully, give answers to these questions. And perhaps, one final answer to the one question that often nagged him while he tried to sleep.

The Cessna landed smoothly on Porter's property and the ranch house could be seen in the distance, as the plane slowly taxied to a stop.

"We're here."

"What a nice flight," said Angie.

"I was never nervous," Lynn lied.

"I love this place," Jen said. "Your ranch house looks so beautiful."

"My home is your home, so please relax and enjoy it."

Everyone grabbed their bags. Porter helped to carry some luggage and led them toward the rear entrance to his home. They all walked in, carrying their bags inside the entry way and Porter offered them seats inside the Great Room.

"Could I bring everyone something to drink?" Porter asked. "I have some iced tea, soda, or beer if any of you are interested."

"Diet soda of any kind is fine with me," Angie said. She dropped her bags.

"That sounds good," Lynn agreed.

Jen smiled. "I think I'll have that beer." She looked at her friends and shrugged her shoulders.

Porter was only gone for a few minutes, when he returned with a plate of chocolate chip cookies, all of their drinks and an iced tea for himself.

"Here you go," he said, "and if you want more, please help yourself. Don't hesitate. Take whatever you want, when you want."

They all spoke at the same time. "Thank you, Mr. Steele." They looked at each other and grinned.

"Jinx!" Lynn shouted.

"Oh my God. Are you twelve, Lynn?" Angie joked.

They all laughed like they were young girls again.

"You're very welcome." Porter took a big swig of his cold tea and stood. "I will be right back. I'm going to take your bags to your rooms and when you're done with your drinks, I'd like to show you around this place."

"We'd love to see it," said Angie.

Porter left with their bags. He carried them to their rooms. He closed the door to Angie's room and sat on the edge of the bed. His nerves were suddenly exposing all of his uncertainty. Porter wiped the sweat from his forehead and took a deep breath. *Jesus Christ, what is wrong with me. I never got this nervous over my caseload.* He stood, walked in a circle, placing his hands over his face. *Get yourself together, Steele.* He remembered more than one commander of his in the Green Beret who repeated this order. He took one more deep breath and opened the door.

Jen was whispering. "This place is so beautiful."

"It's decorated in that southwestern style," Angie said. "I love it."

Lynn asked, "I wonder if this was done by Porter's grandfather, or if he and Ellen had a hand in decorating this place? It's so homey."

"I know Parker Steele built this home many, many years ago," Angie recalled. "I'm sure Porter has added on. Some of this handmade furniture looks priceless."

Jen pointed over at the stone fireplace that was at the far end of the Great Room. "That thing is massive. Look at the size of those stones."

Lynn stood and walked towards it, scanning the entire room. "It is huge but still feels warm and cozy."

"When you're all alone, though?" Angie wondered. "It would be scary to live here by yourself, wouldn't it?"

Jen joined Lynn by the fireplace. "It would have to be lonely. He's so isolated. I'm sure it would be too quiet for me."

Porter returned shortly and noticed Lynn and Jen standing near the fireplace. "My grandfather and one of his good friends built that all by themselves."

"It's stunning," said Angie.

"The slate mantle came from a piece of stone he found right on this property."

"He must have been a very talented man," Lynn complimented.

"It's funny you should say that," Porter replied. "My grandfather did much of the work on this ranch. Not because he always wanted to, but because he simply had too. There was a time when people did everything on their own. There was not always someone else to do the work for you. I guess that's where the saying jack of all trades comes from."

"I can understand that," said Jen. "You learn how to do things quickly when you have to do it by yourself. Trial and error, I suppose."

"None of you would have probably known this, but my grandfather raised me on this ranch up until the time I went into the Army."

"How interesting," Angie replied. "You must have been close to your grandfather."

"I called him Papa," Porter answered. "This is something that Kristine probably would have never mentioned, but my parents died when I was only eleven and Papa Steele took me in and raised me the best he could. Right here. On this ranch."

"May I ask what happened to your parents?" Lynn wondered.

"You can, but I would've never given you an answer if you had asked that question before we flew here."

"You wouldn't have?"

"Let's just say none of you would have gotten on that plane with me to fly here."

Lynn apologized. "I'm such an idiot...I'm so sorry I asked."

"That's fine, I would've told you sooner or later. My parents were killed in a small private plane crash when I was a young child," he explained. "As a matter of fact, I was here at this ranch visiting Papa on summer vacation, when my parents flew here to pick me up. On the way their plane had engine failure and went down. They weren't able to survive the impact."

"I'm so sorry," Lynn said.

"That was a long time ago. A very long time ago," Porter ruminated as he looked around the nostalgic family room his grandfather left him to enjoy. "Let's take a walk around the house. I want to show you the bedrooms you'll be staying in and where the washrooms are and, of course, the kitchen. Anything you want here is yours. Papa Parker would want you to enjoy his wonderful home."

"Thanks so much."

"Yes...thank you, sir."

"Thank you, Mr. Steele. You're too kind," Angie agreed.

There was one conversation that had not taken place yet. It was one that took courage. Although the women missed Kristine very much, they were not sure if openly talking about her in front of Porter would cause him more grief or make him feel better. These were questions that had to be tested. Porter wanted them to make this trip to his ranch for a specific reason. Surely, he was not about to ignore conversations about the two people he loved more than life itself. Angie, Lynn, and Jen felt the time would come and Porter would open that door and allow them in. Talking about the people he loved would only help him recover after all these years. He knew it and they knew it. All he could think about, as he gave the three a tour of his home, was how different this weekend would have been if Ellen and Kristine could have been here.

Porter continued the ranch tour by driving them around the property, showing them the beautiful red rocks of the Arizona landscape. When they returned, he had a surprise for them. Porter saddled and haltered three of his favorite horses, hoping the ladies would want to feel the true spirit of the ranch. He saddled his Appaloosa, King, and led them down the trail. He encouraged them to follow him on a relaxing and peaceful ride. Porter's horses loved people and were well trained. They followed Porter and King, wherever the trail led. The horses knew, without much guidance from the ladies, exactly what to do and where to go. He wanted Kristine's friends to get that Western feel for his ranch. To feel the soothing calm his horses offered. A feel for his life here. He hoped they would begin to understand that everything he owned now took on a whole new meaning, since the death of Ellen and Kristine. All of his possessions could no longer be shared with those he loved.

Porter wanted these three to feel something personal. He needed them to feel his loss, for a reason. Not to be callous and bitter, but to place their minds in the proper perspective. Porter hoped that Angie, Lynn, and Jen would begin to share with him their own losses. Their regrets. Their aching. He knew their lives were never the same after they were brutally raped sixteen years ago. He wanted them to open up and begin to express what those acts of violence did to their lives. If they were not able to express the aftereffects of that grim night so long ago, he could not seriously discuss his proposed solution. Without the three of these young women totally reliving the misery they suffered at the Hard Times Tap, his remedy to cure a lifetime of pain would certainly be viewed as a form of evil. Even bordering on insane. Porter allowed the women to unwind, enjoy their privacy, and get ready for the evening. Tonight, would be the beginning of an important, although surreal, conversation.

EIGHTEEN

IT WAS SIX O'CLOCK in the evening and Lynn, Angie and Jen came walking out of their bedrooms toward the kitchen, where they heard Porter hard at work making dinner.

"Can we help with anything?" Angie asked.

"No. I'm fine. Just about ready. You three find a seat in the dining room and I'll be right there."

They made their way to the dining room, where they found a beautifully set table and a bouquet of fresh flowers sitting in the middle. The women looked at each other like they were pleasantly shocked. Men like this were hard to find.

"It's so nice," Jen whispered.

"Beautiful," Lynn added.

Porter started bringing various types of food into the dining room, where he had a buffet style serving table set up. It looked like a true rancher's meal.

"There's plenty to eat."

Angie smiled. "I sure hope there are more people coming for dinner."

"Just the four of us."

"We're going to have to work the ranch to wear off this meal," Jen said.

"If that's an offer, I accept," Porter grinned.

"You seem awfully handy around the kitchen, Mr. Steele," Jen complimented.

"Ranchers tend to be good cooks," he said. "I know the sight of a man that cooks this kind of meal is rare, but if I want to eat, I have to do it myself."

"Fast food joints don't seem like your style," Angie said.

"It would be difficult to try and compare one of those burgers next to one of mine," Porter bragged. "Go ahead and get started, ladies. Please, don't be shy."

"Thanks."

The group ate and talked, laughed, and even cried, but there was something missing at the table. There were people missing. Porter couldn't help noticing it and neither could Angie, Lynn, and Jen.

Angie broke the invisible, yet brittle, ice. "I can't help but think that you asked us out here for more than just a visit to your ranch. With all due respect, why now after all these years?"

"You're right. There is more, but I'm not ready to discuss the reason I asked you here. Not quite yet."

"I guess the curiosity is going to eat at me even more now," Lynn said.

"It's only fair that I give you some understanding as to why I wanted you to agree to this reunion."

"Why, after so many years?" Lynn asked.

"Because the pain of waiting has grown unbearable. I have some serious questions that I need answered, from all three of you."

"We're here to help. We want to answer any questions we can," Angie said.

"Before I begin, I need one assurance."

"What do you mean, assurance?" asked Jen.

"I need one hundred percent honesty from all of you."

"I'll give you that," Angie vowed.

"Thank you. I need a promise from each of you that from here on out, until you fly back home, you will give me the whole truth. The real truth, to each of my questions."

"I promise."

"I do too," Lynn said. "We owe you that much."

"Then I'll begin," Porter announced. "I need to know exactly how your lives are going right now and how the violence that happened to you back in 1999 changed your lives."

"I'll start," Jen said. "Here is the truth. You want the whole truth?"

"I do. I need the whole truth, however painful."

"My life is total shit," she admitted. "I don't blame Kristine for what she did...and I'm sorry to be so blunt, but I've thought of suicide more than once myself. I can't say for sure what has stopped me. I'm an alcoholic. I have been for years. I can't deal with what happened back at that bar. It was so long ago, I know. Since I was drugged and raped, I've suffered from depression, PTSD, and anxiety. I'll admit that I'm basically a hopeless drunk. My suicide has been a slow process with alcohol."

"Angie, how are you coping?" he asked.

"You didn't mention that the truth would make me feel better, and it doesn't feel like it's going to, but I'll try," she said. "I have been able to throw my entire life into my businesses. Truth be told, I can't even enjoy what I love most, because of the pain and hurt caused by that night. I suffer from some of the same things as Jen, and I'm sure Lynn, but my main problem is with eating disorders. I just can't live without driving for perfection. And I certainly do not mean that in a good way. I hope my businesses will keep me so busy that I forget about that terrible night, but every night when I go home, alone, I remember. There's no forgetting. No escaping."

"And what about you, Lynn?"

"The same story, but different story line," Lynn began. "Since the rape, I've been a prescription drug addict. That is the very first time I've said it out loud, because I've never wanted to admit it. I always had a good excuse for popping pills. To forget the rape, I eased my pain with pills. After my husband's death…"

"I'm so sorry you had to go through that, Lynn," Porter interrupted.

"Thank you. When he died my pill habit got so much worse. I was alone to raise three kids. I worked at a hospital…great place to steal pills, right? That made feeding my habit that much easier. I had become such an organized freak after the rape. I know it was anxiety. I had every moment of my day, every moment of my life really, planned out. So, there was not a single minute of the day that I would allow myself to remember the rape. I did everything to forget. After my husband was killed, one single day felt like it was a month long. I wondered why it couldn't have been me. I told myself that the kids deserved to have their father around as their parent, not me. I could not concentrate. I could not focus on my kids, my work, and my responsibilities. I still can't, if I am honest. My parents have my kids most of the time."

Porter treaded as lightly as he could. "Relationship problems for everyone, I assume?"

"That goes without saying," Angie said. "I haven't had a meaningful relationship with a man for over five years. And I'm almost forty now. The thought of ever finding someone to marry, or having a lasting relationship, never crosses my mind. I just can't allow myself to go there."

"I have to agree," said Jen. "I've been divorced twice. I married men for all the wrong reasons. My drinking got me divorced from my second husband. I'm convinced he would have stayed with me, and probably had kids, if I hadn't drank myself into divorce court. I've got fired from my jobs. I don't feel that I'm good enough to be in a lasting relationship, so I just avoid men altogether."

"My problem is a little different than theirs," Lynn said. "After my husband died, I just felt that I couldn't bring another man into my kids' lives. No one else was good enough. Hell, I didn't even think I was good enough for my husband. I hid my pill problem from him for years. He only knew about that for about six months before he was killed. He was so good to me. He was trying to help me through it. Now, I feel like if I ever got serious with another man it would be a total betrayal."

"It is your turn, Mr. Steele," Angie said. "We want to know how you've been handling this."

"I can't get past all of the guilt," he answered. "It's bad enough that Ellen died of cancer, which I had no control over, but I cannot get past the fact that because I did nothing to protect Kristine, she suffered for years in silence."

Jen leaned forward. "But you didn't know."

"I know… I know that deep down, but I still feel like I should have known. It was my job to know. I should have seen the signs."

"How could you have?"

"I was blind to so many things," Porter admitted. "At work I was fully aware of what was going on around me but, in my personal life, I just assumed Kristine was adapting to her life. She was fighting the blues, I thought. Until the end of course, when it was already too late."

"She tried protecting you and Ellen," Angie stated.

"Even after I found out about the rapes, I didn't know what to do. I felt helpless."

"There was nothing you could do."

"Burying the truth was not good enough…not good enough for Kristine, or any of you," Porter said. "Look what you've all gone through. Secrets made you sick. None of you have been made whole again after what you suffered through. I never sought retribution on behalf of my daughter, or any of you for that matter. Fathers are supposed to protect their families."

"Mr. Steele, you're putting way too much of the responsibility for what happened to us on your own shoulders," Lynn said. She could see he was hurting. They all could see it.

"So, who do you think is to blame?" he asked.

Jen said, "I hate to admit it after all these years, but you could argue that part of the blame lies with us. That's hard for me to say out loud, but we were young and stupid, and we should have never thought about going into that place."

Angie sighed. "That's so hard to hear, now. But it is true."

Lynn began to cry. "Being part of that one bad decision is still so raw. It eats at me."

"If it brings you any peace whatsoever, Kristine was the one person in our group that argued the most against going into that bar that night. She thought of you and actually said, 'my dad would be furious if he thought I was about to do this,'" Angie confessed. "She went along with the group, but reluctantly."

Porter tilted his face downward into his rough hands and rubbed up and down as if he were trying to scrub away the guilt from his brain. He paused for a moment and lifted his head high with resolve.

"I will not accept that. Under no circumstances will I ever accept the argument that you four girls did not have the freedom, or the God-given right, to walk into any place in this country without being assaulted the way you were. I know as a parent, I wish you had not made the decision to go into that bar, but I blame four men, and only four men, for what happened to you girls on that night. None of you are to blame. Not one bit. If this is the first time you've heard that, I owe you an apology for never making that clear. None of you are to blame for what occurred to you and you have to know that. These were violent, inexcusable crimes against you. You were helpless. You all must accept that truth to live in peace the rest of your lives. If you do not come to grips with that one single truth, this guilt you have will eat you alive. Forever."

"I want that peace, but I don't see me ever having it," Jen worried.

"What do you all truly think about those four men that did this to you?"

"That's the memory I've buried the deepest," Angie answered.

Porter saw Jen instinctively make a fist. "I hate them with a passion."

"Honestly, I could have killed the guy that raped me if I would've been able to," Lynn admitted for the first time to anyone.

"We were helpless...drugged...if I would've been able to defend myself, I know I would have fought to the death," Jen said. "I mean, let's face the truth here. I know if I would've had the ability to stop my attacker, even if that meant killing him, I would have done it."

"I agree, one hundred percent," said Angie. "We just didn't have the means. We weren't capable. There was nothing in our lives, well, speaking for myself, nothing in my life that would have ever prepared me for defending myself in that moment. We were at their mercy."

"And it is one major fucking pain in the ass," said Jen. "Sorry for my language."

"Don't worry about it," Porter said. "That's a word I've thrown around this ranch many times in anger over the last several years."

"For so many years I've imagined terrible things happening to my rapist," Angie confessed. "I always hoped he died of a drug overdose, or was killed in some violent way, or even found himself at the mercy of someone else and never got it. I wished he suffered somehow. I know that sounds cruel, but that's how I've felt for so long."

"I don't think it sounds cruel at all," Jen replied. "There were times over the years I actually had dreams...very real, vivid dreams, where I came face to face with my rapist. I dreamt I killed him myself. These dreams have gone on for years. They're so intense. I wake up shaking. At the same time, I feel this sense of relief. Closure, in a way. It's a bizarre sensation."

"My God, I've experienced those types of dreams, too," Lynn said. "I have this one dream where I'm so powerful. So strong. Indestructible and fearless. On a bright sunny day, I casually walk through the front door of the Hard Times Tap and there's only one person sitting at the bar. Just one. It's my rapist. He turns to me and says, 'I knew you'd come back for me.' I say nothing. I raise my right hand and shoot him right between the eyes."

"Jesus Christ, Lynn," Angie said. "Then what happens?"

"I wake up in a cold sweat. I feel like I've just run a marathon. My heart beats so rapidly, yet I feel okay with what I'd done. I never felt bad about it. It's like I feel bad later, because it wasn't for real."

"I rarely remember any of my dreams," said Angie, "but I do think about retaliation when I'm awake. I guess I'm just wishing, daydreaming. I find myself, especially at night when I'm home alone, thinking about revenge. I don't think giving men like this a prison sentence would have been good enough for me anyway. Just think if these guys had been prosecuted back in 1999 and went to prison. They'd probably be out all ready, back on the street, committing more crimes. I'd bet they're all still criminals today, even at their age."

"You would be right about that," Porter confirmed.

"You know that?" asked Angie. "For sure?"

"I know everything about all four of them. I know their names. I know where they live. I know what crimes they've committed. I know they served time for many years and are back out on the street. I know where they hang out and waste their miserable lives."

"I thought you were done with police work," said Lynn.

"I am done with police work," he replied, "but this isn't police work. This is my own work."

Jen leaned forward. "I'm interested in knowing what you know."

"Me too," said Angie.

"Do any of you want to know their full names? Would any of you be opposed to seeing current photos of them?"

"I'd like to see them," Lynn warily replied.

"And, what about you two?" Porter asked, while looking at Angie and Jen.

The women looked at each other, searching for support. Angie answered. "We'd like to see them."

Porter stood from the table and as he walked away, he threw his napkin onto the top of the buffet. He was only gone for a moment when he returned to the dining room with a large three ring binder. The women looked at each other and then back at Porter. He continued to stand, took a deep breath, laid the binder on the table, and opened it to the middle, where he stored several photographs. There were photos of people, businesses, homes, and motorcycles. Porter had done his homework, alright. He may have been retired, but he certainly had not retired his investigative skills. Porter had been building a case of some sort. Building a history for some future event. The women could see what he had been doing but couldn't figure out why he was doing it. They gathered around him to look at the three-ring binder.

"These are the men that assaulted you three, and Kristine, on March 6, 1999," Porter said. He pointed to a photo of Jen's attacker. "This is Jake Severs, aka Stump, as he's known. Severs was probably the youngest in the club. He's also one of the dumbest. Probably a sociopath. I'm not a psychologist, but that's my diagnosis. He would do whatever he was told to do and taking risks is pleasurable for this guy."

Porter then turned the page and pointed to another suspect. "Then there is Mike Carlin, aka Bear. Sorry to be so explicit, but this is your attacker, Angie. He's the leader's right-hand man. He is what I would refer to as the enforcer of the club. He is big, he is strong, and he is ruthless. Carlin is also aggressive toward other bikers. He has no conscience. He always focused on working his way up to the top of this chapter. Women, to him, are only put on this earth for one reason. His pleasure. He doesn't consider them human. He has no respect for the female species, whatsoever. Women are only playthings to this man."

Porter turned the page again and pointed to a photo of Lynn's suspect. "Once again, I apologize for my bluntness, but this is your attacker, Lynn. His name is Nick Emerson. They call him Hammer."

Before he could continue, Lynn ran from the room to the nearest restroom, just down the hall from the dining area, where she could be heard vomiting. Angie and Jen felt terrible, because they were feeling nauseous as well. They both ran to help her. Porter went into the kitchen, grabbed a towel, soaked it with cool water, and took it to Angie, so she could help Lynn.

Porter knew he was being harsh, but he couldn't think of any better way to explain what happened to them and who the perpetrators were. This was the first time they were hearing such detail about their attackers. Porter was painfully reminded that the truth could be as ugly as hell. The three women bravely returned to the table.

"I'll stop right now if you want me to. Please, just tell me when you've had enough."

"Go on, Mr. Steele. We need to know who these men are," Lynn said.

"Nick Emerson, aka Hammer, is one vicious prick. He's a motorcycle nut. That's common in this group. He's extremely violent, a known street brawler, and has no respect for women," Porter said. "Needless to say, none of them do."

Porter pointed to the final suspect. This was the one man that caused him tremendous pain to even speak his name, but he had to. "This is Kristine's rapist. He's the leader of the South Vegas Hell Rider's chapter. His name is Danny Trask, often referred to by his moniker, D.T."

"What does D.T. stand for? I assume those are his initials?" Angie probed.

"Actually, they represent something more sinister. Something more gruesome. Danny Trask has had the nickname Double Tap for many years now. So, D.T. is actually short for Double Tap. It's a nickname he does not like, but some bikers call him that anyway. Many law enforcement officers refer to him that way as well. And there is a good reason."

"Where did it come from?" Jen asked. "What does it mean?"

"Double tap is a common term used by firearm instructors. Imagine shooting a target with two bullets, in rapid succession. Bam! Bam! One right after the other. You tap that trigger twice, quickly. That is what is often called a double tap."

"There must be a good reason for that nickname," said Angie. "I even hate to ask."

"Here's the quick version of that story. Danny Trask is suspected of killing at least four rival gang members, several years ago. Unfortunately, he got away with it. He was never arrested and prosecuted. Quite frankly, who knows how many people Trask has killed? The men we suspect him of killing appeared to have been shot in the exact same manner. Twice, in rapid succession. One round to the chest first, we assume. Then a second round to the center forehead. That's how all his victims were found. Same modus operandi. Same firearm used in all four murders."

"How did he get away with it?" Lynn asked.

"For a couple of reasons, really. Don't get me wrong...this is not a compliment, but Trask is by far the smartest guy in this crazy bunch. He is highly educated and from a very successful family in the business world. If it weren't for the fact he was born with a tremendous amount of criminal DNA, this man had the potential to run his own company. He just didn't have the character to travel the high road in life. The second reason he got away with it was because of the biker brotherhood's code of silence. These men are hardcore. They typically don't rat each other out, unless there is a really damn good reason. Like, when their own ass is on the line. Then, some of them will sing like birds."

Porter was now beginning to feel comfortable enough with the three women to explain his questionable behavior. How would they respond? Was this a terrible mistake on his part? Was he about to take a plunge into the deep end of that risk pool? Would his words cause more harm than good? He was about to find out.

"You are probably wondering where all of these revelations are leading?"

Lynn was honest. "I'm somewhat afraid to know where this is all going."

"Let's deal with the truth," he said, "because the truth is the only thing left that will free you from the bondage of misery you all admit you've been suffering."

"I'm here to face the truth," Angie demanded. "No matter how ugly."

"The truth is painful. Unfortunately, there is not a single person in this world that will bring justice to those men that raped you. And of course, Kristine. Sixteen years is a damn long time to suffer. No one... no one but you and I can even talk about justice. Those men you see in this very binder will never face arrest. Those men will never face prosecution. Those men will never face prison time. Those men will never pay any price to you, or to society, for what they did to you. They will never answer for their sins. Ever. Those men will not even be subject to self-ridicule, because that would take a conscience, which they have proven time and time again they do not possess. You three young women are nothing but a distant memory. A joke to them. A perverted fantasy within the sick minds of Danny Trask, Mike Carlin, Nick Emerson, and Jake Severs. Those four men have committed innumerable crimes and will continue to commit them as long as they are breathing. There is no doubt in my mind, after all these years of mental torture, our lives will only be repaired and renewed when their lives come to an end."

"You mean...someone should kill them?" Lynn gulped.

"Who? Who will do it? You, Mr. Steele?" Angie probed. "You're willing to kill them for us?"

"Aren't you two listening to what he is trying to say? He clearly means us," Jen said. "We are the someone in this scenario. We are the victims here."

"I'm telling all of you, in no uncertain terms. When survivors such as you, and me for that matter, stand up and fight back against hateful criminals, it is then, and only then, any of us will be made whole again. If we don't take a stand and fight back, who will fight for us? If we bury the past, every last ounce of our spirits will slowly die with time. Until our bodies take their last breaths."

"I have felt that way over the last sixteen years. I must confess, finally, out loud," Angie said.

"Spirit...what spirit?" Jen replied. "The last spirit I remember was that glass of wine I had in the airport before flying out here."

"There's no way I could kill someone," Lynn revealed. "I just don't know if I have it in me."

"This is an extremely serious undertaking, so I don't want any of you to have second thoughts," Porter explained. "I don't want you to simply think of this as killing someone, just anyone. That thought process is much too simplistic. None of you are killers. You are not criminals. But this would not be a crime in my eyes. It would be an eye for an eye. Innocent victims fulfilling a just sentence upon their attackers. This is an act, which is justifiable. Does a judge commit murder every time he sentences a criminal to death? No, of course not. But we don't have a judge to step in for us. Those days are gone. We are the silent survivors that have been told, too bad so sad, get over it. There are no white knights in shining armor to step up and defend your honor. You have been left alone, in this deserted wilderness, expected to somehow view your life as worthless. You are expected to move on, quietly, put it out of your mind and just shut up and go away. To be eaten alive by the cancer of shame and guilt."

"Can we justify this in our minds?" Jen wondered. "That's the question I struggle with."

"That's a good question," Angie replied. "I have no problem justifying it in my heart. But in my mind, I'm confused."

"How can we justify this, Mr. Steele?" Lynn asked.

Porter answered with a stoic confidence. "I believe in lex talionis."

"Lex what? Say that again."

"Lex talionis. It is Latin for the law of retaliation. You have heard of an eye for an eye?"

"Revenge?" Angie acknowledged.

"A pacifist would argue that this is too harsh…that we must turn the other cheek," Porter claimed.

"We have turned the other cheek," Angie argued. "For years, we have turned the other cheek."

"Yes, you've turned the other cheek for at least sixteen years. How has that worked out for all of you?" Porter asked. "Show me a pacifist that would refuse to defend his loved ones to the death, in the heat of a violent crime, and I will show you a coward, hiding behind a utopian fantasy that allows him to sleep at night like an ignorant sheep."

"But would this be an eye for an eye, as you put it?" Lynn asked. "I thought that meant equal justice. Does the punishment of death fit the crime?"

"That question is based on a naive theory. Since these four men did not kill you, then we cannot sentence them to death?" Porter considered. "That would not be an eye for an eye, correct? Is that what you're saying?"

"That's what has me leery," said Lynn. "I worry that we'd be taking things too far. Too extreme."

"Didn't those animals go too far, when they caused the death of my daughter? When they ruined your lives?" Porter argued. "Can someone perpetrate a crime so heinous on another human being that it causes them to end their own life?"

Angie agreed. "Now that is an argument I can definitely wrap my head around."

"Take the criminal that commits murder and is only sentenced to life in prison," Porter said. "That is not truly an eye for an eye…

although the sentencing judge would have to argue that his sentence fits the crime. If he doesn't make that argument, hasn't he abandoned true justice? Without equal justice there's no justice at all. Who can define true justice?"

"That makes a lot of sense," Lynn admitted.

"Pure logic," said Jen.

"I would argue that the three of you have suffered, over the last sixteen years, more than a victim who suffers the fate of death. Some people believe that death is the ultimate crime against a person, but I say life without justice at all is more punishing on the victim. Death is relief from the pain and suffering. Death liberates the dying from the suffering of a lifetime of pain. Dealing with those four animals, once and for all, will not only bring about lex talionis for you three and Kristine, but it will also save countless other victims from suffering the same fate. Unfortunately, there were others raped before you."

"We're going to have to discuss this in private," Angie said. "We will have to really dissect everything we've discussed here tonight. It is overwhelming, to say the least."

"That's understandable," Porter replied. "I know I've just turned your worlds upside down and I apologize."

"That's okay," Angie said. "We get it. Now, we understand why you called us here. We're just a little stunned."

"I do want you three to know something very important," Porter explained further. "Lex talionis will happen. Justice will be served, in one form or another, even if it's only for Kristine. Because she has no voice and no vote. I am her only decision-maker."

"We won't be able to give you an answer today or even tomorrow, but we will give you a definitive answer."

"That is all I can ask for. Thank you," Porter said. "Tomorrow morning, I want you all to stay together and take the time you need.

Take the morning to ride the horses, walk the property. Do whatever you want to relax and think about what we've discussed. This is a big decision. Then, have your bags packed and ready to go by noon. We'll fly back to Chandler at that time. I have some business to attend to in the afternoon in Phoenix, so I'll have you back at the airpark by about two p.m. If I remember correctly, you'll need to catch your flights home the following day?"

"That's right," Lynn said.

"How do you want to communicate with us after we leave?" Angie asked.

"After the three of you make your decision, Angie can write me a brief letter with your answer," Porter explained. "If you want absolutely no part of this, simply make it clear that you refuse my offer. You will go back to living your lives as they now are. If you want to be part of this, please remember, it means that all three of you have decided to be a part of it. It has to be all of you, or none of you. Then, I will write you one more time with another invite to meet with me. I don't have an exact date and time set for that meeting, but if you say yes, plan meeting sometime in December. During that meeting, my entire strategic plan will be laid out for you. In clear, plain English."

"We understand," Angie spoke for the three. "We have a lot to think about. Thank you for giving us the time we need."

"Yes, thank you," Jen and Lynn reacted.

"Now, if you all will excuse me, I have some horses to attend to," Porter smiled. "I can get them ready for you, if you want to take a nice evening ride. Or you are welcome to watch some television and just relax. By the way, there's some dessert out in the kitchen. You'll find it in the refrigerator."

NINETEEN

PORTER RECEIVED A LETTER from Angie just one week after he had flown them back to Chandler, so they could catch their flights home from Phoenix. He was quite surprised to hear something from them so quickly. That could mean one of two things. Porter was not sure what to expect, but either way he was prepared. He opened the letter and found it to be brief, yet directly to the point:

> *Mr. Steele,*
>
> *Thank you for our recent weekend at your ranch. We appreciate your offer for a return visit. In regard to our discussion, we have all decided to accept. The first week of December would work best for us. I will wait for your response with the details.*
>
> *Angie*

Porter was not sure what to think of the letter at first. He was surprised at their answer. They must have been hurting even more than he could imagine. His discussion with them must have ignited a strong sense of justice. He wrote them back that evening explaining the next step in his plan. Porter advised them that during the first week of December,

Angie and Jen were to fly into Denver. They would be met at the airport by Lynn. Lynn would drive the three of them to a small airport, just south of Denver. He went on to explain to them that he had a very good friend, Sean Wallace, who would be flying his private plane to the airport to pick them up. From there, he would fly them to his vacation home in Durango. The visit in Durango would be roughly one week in length. Porter explained to Angie that Sean was a skilled pilot and that he would be assisting Porter in a variety of ways during this event.

Once they arrive in Durango, the entire operational plan would be laid out in great detail. At the end of the week, the three women would be flown back to the same airport. Lynn would drive Angie and Jen back to Denver International for their flights home. They were to consider this trip as simply three good friends spending a week-long visit at a friend's vacation home. Any outsider would perceive their behavior as a logical chain of events.

The logistics surrounding every human element connected to this strategic plan, would eventually be burned deeply into their minds. Porter and his friend, Sean, would become mentors to these women. There was a lot of planning involved in this final act of justice and mistakes had to be negated by way of serious, repetitive training. Porter knew that any errors along the way would be the undoing of them all. He was convinced that if his plan worked to perfection, without any miscalculations, the justice that eluded these women for the last sixteen years would finally be achieved. Maybe, just maybe, they stood a chance of finding a renewed sense of purpose in their lives. Porter made the flight plans that he felt would be the easiest on the three women.

WHEN DECEMBER ARRIVED, Jen flew into Denver International from Milwaukee, while Angie flew in from Kansas City. Lynn drove to the airport from her home in Denver and awaited their arrival. Lynn picked up the women, and their luggage, and they drove southeast to a much smaller private airport. There was one minor change in plans. They would be met at that airport by Porter, instead of Sean. Porter decided it was best if he flew from his Arizona ranch to pick up the women. He had a reliable connection there. The airport was easy for him to navigate, and Lynn would be able to park her car there for the week without any problems.

PORTER ARRIVED ON TIME and fueled up his Cessna, and their flight to Durango began. After a smooth and stress-free flight, Porter landed his Cessna at the county airport. His good friend, Sean Wallace, was eagerly waiting. After a brief introduction between Sean and the women, the five of them loaded into his Land Cruiser and began the drive to his vacation home for an intriguing seven-day retreat.

They would soon learn that this would not be much of a vacation. Their days would be packed full of hours of planning and preparation. Once they arrived at the front gate of Sean's property, and approached his log home, the women were in awe of the sheer magnitude and beauty.

Lynn stared upward. "Your home is magnificent."

"Thank you," Sean replied. "It's a long story as to why I built it and how I ended up here."

"I gave them the brief version on our flight here," Porter smiled.

"Thanks pal," Sean grinned. "I won't have to waste anyone's time with the details. Just enjoy your stay."

"My God," said Jen, as she stared at the tree trunks framing the entrance to his log home.

Sean parked his Land Cruiser in the driveway, and everyone got out, grabbed their bags, and headed toward the front door. As the women entered, their eyes were immediately drawn to the beautiful wood ceiling that rose up toward its peak with breathtaking splendor.

"The first thing I want everyone to know is my house is now your house for the next week," Sean announced. "Porter is like a brother to me. Anyone he invites to my home is like family. Please take advantage of everything here."

"Thank you so much," the women answered.

Sean led them inside. "I'm going to show you where all your rooms are, so you can put your bags away."

"After Sean gets you familiarized with your bedrooms, please meet me in the Great Room," Porter directed. "I think it is very important that we get started straightaway. A week may seem like a long time, but you'll find that it will fly by."

"Sounds like a poor attempt at pilot's humor," Sean grinned. He began to lead Angie, Lynn, and Jen to their rooms. On the way, he pointed out the Great Room, where they would soon meet. As Sean led them down the hallway he hollered back at Porter. "How 'bout thirty minutes and they meet us in the Great Room?"

"Perfect," Porter answered. "Thirty minutes."

Inside the Great Room, there was a large round hickory table set up with paperwork. Maps, and a wide array of documents containing important names, addresses, and criminal record information filled the table. There was a detailed, written strategic plan of operation. When the three women walked in, they felt as though they just entered a corporate business conference. They looked at each other in disbelief. This was no simple undertaking. This was a highly thought-out plan of attack against evil, and Porter was Commander-in-chief.

"I would like each of you to grab one copy of each of the documents on that table and get comfortable on the couch," said Porter. "We're going to have a lengthy and highly confidential discussion."

"Where's Mr. Wallace?" Angie wondered.

"Sean's not going to be part of this discussion. He'll join us later."

The ladies looked around and Sean was nowhere to be found. They could hear his Corvette revving up in the garage, and within seconds the car was speeding away. Porter wanted Sean to be a quiet player in this operation. This was intentional, due to the fact Porter wanted there to be some legitimate plausible deniability on Sean's part. At least as much as possible. There were certain things that Porter wanted, even needed, from Sean: his home in Durango, his knowledge of the permanent disposal of objects, his impeccable flying skills, and his unwavering loyalty. What Porter did not want, in any way, was for Sean to own culpability, or guilt, for what was about to happen.

Porter stood in front of the three women and began his presentation.

"Is everybody comfortable?"

"Yes," they harmonized.

"Let's begin," Porter started. "What you have in front of you is a tremendous amount of information. This has to be read thoroughly. I would like all of you to go over this at least once by the time you go to sleep tonight. We'll discuss it at length tomorrow, because what you're about to read will be the foundation for all of our training."

Lynn looked puzzled. "Training?"

"Yes, of course," Porter answered. "There's no better way to perfect certain behaviors and increase performance. Physical training. Hands-on training. Repetitive training."

"I totally agree," Angie said. She knew through her high level of fitness training over the years that Porter was right on point.

"Everything you have in your hands is essential to learn. This is the only way that this strategic plan is implemented successfully."

This was not the Porter Steele they thought they knew. This was not the sweet father of their best friend from college. The man they remembered as young college students in their twenties. Porter was beginning to appear to them as he once was. A man they never knew. The special forces soldier, Green Beret, which they had only heard stories about, so many years ago from Kristine.

Porter was a perfectionist, a strategist, and a performance-driven leader of men. That was how Kristine often described her father, although she was not exactly enthused with those attributes. At least not when she was only twenty years old and a struggling college student. His disciplined ways came off as rigid and demanding. But now, in this environment, sixteen years later, when life and death were at stake, these women were awestruck with his leadership skills. They felt safe. Protected from further harm. They realized that his discipline and expertise were the only answer to their persistent, gnawing mental health problems.

"Take out the document with the title, *The Plan*," Porter directed. "You are going to be reading this in its entirety, but for right now I'm going to give you a summary of how this is all going to go down. Stop me at any time if you need clarification or have any questions."

The women went silent and focused. Porter's lecture began:

"This operation will take place on March 6th of next year. I don't have to explain the significance of that date, but symbolism is important when preparing for battle. And that is exactly what this will be. It is a battle to recapture your lives. Your spirit. Your self-esteem. That means we have the next three months to educate ourselves on this entire operation, learn what important tactics will keep you alive, and complete firearms familiarity and repetition training. You will also spend the next three months getting yourself into excellent physical condition. Think of that as an extra added benefit, right Angie? I'll be speaking to you about designing a fitness program. A strong mind and body will be essential. It will help you overcome any unexpected adversity. On that date, we will be flying into a private landing strip owned by someone I know. This person is an old, but reliable, contact I had in police work. I'm not at liberty to identify him, but let's just say he has a tremendous amount of insight into the Hell Riders and has no love loss for Danny Trask. He will keep his distance and remain oblivious to why we are flying in there and I think it's best to keep it that way. He also wants to remain at a distance but agrees to do specific things if asked of him. He will only know minor details of the overall operation. The less he knows, the better. There are specific times in which each target will be hit. You will read more about the details, and we will go over them several times as we train. My Intel shows that each Hell Rider target will have a high probability of being at a specific location, at a specific time, according to their repetitive behavior and routines. They have been monitored for a while now. Those locations will be surveilled prior, so I will know for a fact that the Intel is solid. When we set out the day of this mission, I will be driving all of you to your targets. One directly after the other. The strikes will all be done within minutes of each other. All targets will be terminated within a window of twenty-two minutes. We will all stay together during the operation. No one will ever be left alone, except during the individual strikes. There is one very important reason why. It is because you will all be utilizing the exact same weapon during this operation. That means one firearm, not three. The weapon of choice will be a SIG Sauer P290RS. I feel it is the perfect weapon for the operation. First, it's a 9mm, with a small grip. Second, it's lightweight and easily concealable. Third, it will have excellent night sights and carries eight rounds of ammunition. This specific SIG is also untraceable. All numbers have been removed. The order of the strikes has been determined based on travel times, target behavior, and your safety. The following is a timeline that you can expect. Lynn, you will strike your target first. You will be quick and certain. You will waste no time at the target's location. After the target has been eliminated, you will quickly collect the two shell casings from the rounds fired. There is a vital reason for that, so it's important you do not leave them behind. I have a container the casings will be kept in. Once back in the vehicle, I will drive directly to the next target. Jen, you will exit the vehicle and go directly to the strike location and you'll eliminate your target. Again, collect the two casings and promptly return to the vehicle. From there, we will go to the third and final target location. Angie, you will proceed to your target and perform your strike. This will be the final hit of the three primary targets, which involves the three of you. Once you've collected your two casings each and return to the vehicle, we are driving straight back to the private landing strip. At this point there is one caveat. After reaching the airstrip, we will be met there by Sean. He will be flying the three of you to my ranch. Sean will then continue on to his home in Durango for some very important and necessary business."

Angie interrupted. "What if in the panic of the situation, or even just because of darkness, we can't find those brass shell casings?"

"First, none of you will be in a panic. But I do agree it will be dark," Porter explained. "If some of the casings are left behind, it actually won't pose a significant problem. But we will need some of the six casings. The issue surrounds the importance of specific and necessary evidence, which I will explain in detail later."

"What are you going to do after we fly off with Sean? We aren't leaving Las Vegas without you."

"You're going to have to leave without me. It has to be that way. I'll take possession of the SIG the three of you will use and I'll also take possession of all of the spent shell casings you'll retrieve after the hits on your targets are completed. I'll repeat. I'm not worried if you don't recover all six casings. By the time the bodies of the eliminated targets are found, which could be anywhere from eight to twelve hours, I'll be completing my responsibilities. And, hopefully inside my plane leaving Las Vegas."

"Then what?" asked Jen.

"I'm going to fly directly back to my ranch to check on the three of you. I may have to fly up to Durango first. That will depend on Sean and if he needs any assistance. I will make that decision while I am in the air."

"What's so important that you have to stay in Vegas once the three targets are dead?" Lynn asked.

"Aren't you just adding to the risk by sticking around another day?" Angie questioned. She thought she knew the answer but waited to hear his response.

"I have to remain in Vegas for a brief time. There is one very important thing I must do before I leave. None of you need to be privy to those exact details. But if I leave with you three directly after your hits, the final phase of this plan simply will not work. That could destroy the entire operation. I'll explain why at the proper time."

Jen pressed Porter for more details. "This is about Danny Trask, isn't it?"

"You're going to take out Trask yourself," Angie speculated. "For Kristine?"

"This isn't the appropriate time for me to discuss this part of my strategy, as I said, but I promise you'll all know soon enough about my entire role in this operation."

"When will you get back to the ranch?"

"If all goes well, it should be the following day."

Lynn stood to get a glass of water. "What happens then?"

"You will all need a few days to decompress. Believe me, your mind and body will be out of sorts from the rush of adrenaline," Porter warned. "The adrenaline dumps you'll all experience can do really weird things to the human body and mind. You'll need a lot of rest and time to completely chill out. Re-boot your systems. Get rid of all that pent-up hyper-nervous energy."

"How can we relax after an operation like this?" Jen asked. "Will we ever be able to?"

"The best way will be to think of it as the first day of the rest of your lives."

"What about all the evidence?" Angie wondered.

Porter could tell that Sean was returning home, because the garage door had begun to open. "Our friend here, Sean, will have everything destroyed. Incinerated. All our targets' criminal histories, scouting reports, Intel, photos, maps, strategic planning documents, training techniques, surgical gloves, and every last stitch of your clothing. It will be gone. Ashes. Particles blowing in the wind."

"What about the gun and shell casings?" asked Lynn.

"A discussion about those important pieces of evidence will have to be for another day," Porter reminded, as his lecture on the proposed strategic plan of operation came to an end. "Sean's home now. Let's all take a well-deserved break. Wrap your head around this initial assignment. You will have a lot of reading. There'll be a lot more to discuss as the week goes on."

Porter considered Angie as the natural leader of this group, although it was clear to him that she had significant problems of her own to overcome. He got her attention.

"Angie, I need to meet with you in Sean's study. Alone, please."

"No problem."

They walked to the study and sat down on two burgundy leather chairs. The study was actually a business office. Sean kept all of his documents from the sale of his construction business, client contacts, old home blueprints, and financial papers, locked up in a safe inside.

"I need you to step up and take a leadership role," said Porter.

"Why me?"

"I have known you the longest. You were Kristine's best friend," he said, "and you're the apparent leader of this group. That's obvious not only to me, but to Sean as well. He said he noticed it immediately."

"What do you need me to do?"

"We have just under ninety days to prepare for this operation, and it will be tactical," Porter stated, "so three months is not a very long time to prepare someone, anyone, especially people that have no military or law enforcement experience."

"And we are women?" Angie suggested. "Isn't that what you were thinking?"

"I wasn't thinking that, no," he answered. "I have worked with some excellent women in my career. I trusted my life to them."

"So, what's the issue?"

"I'm asking the three of you to enter a world you know nothing about. You aren't professionals. You're being asked to do something that you would have never done in your wildest dreams. Frankly, I need to know if the three of you are tough enough. Not just physically tough, but mentally tough."

"I think we are," Angie replied. "In my CrossFit gyms, most men can't keep up with me. I have to admit though; I don't know how we'll respond after taking someone's life. Even if that someone is a ruthless criminal. You trust us. That's what counts."

"I need you to take charge for the next three months of not only your own physical fitness, but the fitness of Lynn and Jen as well. When it comes to the psychological issues, they must be addressed before this operation takes place."

"Whatever needs to be done, I'll see to it that it gets done," she said. "What do you have in mind?"

"First, you will have to design a strict, and specific fitness program. It needs to be intense for the next two and a half months. Lynn and Jen will have to stick to it. You'll have to incorporate weightlifting, core strengthening exercises and aerobics. I know that you are way ahead of Lynn and Jen, but they'll have to become fully engaged and use every minute of the day, from here on out, to get into the best shape of their lives."

"Go on."

"You all must get on a stringent, healthy eating regimen."

"What are you saying?" Angie smiled, because she knew what Porter was insinuating.

"Sorry for any implications but I don't mean just to lose weight. But you all must be healthy, strong, and energetic. This operation will take stamina and a very steady hand."

"These are the things I teach every day. These are the areas of my expertise."

"Finally, and please do not take this the wrong way..."

"Go ahead, you can't say anything that will hurt my feelings. I know what you're thinking."

"The three of you must work very hard at getting your heads in a good place. Mental strength is just as important. Maybe even more."

"You mean like my eating disorder?"

"You have to take control of that issue, even if it means seeking the necessary psychotherapy. If I told you how many times I have wished I could have recognized the help Kristine needed so desperately."

"And Jen and Lynn?"

"Jen has to stop drinking right now. Not tomorrow or next week. Once, and for all," he answered. "She cannot have even one ounce of shakiness in her hands during this operation. Lynn has to get off the pills for the exact same reason. I can't have her flying high when she's holding that SIG Sauer in her hand. Her reaction times would be way down under the influence of those pills. I don't care what kind of help those two need, I'll cover the cost. But professional help is necessary. They cannot lie to themselves anymore, or it will get them killed."

"I couldn't agree more. I understand, and I know they'll understand. This is just like all of those competitions I've competed in over the years. You have to be at the top of your game, physically and mentally, or you'll end up losing."

"Losing at this game can mean the difference between life and death. The men we are dealing with would kill you in an instant. You three, starting this very minute, must think of yourselves as detached, robotic, fighting machines," said Porter. "If you let your minds slip into victim mode at any time during this operation, you will be asking for mistakes to be made. Mistakes create chaos. And chaos will get you killed."

"I'll start working tonight on an exercise program for all three of us. Also, a healthy food plan."

"Do you want me to talk to Jen and Lynn about the mental health issues?" he asked.

"I want to talk to them first," she answered, "but, if they seem hesitant...if they seem unsure...I'll come to you and the four of us will sit down together and hash this issue out."

"Angie, you remind me of a young woman I used to work with," Porter reminisced. "She was as tough as nails."

"Who was that?"

"She was a sergeant that had a lot of responsibility in taking down the Hell Riders several years ago. Operation Iguana. Martina Savala was her name. I called her Marti. She ended up getting promoted to Lieutenant because of her work on that case. Savala was a strong-willed fighter. She reminds me a lot of you."

"Do you still hear from her, or see her since you've retired?"

"Unfortunately, Marti was severely injured just one year after I left the department. She was shot by a twenty-year-old gangbanger during a SWAT raid. She was forced to take a full disability. Makes me sick just thinking about it."

"I'm sorry to hear that. And I do appreciate any comparison to strong women. But I hope this isn't an omen of things to come."

"If the three of you follow my exact orders, and none of you deviate from your preparation and training, I guarantee one hundred percent success."

"We trust you with our lives," she said. "Isn't that enough?"

"I may have failed my daughter, but I won't fail you, or Jen and Lynn."

"So, what's next for the three of us?"

"Tomorrow morning Sean and I are going to introduce you to something that will become your closest companion. Your best friend, you could say."

"And that is...?"

"The SIG Sauer P290RS."

"The firearm we'll be using?"

"Exactly."

"We'll be shooting it?"

"No...not quite yet," he said, "but you will spend the day getting familiar with everything about it."

"I'm anxious to get started."

"Go back and have a talk with Lynn and Jen about the importance of getting their heads on straight. No more alcohol...no more pills...no more ups and downs, Angie. The roller coaster ride is over. I want you all healthy. Think of getting healthy as the beginning of a new start. New women. New lives. It is long overdue. They need to know the importance of being in a sober state of mind. You cannot be sidetracked by your anxieties. Remember, the cost will be taken care of by me, but they must seek treatment starting next week when you get back home. Also, I would suggest getting started on customizing your fitness plan and healthy eating regimen, tonight. I would like to see a written plan, before you go back home."

"I'll have it to you before we leave here."

"Tomorrow is the beginning of a new day for all three of you," Porter promised.

"That's a good way of looking at it. I truly believe I'm ready for a big change. We all are."

"I'll see you in the morning. Eight o'clock sharp. Breakfast will be on the table."

Angie looked at Porter and didn't say a word. He looked back at her. She was staring deep into his intense, dark eyes for something. But what? Perhaps she was searching for a sign of reservation. An inkling of doubt. She didn't doubt him for a second. That wasn't her concern. But for the first time, in an extremely long time, she looked into the eyes of a man with unparalleled resolve. A man with laser-like focus. A man fully determined to turn his personal pain into their personal peace. Angie stepped toward him extending her arms. Porter, with the love of a father, embraced her as he would have embraced his own daughter. He missed the loving touch of Kristine. He missed the warmth of Ellen's hand in his. Porter missed being depended upon. He needed to give of himself. Relieving these women of a lifetime of misery had now become his sole mission. Tomorrow, that mission would undoubtedly begin.

TWENTY

THE WOMEN AROSE before eight a.m. and made their way out to the kitchen. At the table was an array of breakfast food, already prepared. There were pancakes, hash brown potatoes, eggs, sausages and two separate bowls of fruit, including blueberries and strawberries. Coffee was brewing and milk was already poured. The girls felt like they were at a world class bed and breakfast.

Porter walked into the room. "Good morning. I hope you all slept well."

"Good morning," was said in unison. "We did."

"Enjoy your breakfast," Porter insisted, "and then I'll have something to give to you."

"Everything looks so good," said Lynn.

"Ranchers have a special place in their hearts for breakfast," he grinned. "It's the only fuel we get before a long day of work begins. We usually work right through lunch."

On the counter, next to the kitchen island, Angie noticed three separate boxes. They weren't wrapped, but they were all identical in shape and size. She assumed that Porter was referring to these when he said he had something to give to them. According to Porter, today was the first day of training, so whatever was in those boxes must have been important.

"Sean's out in the garage getting something ready for us, so take your time eating," he said. "I'm going to go check on him and then I'll be back to show you something you'll need for the training."

The women were intrigued by Porter's secrecy, but they also knew that whatever the objects were in those boxes, they'd be as practical and utilitarian as the man providing them. The three of them sat, relaxed, and enjoyed their overly abundant morning meal. They could hear Sean and Porter talking and working out in the garage. They were preparing something for the women, but it would only be a wild guess at this point as to what was going on. When they were finished eating breakfast they sat, drank their coffee, and waited for whatever was about to come.

Porter entered the dining room. "I need you out in the garage."

They stood and deliberately walked, single file, toward the garage. Sean was waiting. Porter grabbed the three boxes off of the counter and followed them. The women entered the garage and immediately noticed three silhouette targets, standing side by side, along the north wall.

Porter got their attention. "Today is the beginning of your preparation for Operation Justice. March 6th is not too far away. Inside these boxes are the most important training tools you will receive. These are the tools that will prepare you for success."

Porter handed each of the girls a box. "Go ahead and open them."

When they opened the boxes, they found three replicas of the SIG Sauer P290RS, made out of an unknown polymer type material. "Don't be afraid to handle them. These guns will not fire."

The women removed the training weapons and set the boxes aside. "What are these?" Angie asked.

"These will be the training tools that will become your best friends over the next several days," he answered, "and until the real SIG Sauer is placed into your hands, these are the next best thing."

"What'll we do with these?"

"Each of you are going to handle it. Carry it. Caress it. Raise it. Lower it. Point it. Talk to it if you have to," Porter laughed, "but you will become so familiar with the SIG Sauer, you will long for it when it's not in the palm of your hand."

"What's this right here?"

"That's a laser sight," Sean replied. "You'll use that today. Remember, we initially utilize these because they cannot fire. So have no fear, whatsoever, handling these training firearms. These are for phase one training only."

"We made these from a 3D printer," Sean explained. "If we wanted to, we could have made these firearms completely functional."

"So, what's next?" asked Angie.

Porter showed each of them how to grip their training firearm with two hands. Their strong hand gripping the gun with tension, primarily on the middle and ring fingers. And the weak hand supporting the strong hand, by gripping the middle, ring, and pinky fingers, firmly, yet comfortably. With one of the training SIGs in hand, he demonstrated the Weaver stance. He placed his firing side foot slightly to the rear and his non-firing side foot toward the target. He had them get a feel for the stance, and work on balance and comfort level, before moving on to the next step. They would be spending a great deal of time on stance and grip during their training. Porter knew that each of the women would have a different comfort level with the stance and grip. He knew practice and repetition would alleviate those issues. They worked for the next hour on stance and balance alone. Both men helped each of the women with issues they were having, so they would begin to feel comfortable.

"We want you to stand here and feel the gun…feel the weight…feel the grip…feel the trigger position," Porter said. "Move around with it. Work on your stance. Raise it up, then lower it to your side. Walk with it…handle it. We want you to get use to the feel of it in your hand. By March 6th I want the SIG to feel like a watch on your wrist. Like it belongs there. Like something you forget you're wearing. I want it to be a living part of you."

"Which is your strong hand?" Sean asked.

"Left," Angie answered.

"Right for me," Lynn said.

"Right," said Jen.

"Get used to having it in your strong hand for now. You'll work on your weak hand later."

Porter walked over to the three standing silhouette targets and asked the girls to follow him.

"With the laser sights on, I want you to focus your laser on the target directly in the center mass area." Porter pointed to center mass. For training purposes, he had circled a six-inch area with a red permanent marker, which was dead center mass. "And also, the forehead. Right about here," he said as he pointed to the area directly above the bridge of the nose, between the eyes, which he had also circled in red marker. "These are the only two areas you need to concern yourself with."

"How do you get this laser on?" Jen asked.

He showed them.

"Now, I want you to stand seven feet back from the target. We've put tape on the floor. With your strong hand, and the SIG down at your side, I want you to raise it up and put the beam of that laser directly into the center mass circle that I've drawn for you. Keep that shooting arm straight. Your weapon is an extension of that arm. I want the raising motion to be smooth, but so precise that eventually you will be able to quickly raise your weapon and place that laser dead center mass right inside that red circle, without even thinking about it."

They all tried it once. They laughed.

"Is that it?" Jen asked.

"No, that is not quite it," Porter grinned. "Sean and I are going to go into the house and discuss some training issues. I need the three of you to do that exact motion five hundred times each. Break it down as you see fit. Five sets of one hundred. Ten sets of fifty. Whatever it takes. Angie, you're in charge. Let me know when all of you are done. Because when you're done with that, I want you to practice doing it with your eyes closed. Feel the motion."

"Holy shit!" Jen yelled.

"What's the problem?"

"No problem," Jen smiled. "I just hope I'll have an arm left to use when I'm done."

Sean started laughing. "You'll be fine. We have ice packs for that."

"When you're two months into this preparation, you'll be in the best shape of your life," said Porter. "That shooting motion we want from you will become second nature."

The women spent the next two hours working on their stance, grip, balance, and that specific controlled movement. Five hundred times, raising their 3D firearm replicas up and down, up, and down, pointing the laser beam into the red circle, center mass. They helped each other train. Their arms hurt like hell. Their shoulders hurt like hell. Their backs hurt like hell. The repetitive motion made the three of them realize that they had muscles in their bodies that had never been used before. Even Angie recognized the muscles that formed her beautifully sculpted body were different muscles, which had been used in different ways.

When they were finished with the five hundred reps, Angie went into the house and told Porter they were done. She seemed relieved, and happy they had gotten through it. When Porter came back out into the garage, Lynn and Jen were visibly thrilled that the training was over. So, they thought.

"Nice work. Now, I want you to do one more set," Porter ordered.

"One more set?" Lynn moaned. "One more set, of five hundred?"

"No, just two hundred fifty this time. But these will be different."

"How so?" Angie asked.

"For this set, there will be two separate motions. First, I want you to bring the firearm laser up from your side, into the center mass circle, just like you have been doing. And then, immediately after the laser touches the center mass circle, I want you to raise the firearm up slightly higher. Place the laser beam directly into the red circle on the target that is right between the eyes of the silhouette. Above the bridge of the nose. Without hesitation, counting one and then two. One to the chest and two to the head."

"Two hundred fifty times?" Jen asked. "Seriously?"

"Yes, seriously. Two hundred fifty times. Center mass is one and then center of the eyes is two. Consider each placement of the laser as a *tap*. Tap once to the chest and tap twice to the head. Make it as fluid of a motion as possible. Think smooth transition between taps." Porter took Angie's training firearm from her and performed the two-step motion for them. "Count one tap and you should have the laser at center mass. Count two tap and the laser should be above the bridge of the nose, right between the eyes. Just like this."

Porter performed the motion five times in a row, raising the firearm from his side, up to center mass, then from center mass straight up to the center forehead. "One and two. One and two. One and two. One and two. One and two."

Angie's training firearm was given back to her. Porter continued. "Eventually, as we work on the time gap between the first tap and the second tap, it will be hardly negligible. Always think to yourselves, *Double Tap. Tap-Tap. Bam-Bam. One-Two.* Get the counting motion down in your head. Whatever is easiest for you. Go ahead and begin practicing. After two hundred fifty repetitions you will be done for the day. Sean and I are taking you out for dinner tonight. We will discuss the training regimen for the rest of the week."

"You're planning on feeding us, I hope. And I mean literally feeding us. Cutting our meat and putting it up to our mouths," Jen laughed, "because I won't be able to raise my right hand that high."

"I'll have to do everything with my right arm," Angie joked. "My left arm is already numb."

"Won't we all look funny at a restaurant with slings on our arms?" Lynn asked. "With two grown men cutting our meat and feeding us."

"You'll be fine. Stop whining," Porter said, as he faked his rough drill instructor character. He smiled at the women's sense of humor.

The three went back to training. Just two hundred fifty more reps and a good meal at a restaurant waited. An hour and a half later the women were done. Their arms were shot. Their shoulders were pounding. Showers were in order, ice packs for their arms were a must and thirty minutes of simple relaxation was on their list of essentials before heading out to the restaurant. These new warriors in training were exhausted, but hungry for sure.

"You three let me know when you're ready to go and we'll head out," Sean said. "I'm taking you, and my friend Porter, to my favorite restaurant. Dinner is on me tonight. You can relax, eat all you want and enjoy the evening. I have Ibuprofen for dessert."

"I second Sean's motion for a nice relaxing evening," Porter added. "I know I've startled you with an intense beginning to your training. Relax tonight, because tomorrow is a brand-new day. I can't say it's going to get any easier. As a matter of fact, it will get harder. This was just a small taste. Your training has only begun."

OVER THE NEXT THREE months the women painstakingly prepared to become a trilogy of force behind their impending coup de grâce. Angie designed a fitness regimen that Lynn and Jen could do at their home cities of Denver and Milwaukee. The three of them religiously stayed in constant contact, reviewing workouts, discussing food prep, encouraging each other to push forward and never stop their progress.

As the days and weeks passed, their exercise program was making an obvious impact. Angie had started Lynn and Jen off at the ranch with daily walks of only a half mile. This continued at their homes. It soon turned into a mile, then two miles. Within the first month all three women were running four to five miles a day. They were hitting their local gyms four times a week for the first month. Angie set up a program to build large muscle groups, which strengthened their cores. Cable rows for the large back muscles, squats and leg presses for their quads and hamstrings, lateral raises and shoulder presses began to give them a strong sense of stability. Bicep curls and pushdowns for triceps strengthened arm muscles that these women never even knew existed. Angie had them working their abdominal muscles by performing leg raises, sit-ups, crunches, and planks. Building their cores was the ultimate goal, according to Angie, so they had a foundation of stability, strength, and agility. She had them working on their balance, standing on the BOSU ball with one leg and doing Plyo-box jumps for agility.

Porter was a stickler when it came to a well-rounded fitness routine that would prepare these women for battle. He couldn't shake his Green Beret roots. Angie knew how to do it and get it done. This type of training was in Angie's wheelhouse, and she felt a sense of pride developing her friends into strong, fighting machines.

Food was the fuel for energy and Angie had her friends thinking of meals as sustenance and nourishment, not just a fast fix after a long day at work. They were eating lean beef, pork, and chicken, fresh fish, vegetables, and fruit. There was no more digging into cupcakes and doughnuts every time someone at work had a birthday. Their desired treats became almonds, strawberries, and blueberries. The cravings for sugar disappeared. With the help of Alcoholics Anonymous, Jen purged her body of alcohol, giving her a new outlook on life. Now, with assistance from a well-researched psychologist in the Denver area, for the first time in years Lynn lived without the vise grip hold that pain pills had on her.

As Angie prepared her two allies, she too had an epiphany. She began to follow her own advice, and food became something she managed. She was able to get help from a counselor in Lawrence that specialized in eating disorders. No more shame. No more secrets. No more self-loathing. These women began to connect with each other and accept their new lives, like long lost sisters who found each other after a lifetime of searching. They felt alive again. They felt reborn. They had become warriors in creating their own destiny. Their determination and strenuous work ethic was leading up to one major revelation. Freedom.

Three days a week, these women were going to local shooting ranges, perfecting their double tap training routine. They practiced short range firing drills at silhouette targets, focusing on direct hits to center mass and center forehead. They kept track of their hits, bringing home their paper targets to monitor their progress as the weeks went by. They marked specific targets they were using, so they knew when they had shot the targets with their eyes open and when they were closed. This became very important, because it gave them working knowledge of how proficient they were becoming. They were able to calculate improved muscle memory, within the movement of their arms during firing, and the precision with which they repeated the double tap sequence. They needed this repetitive process in order to develop precision. The firing motion had to become instinctual. More than just improved performance, they needed these techniques to become ingrained into their collective DNA. They could hear an internal spoken whisper, *tap twice*, while they slept.

The women traveled several more times between December and March to Porter's ranch for tactical meetings, progress reports, and firearms proficiency training. When their training was complete, there was only one thing left to do. Angie, Lynn, and Jen were now fully equipped for the long-anticipated reckoning. That solemn day in March was soon approaching.

TWENTY-ONE

IT WAS LATE MORNING on March 5th. In slightly more than twenty-four hours the day of reckoning was about to begin. Angie and Jen flew into Denver where Lynn patiently waited. After being retrieved at Denver International by Lynn, the three of them made their way south to a small private airport, where Porter was anticipating their arrival. With his Cessna fueled and equipment checked, and the women ready to go, he packed their bags on board and made his way down the runway. Destination, ranch.

"How are you all today?" he said as they prepared for takeoff.

"We're doing well," Angie answered for the three of them. "Can't you tell, Porter? Just look at us."

"You're looking fit," Porter complimented. "You took your exercise regimen to the next level. It is obvious."

The women were focused. Even stoic. He noticed that their demeanor was unlike their first visit. They seemed like three totally different women. They had an air about them that communicated they were all business. Their physical appearance had changed considerably, since the first time they had met to begin training back in December. That was only ninety days earlier, but how much they were able to develop in just three months was astounding. The looks on their faces were now ones of strict professionalism. They meant business. He noticed that all three of them had dyed their hair a deep dark brown, bordering on black. That was Angie's idea. Porter noticed a dramatic change in their body structure, as well. Angie was always a fitness devotee, but Lynn and Jen had shunned exercise as they grew older. But now, even in their late thirties, they were in excellent physical condition. He was amazed at their progress in such a short period of time.

Porter recalled overhearing a private conversation at Sean's home between Jen and Lynn, where they both discussed how tired they felt. They were concerned about being twenty to twenty-five pounds overweight. The extra weight had drained them of energy. They talked about how hard it was to get a handle on a healthy diet. There was no time for exercise. Now, those problems seemed light years away. Angie told Porter that Jen had lost twenty-five pounds and Lynn, a staggering thirty. Not only had they lost weight, but it was also apparent that their biceps, triceps, forearms, and legs were well-developed, even sinewy, from months of weight training and weight loss.

During the flight to the ranch, the women discussed their workout regimens and were proud of how they were preparing for a marathon in the summer. Porter was impressed with their dedication. He couldn't help but think that he would have been honored to fight alongside of them as a Green Beret. Their posture, their demeanor, and their overall bearing, was visibly superb.

The flight to Porter's ranch was silky smooth, even tranquil, which made it pleasurable for all four of them. Any tension that may have appeared in the women, three months earlier, had dissipated, giving way to an odd sense of relief. There was a tangible sense of resolve among the women. An irrefutable feeling of comradery. This is exactly what Porter had hoped would happen. A sisterhood, like the brotherhood he developed in the Army, was palpable. He knew the austere training would give them a psychological edge during this operation. He remembered boot camp. Even though they didn't speak of it openly, each woman in that airplane felt the exact same way. They knew they were well prepared for what lay ahead.

When Porter landed at his ranch, it didn't take long for the women to notice Sean's Cessna Caravan wasn't parked off to the side of the runway. They hoped he would be there. The women had come to respect Sean, because his loyalty to Porter was undeniable. And because of this rare quality, they all knew that his commitment extended to them as well. Porter parked his plane off to the side of the runway. The women exited with a noticeable spring in their steps. Light on their feet. Stable and sure of their movements. Happy to be back at the ranch. There was an overall feeling of calm. A serene quality, emanating from their silence, like a faint mist on a cool spring morning. Porter grasped that sense of peace. Holding on to those moments, which always took him back to Ellen, and Kristine. To discard his emotions would be like throwing away a life already lived. These women were prepared, both mentally and physically. Now it was time for Porter to give Angie, Lynn, and Jen the spiritual relief they so desperately deserved.

Tomorrow was not the end. Tomorrow was the beginning. Four unassuming people came together to form a steadfast cast of characters, with the sole purpose of fulfilling a simple, yet pure, form of justice. Overdue justice. They had become a living human collage of emotions, destined to be the unspoken voice for redemption. One single voice, determined to avenge a festering secret. Resolute. Releasing a truth to power. Revenge. Without anyone ever knowing. As they entered Porter's home, the group walked into the welcoming Great Room, sat down at a warm, inviting, antique oak table, and quietly listened to each other breathe. Their silence was deafening.

MARCH 6TH ARRIVED, along with a bright morning sun, glittering off of the red rocks. The women had slept well and were ready for the final phase of their operation. None of them thought of turning back. Porter fixed a good breakfast, providing much needed energy for a long day ahead.

"Good morning, ladies."

"Good morning."

"When you get through with breakfast, I have something for you in my den. I'll be in there reading the paper and having some coffee, so please join me after you get through. No rush."

"We will, thank you," Angie answered.

Twenty minutes later the women walked into Porter's den and found him opening three large boxes, which he had setting on the couch.

"What are those?" asked Lynn.

"These are your work clothes for tonight."

All the women stepped closer and found clothing that was bland at best and downright boring at worst. Laid out on the couch were three dark navy blue, nondescript track suits, with their logos blacked out, three pair of black sports socks, and three pair of black running shoes. The sizes were all correct, which caused the women to smile. They didn't think of Porter as the type of man that would be able to select the right sizes in women's clothing, especially since their bodies had gone through such a transformation. He surprised them with his pinpoint accuracy. *Now that's a good detective,* Angie thought. Details were his specialty, so they should not have been shocked. There were also three pair of surgical gloves, shoe covers and, odd as it may have seemed at the time, three black nylon swim caps.

Jen held her swim cap up in the air laughing. "What in the hell Porter, we don't have time to go swimming."

"Those are definitely for function over style," he laughed. "Keeps your hair up...high and tight. I don't want any strands of your newly colored dark hair left behind at the scene."

"When do you want us to put these on?" Angie asked.

"Not until right before you exit the vehicle. Before you begin your approach toward your targets."

"Remind me never to let you buy me any evening wear," Jen joked.

"Did I strike out in the fashion department?"

"Let's just say, we should have done our own shopping," Lynn laughed.

"Don't worry about these outfits," he replied, "because you'll never wear them again. In fact, you'll never see them again after tonight."

"Aha. Understood," said Angie. "We are quickly getting the picture you're painting."

Under the clothing, lying on the couch, were three black sport bras and matching spandex shorts, all to be worn directly underneath their tracksuits.

"You won't get to keep these either."

Porter walked away from the couch and went over and sat down behind a large mahogany desk. It commanded attention. It communicated that sense of power and resolve. Confidence. The three women sat on the couch, facing Porter, as he reached into the drawer to the right side of the desk and pulled out a small gun case. The women knew what he was about to reveal. Inside the case was the SIG Sauer P290RS. He gently lifted it out of its container and held it, as if it were on display. The women stared.

"This is the weapon that will be used tonight."

"I assume it functions up to your standards?" Angie asked. "Are you satisfied with it?"

"Yes. And the serial number and any other identifying marks have been removed."

"You'll be holding onto it for us, correct?" Jen confirmed.

"Yes," Porter assured. "I will be the only one in possession of this firearm up until the time each of you are ready to exit the vehicle and use it against your target."

"And after the three targets are eliminated?"

"I'll retain possession of it for a very important reason. You will never see it again. Gone. Kaput!"

"And that important reason is, Danny Trask?" Angie pressed. He still had not explained himself.

"Without going into detail, I will not be using this weapon to kill Trask, if that's what you're implying."

Angie knew that Porter was not going to reveal his specific plan before the women were done eliminating their targets. She knew all along that Porter would deal with Trask in his own way. In his own time. She made it clear to him that they were all on the same page. "That's all we need to know, right you guys?" She nodded to Lynn and Jen.

"We leave here tonight at eight p.m. sharp. The three of you will be flying with me to the safe house in southern Nevada. The house is maintained by an old friend of mine and there's a small runway on the property. I will mention it's not a long one, but we should be able to land and takeoff with a little luck."

"What about Sean?" Angie wondered. "Where is he going to be?"

Just as that question left Angie's mouth, they heard that familiar sound of the engine of his Cessna Caravan landing on Porter's runway.

It began winding down and taxiing to a stop. Shortly after, Sean walked through the front door. He was heard talking to someone. Sean's voice bellowed. "Porter, where the hell are you?"

"We're in here."

They all stood and walked out to the Great Room, where they were greeted by Sean and a new face. An old friend of Porter, which none of the women had ever met. They were startled to be introduced to a brand-new player in this operation. This caused immediate concern.

"Hello, Sean," Porter said. He turned to the women. "I want you to meet an old, but very good friend. We served in the Army together. This is Jose."

"It's nice to meet you, Jose," Angie replied. The women didn't know Jose and as far as they could remember, Porter had never mentioned the name Jose in any of their strategic planning sessions. Deep down, all three women were concerned that now there was a new, and unknown element added to the equation. One they had not been told about. It was risky to add more people, at this late time, to their operation.

Porter could see the angst in their faces. He anticipated this.

"Jose is a longtime friend of mine. A loyal friend. We were in the Green Beret together. We share a special bond. That bond is sacred. Unbreakable. There's a reason I'm not telling you his last name."

"Why's that?" asked Jen.

"Because it's not necessary. Jose would like it to stay that way, so it's best for all of us that we keep it that way. Jose is one hundred percent loyal to me, which means he is completely loyal to you. But becoming friends is not necessary."

Angie felt she needed more details. "What will he be doing, exactly?"

"He will be driving my Tahoe out to the safe house for me this afternoon, so it is there and ready for us tonight. After the operation is completed, he'll be driving it back to the ranch. That's about all he'll be doing. He knows little about the rest of the operation occurring tonight. Other than some surveillance, gathering some Intel, he won't be involved. And what he does know, he will soon forget. If you know what I mean."

"What operachun? What are you talking about? I know nudding of any operachun. I only drive Señor Steele's el carro there and back. That is all I do. That is all I know," Jose laughed at his comical attempt of an overexaggerated accent and terrible use of the Spanish lingo. He was trying to calm their fears with his dry sense of humor.

Porter smiled. "Jose is somewhat of a comedian as you can see." It became obvious that he was trusted by Porter, and they received that message loud and clear.

"Okay team let's move on," said Porter. "Tonight, after we take off, Sean will be flying his Caravan to the safe house as well. So, both of our planes will be parked there. As you know from the operational plans, when the mission is complete, Sean will be flying the three of you back to my ranch. I'll be returning approximately eighteen hours later, even sooner if all goes as planned. I'll fly home in my own plane, and Jose will be driving my Tahoe back to the ranch for me. Any questions about that?"

"We're all good," Angie said, nodding.

"Excellent. We have a few hours of down time. The kitchen is open if anyone gets hungry. Enjoy some television, reading, or you can even take a nap. Review your assignments. Also, recheck all of your equipment and be prepared to fly out of here by eight p.m. sharp."

"What time are you leaving, Jose?"

"Six o'clock, boss," he answered. "That'll give me time to get there before you do."

"Perfect. I'll meet with you, and review things before your final surveillance run."

IT WAS EIGHT p.m. and Porter, Angie, Lynn, and Jen made the one-hour flight to the safe house, just south of Las Vegas. This gave them plenty of time, due to the time change. The narrow dirt runway was short and bumpy, but they landed safely and parked the plane behind a large outbuilding, which was used as a small hangar at one point in time. Inside the hangar, Jose had parked Porter's Tahoe, to be used later.

Sean's plan was to arrive at the safe house at approximately eleven p.m. Although that seemed very late, his only mission tonight was to pick up the women, after the operation, and fly them directly back to Porter's ranch. He didn't want to get to the safe house too early and sit around, twiddling his thumbs, while his beautiful Cessna Caravan sat out in the backyard. A shiny new plane was hard to hide from suspicious eyes.

At ten p.m. the women began to put on their work clothes. Everything from head to toe was considered important for this operation. Porter was trying to do everything possible to keep them comfortable, not to hinder their shooting abilities. But he also wanted to reduce the risk of leaving behind any trace evidence at any of the three target sites.

At roughly ten-twenty p.m. Jose took the Tahoe and made one last surveillance run. He needed to verify that the three targets were at their usual locations. He only had approximately twenty-six minutes to accomplish it. Jose needed to return by ten forty-eight p.m.

PORTER HEARD JOSE pull up behind the safe house and enter through the back door. He met him in the kitchen. "How do the targets look?"

"They're all exactly where you expected them," Jose reported.

"Give me a quick rundown on all three men."

"Target number one, Hammer, is in his garage, as usual. There's one light on, but it's localized around the area where he works on his motorcycles. The light does not extend to the outside, so it's strictly focused on his work area. That means it is very dark outside, around the exterior of the garage. As usual, he has the man door wide open, for airflow. He's hard at work on one of his Harleys."

"What's going on with target two?"

"Stump is inside the south side of the duplex where he lives. The neighbor on the opposite side of the duplex is right where she is every Friday night, gambling at Caesars. She never gets home until well after midnight. Stump is just walking around, drinking, and lifting weights. He listens to hard rock when he works out. He drinks and lifts late at night. The music is loud."

"Some prison routines are hard to break," said Porter. "And target three?"

"Bear. He's in his trailer, alone as usual. There is one streetlight at the end of his driveway, but other than that it is dark. He's in his living room, with one lamp on, watching television and drinking a whole shitload of beer. His entry door is open, but there is a screen door that is still closed but probably unlocked. I couldn't risk checking that. I'm sure he can't wait to help a young lady in distress. He's such a gentleman."

"Give me the numbers on your drive time."

"Once you leave here, it will take roughly eleven minutes to get to target one's location. You will spend about forty-three seconds there, if there are no issues. It will then take you four minutes to drive to target two's location. Another forty-three seconds there and your drive time to target three's location will be approximately five minutes. After forty-three seconds there, your drive back to the safe house will be a nerve-wracking twelve minutes."

"So, as I initially estimated, if all goes as planned, we will be back to the safe house within approximately thirty-four to thirty-five minutes. That does take into consideration the first eleven minutes to reach target one."

"You'll be lucky if you make it back that quickly," Jose said, worried. "That is a damn long time my friend. You know things rarely go that smoothly."

"I get it. It will seem even longer if the shit hits the fan," said Porter, "but we have to stay calm and focused. If we do, we will be close to hitting our times."

"As you know much better than I do," said Jose, "true justice can take a long, long time."

"When I return with the women, Sean will be flying them back to my ranch, pronto. That means at eleven-twenty p.m. his plane should be started and ready to roll," Porter said. "Coordinate with Sean and make sure that happens. You and I will have to stay here and get through the night."

Jose smiled. "This is the most fun I've had since our Green Beret days, boss."

"Fun?" Porter raised his eyebrows. "I hope to see you by eleven-forty."

Porter called the women into the kitchen. As they walked in, he could see they were chomping at the bit, more than ready to go. They looked professional, fit, focused and, most of all, they looked mentally prepared to meet out the justice that had eluded them for over sixteen years.

Porter looked at his watch, and it was ten fifty-eight p.m., and he could see the lights of Sean's Cessna Caravan landing at the end of the runway. He needed every last inch of that small strip of road to get his plane stopped before reaching the safe house. When he got it parked and hopped out, he passed by Porter, giving him a wink and two thumbs up.

Angie, Lynn, and Jen walked at a swift pace toward Porter's Tahoe, which was parked in the old hangar. The women didn't even look at Sean. They were too focused. They entered the Tahoe in their assigned seats. Porter was in the driver's seat. Lynn sat in the front passenger side. Jen sat in the rear passenger seat. Angie sat in the rear driver's side. This arrangement helped to make the women's movements more efficient and effective, reducing the waste of valuable time. Porter wanted the exit times and return times from each target elimination to be no more than forty-three seconds. It had to be that way, or the associated risks increased significantly. Timing, accuracy, and composure were the three factors that increased their chances of success. He knew that all three of the women were ready to complete the mission.

Porter began the drive to target one. As he arrived at the single-story dwelling, the driveway was short, so he shut off his headlights and pulled in, turning the Tahoe sharply to the left. This allowed the passenger side door to be closest to the target for Lynn, so she could exit the SUV smoothly. Then, reenter quickly after her return from the hit. He couldn't drive in too far, or it would give Hammer a greater chance of seeing the Tahoe. Jose had already removed the fuse to the interior lights, so it was dark when the doors were opened.

Porter spoke. "Are you ready to go?"

"I am," Lynn nodded.

Porter reached up and placed his finger over his stopwatch. "Go," he whispered, then started the clock.

Lynn put on her nylon swim cap, pulled up her hood and exited the Tahoe, leaving the door slightly ajar for her return. Her pace was brisk, but she was not running. Her gait was smooth, as if she were gliding just above the ground. It showed Porter that she was composed, her breathing measured and steady. Heartbeat calm.

When she reached the open man door to Hammer's garage, she could see him working on a motorcycle. His back to her. There was dim lighting, but that was all. That didn't faze Lynn, because she was trained to shoot in the dark as well. Her training with her eyes closed was a benefit. Lynn took one step into the workshop. Within seconds Hammer felt someone's presence and turned around, coming face to face with Lynn. He had no clue who she was, or what she wanted, but he was not at all fearful. After all, he thought, it was just a woman.

Hammer, seemingly at ease, asked, "Can I help you, young lady? You seem lost?"

"Answer a question for me," Lynn said.

"I'll sure give it a try." He stood, threw his oily rag on his workbench, and faced her. He was only five to six feet away.

"Do you remember the college girl you raped?"

"Who in the fuck are…"

Even before he could finish the last words he would ever speak, Lynn raised the SIG Sauer and placed her first round at dead center mass. The bullet entered Hammer's chest one inch above his sternum and one inch to his left, which would've been somewhere near the heart. The force of the round stood him upright, even more vertical than he already was. It thrust him backward against his work bench. Only a fraction of a second passed and she instinctively lifted the SIG slightly higher and placed a round at the top of the bridge of his nose. The round fractured the nasal bone and entered his left eye. Lynn squatted down toward the floor and located one of the two shell casings. She could not find the second casing, determining that it had to have rolled underneath his workbench. She knew instantly not to worry and left it behind. She cupped the casing tightly in the palm of her fist, slid the SIG Sauer into her tight waistband and quickly ran back to the Tahoe. After she entered the vehicle, Porter drove away. He had to get to the location of target two. No time to waste.

Porter looked over at Lynn and whispered, "Thirty-nine seconds. Any problems?"

Lynn never responded. She stared straight ahead, inhaling and exhaling three deep breaths. He knew she eliminated her target.

Angie reached forward and gently squeezed Lynn's shoulder, as if to remind her that they were with her. Porter continued to drive. He only had about four minutes to reach the next target.

"Jen...are you ready?"

"I am."

At that moment Lynn turned and handed the SIG Sauer to Jen. Lynn then handed the one, and only, shell casing to Porter. He placed it into a small plastic bag he had sitting on his lap.

Lynn finally spoke. "I fired two shots. Both were right on target. But I only found one shell casing. There are six more rounds left in the SIG."

"Got it," Jen replied.

Roughly four minutes and thirty seconds had passed and Porter was approaching target two.

The driveway to Stump's duplex was narrow, so Porter went slightly past the driveway and shut off his lights. He slowly backed into the end of the driveway and stopped, facing the front of the Tahoe toward the road for an easy getaway. The north apartment in the duplex was completely dark. Jose was correct, no one was home. Jen could see Stump walking around in the apartment. The stereo was blasting and she could see a weight bench in the living room. He appeared to be drinking beer and there was a light on inside the kitchen, and a lamp on in the living room. Jen put her swim cap on and pulled up her hood.

"You ready?"

"I am."

"Then go."

Porter started his stopwatch again as Jen exited the vehicle. She approached the south side of the duplex and as she got halfway to the door, she could see Stump walking into the kitchen. Within only seconds, he was turning away from the refrigerator and leaning down to look outside the window. Jen told herself, *don't panic*. She thought Stump could see her walking toward the door. She was right. Jen remained calm and knew that although he could see her approaching the house, he wouldn't be able to see her face very well. As she got to the door and prepared to knock, the door flew open, startling her for just a second. Her training kicked in and she took one deep breath. There she was face to face with her rapist.

"You scared me there, little lady," Stump laughed. "Car break down or something?"

"Yes, it did."

"You need me to call someone for you? Or if you'd like, you can spend the night here with me and I can help you get it started in the morning." He grinned.

"May I come in?"

"You sure can," he said and turned his back to her as she grabbed the door and entered.

Stump took several steps into his living room and as he turned back around, he found Jen pointing the SIG Sauer directly at him.

"What the fuck..."

"Do you remember the college girl you raped?"

At that very moment, Stump charged at Jen. He was already drunk and feeling too strong for his own good. She pulled the trigger and the first round entered three inches below his left pectoral muscle. The impact of the bullet caused him to spin to his left. He faced her again, hoping to rush her before she fired another round. His decision was a fatal one. Jen raised the SIG calmly, but rapidly, and fired her second shot, which struck him directly above his right eyebrow, penetrating his forehead. The force drove him backward, where he fell over an ottoman, causing him to get lodged between the wall and his favorite lounge chair. She was able to retrieve both shell casings from the living room carpet and left as quickly as she arrived, shutting the door behind her. When she got back to the Tahoe, she entered the rear passenger seat and sat in total silence, handing the firearm over to Angie.

"Forty-six seconds," Porter announced, driving away. In minutes, he would be arriving at target three's location.

Angie was quiet, pensive, taking some deep breaths. She knew in just a few minutes she would be standing in front of her attacker, after sixteen years. Justice was imminent, but the minutes felt like hours. Porter arrived at Bear's trailer, which was in a dark rural area. The next closest home was over five hundred yards away. One problem was the length of the driveway. It was just long enough to make Porter apprehensive, because he didn't want to stop too soon and make Angie run a long distance on foot. If she arrived at her target's front door, out of breath, it could have a negative effect on her precision. She needed to be relaxed, and accurate, when it came time to execute the shots. Her breathing had to be calm and measured. Porter took a gamble and shut off his headlights, creeping ever so slowly down the driveway, while Lynn watched the trailer through binoculars. Lynn directed Porter on his approach, by monitoring any movement inside the trailer.

Lynn reported: "He's in a recliner. The television is going. There's only one light on."

Porter continued his slow pace. Halfway up the driveway he stopped. "I need to let you out here, Angie. I can't risk getting any closer. Bear is the type of guy that would come through that door with a shotgun if he saw a car without headlights driving toward his trailer."

"That's fine. I'm ready." She placed the swim cap on her head and pulled up her hood. She drew in two more deep breaths, as if she were competing in a Cross Fit competition. Then, she exited the Tahoe.

"A quick, but consistent pace, Angie," ordered Porter. "Remember to breathe."

Angie took off and headed toward Bear's trailer. Her pace was not a sprint, but faster than a jog. Steady. Smooth. It was as if she were gliding on ice. She arrived at the front door. She could hear the television blaring, which gave her some comfort. *He may even be asleep in that chair*, she thought to herself. She knocked on the door, but no one came. She knocked a second time, but again, no one answered. When she looked through the window, there was no one sitting in the chair. Just a television blaring loudly. All of a sudden, she heard a back door open to the trailer and a man's voice was clearly talking to someone. Angie had to move quickly, her time was ticking and she had not even contacted her target yet. As she came around the corner of the trailer, she saw Mike Carlin standing there, with his back to her, talking to his Rottweiler. The dog was as big as dogs get, just as Bear was as big as men get. Angie realized that she had to adapt to the situation. She stealthily approached them both, just as Bear turned toward her. Angie walked forward, denying herself the slightest hint of fear.

"Who in the hell are you?" asked Bear.

"Do you remember the college girl you raped?"

Just as Angie said the word raped, Bear released his Rottweiler. The dog darted straight for Angie, but she calmly raised the SIG Sauer and only hesitated long enough to let the dog get right in front of her, until it reached the barrel of her gun. One shot between the eyes dropped the dog in its tracks. Bear was now seething with anger. His prized Rottweiler, dead. He began sprinting at Angie like a linebacker charging a helpless quarterback. She remained calm and lifted her weapon and fired one round into his chest. The bullet entered directly above his left nipple. The power of the bullet stood him upright, causing him to fall to the left, up against the side of his trailer. As he turned one more time to see where Angie had gone, she was standing right in front of him. She had not moved an inch.

"You never answered my question," she said as he gasped for oxygen.

"I remember...and I remember you liking it, bitch."

Angie fired one last round, with pinpoint accuracy, directly between both eyes. Blood splattered on the cheap aluminum siding. Bear slid down the side of his trailer, coming to rest on the bloody ground beneath his feet. She located two of the three shell casings and returned to the Tahoe. Just as she entered the rear driver's side door, Porter quickly sped away, back toward the safe house. Angie's breathing was much too rapid. He knew something bad had happened. Porter was afraid she was forcing herself into a panic attack.

"Calm yourself, Angie," Porter demanded. "Slow your breathing... twelve minutes to freedom."

"How long?" she asked.

"Almost a minute? That was too long. Was there a problem?"

"Yes, a big problem."

"What?"

"No one mentioned a massive Rottweiler lived with that asshole."

"And?"

"And I had to waste a round on it before I could take out Bear."

"How many shell casings did you retrieve?"

"Two."

"That leaves us with one round left in the gun," Porter said. "That'll work."

Angie reached over the seat. "Here, take these." She handed him the two shell casings. He placed them in his bag. That was a total of five recovered casings out of seven rounds fired.

"Let's get back to the safe house. We're making excellent time, considering the surprise issue with the dog. You adapted to the problem. This will take me less than the projected twelve minutes. I guarantee it. There are three bottles of water right there, in the console, next to you Angie. I want you guys to drink those and try to stay calm. By eleven forty-five, you will be up in the beautiful dark skies over Nevada, on the way to my ranch. Sean is waiting for your arrival."

"He better not have forgotten our real clothes," Jen said. That one light-hearted moment caused discreet laughter inside the Tahoe. It was an odd sensation. It was a moment when one undefinable, even confusing, emotion exposed itself to all three of the women. It was a perplexing state of mind with which they would all have to learn to live.

TWENTY-TWO

AT ELEVEN FORTY-FIVE p.m. Angie, Lynn and Jen transferred from Porter's vehicle into Sean's plane, preparing for takeoff. Sean was in the pilot's seat ready to fly.

"I'll see everybody back at the ranch," said Porter.

"After I drop the women off at your place, I'll be heading up to Durango to take care of everything for you," Sean confirmed. "I'll have everything loaded in the plane that needs incinerated. I want to get it destroyed as soon as I can."

"Thanks Sean."

"You bet. Will you be flying Jose home?"

"I was planning on it."

"If you change your mind, I can fly him home myself the next day."

"I'll leave that up to Jose."

"Sounds good…we're off then," Sean said as he revved the engine to his Cessna, preparing for takeoff.

Porter watched as the Caravan slowly taxied out onto the narrow, dirt runway. Sean needed to get the RPMs up quickly to get his plane off the ground, before he reached the end of the makeshift airstrip. Porter wasn't worried. Sean was an excellent pilot. Within minutes they were rumbling down the runway and lifted off into the sky, on their way to the ranch.

Operation Justice was near the end, but Porter's mission was incomplete. He couldn't relax quite yet. There was more work to be done, and the final phase of his plan was, honestly, in need of more than a little luck. He was well aware of the fact that all of his logistics would fall by the wayside, if Danny Trask did not respond to the lure of Porter's trap. This was the point in the operation where he realized he didn't have a realistic backup plan. Now was the time to find out just how well he knew the instincts of a man like Trask. If Porter was correct with his calculations, the web of justice was about to capture Trask like an unsuspecting insect.

Jose and Porter planned to stay at the safe house until seven a.m. the next morning. That was the exact time the final phase would begin. This part of the mission fell entirely on Porter's shoulders. If Porter failed, Danny Trask would find safe haven, probably in Mexico, and there would be an ongoing investigation into the three Hell Riders' murders. That would never bode well for the three women. And he knew it. What the women did not know, was the fact that Porter had already decided he would confess to all of the homicides if captured. The three women would go on to live a life of freedom from this day forward. Porter had promised them they need not worry. He assured them, on his honor, they would never be prosecuted.

Anticipating Trask's next move would be the key to what would follow. If Trask took the bait, like the rat he was, Porter would successfully cement his original premise into the minds of law enforcement. For this final phase of the plan to be successful, his predicted scenario had to play out perfectly. Porter and Jose decided they needed to try and get some sleep. The early morning hours would arrive quickly.

PORTER WOKE UP from a shallow sleep and got dressed in unremarkable casual clothing. He prepared the evidence he relied upon for the final piece of his elaborate puzzle. A puzzle which he had worked so hard to design. He placed a small leather duffel bag on the dining room table. He then placed the SIG Sauer P290RS inside, along with the plastic bag containing five shell casings. Once Jose got back with his Tahoe, he would be ready to go. Porter had sent him on an important mission. Jose's role in this operation would turn out to be one of the most important. At zero seven-thirty hours, Jose walked through the back door.

"How'd it go?" Porter asked.

"Worked perfect, boss."

"Any problems with the magnet?"

"Not at all. Completely out of sight," Jose smiled.

"You attached it to the frame, correct?"

"I found a place on the lower frame, with at least four inches of road clearance."

"Let's check to see if the GPS works, before I take off."

Porter initiated the GPS monitoring system on his phone to see if the device Jose planted on Trask's motorcycle frame was functioning properly. He found that his motorcycle was still parked at his residence, exactly where it was when Jose affixed the tracking device.

Porter grabbed the leather duffle bag off the table and handed Jose a untraceable burner phone. "When you see me pull away from the house, make the call."

"Will do, boss."

"Remember, Jose, Trask has to believe you are connected to the Vipers," Porter stated. "He has to get on that highway and start heading south, toward the safety of Riverside."

"I'm ready. Let's do this!" Jose shook Porter's hand. Porter held his grip a few seconds longer than he normally would. He stared into Jose's eyes. Loyalty creates powerful emotions. They both knew what the other man was thinking.

Porter headed out to his Tahoe and slowly pulled away from the safe house, heading directly for a predetermined spot to park, wait, and surveil. Just off I-15 south, ten miles out of town. Porter would be waiting there patiently. Did he know Trask better than Trask knew himself? Was the trap set properly? *This has to work*, Porter told himself with a shaky conviction.

As he drove toward his destination, Jose made the call. It was very early in the morning, but if Trask answered, he would surely know how serious the call was. The phone rang several times. Jose was about to disconnect and try again. But then, Trask answered the phone.

"This better be real fucking important."

Jose overaccentuated his Spanish. "Yo bro, is thees D.T.?"

"Who the hell is this?"

"A muy bien amigo from the Vipers."

"What's up, man?"

"Bear, Hammer and Stump are all dead. They were taken out last night. It was a professional hit, my man."

"What the fuck you talking about? Who is this?"

"You need to get out of town now...you're next," Jose lied. "The cops will be finding the bodies soon. You don't want them to find yours too, bro."

"How do you know all this fucking shit, man?"

"It doesn't make any difference how I know. What I do know for sure is you're next."

"What do you want me to do?"

"I'm telling you that the Vipers will let you hang out down here in Riverside for a while. Until things quiet down. That's coming straight from Diablo, bro."

All Trask had to hear was the name Diablo and that helped reduce his paranoia.

"I'm on my way," Trask stated. His past connection to Diablo gave him a misguided sense of confidence. At this point, a safe haven was at the top of his list. Even if only temporary.

Jose hung up and called Porter immediately.

"Hey boss, looks like he took the bait."

"He's on his way?"

"He said he was on his way. All you can do now is wait."

"The GPS should show me where he's at."

"I'll see you back at the safe house when this is all over."

"That is my plan, Jose."

Jose smiled to himself and began to sing. *"Fighting soldiers from the sky. Fearless men who jump and die..."*

Porter laughed and interrupted his song. "Thanks, brother. I will see you if this whole thing doesn't fall apart."

ANGIE, LYNN AND JEN all slept. Their sleep was deep. Unusually deep. Their bodies were exhausted. Their minds were hiding out from the world. Utterly drained of all vigor, rest was the only way to slowly re-energize and readapt to living normal lives again. If that was even possible. One day at a time would have to be their new mantra. There would have to be a method of recovery from something they could not identify. Their bodies and minds were still in a state of shock. Porter knew this would happen and that's why he wanted Sean to fly them to his ranch directly, after the operation was complete.

Post-traumatic stress disorder was an inexplicable, sometimes unidentifiable, psychological response to a traumatic event. It could be short term, or long term. Everyone experiences it differently. They needed to start recovery immediately. The adrenaline dumps, from eliminating their targets, were devastating to their systems. Their bodies and minds would need time to recover from that sort of shock. It was still early in the morning at Porter's ranch. Their rooms were still dark. Their surroundings were eerily quiet, giving them the peacefulness necessary to begin healing.

Sean wasn't there. After dropping the women off at Porter's ranch, he flew on to his home in Durango. There was unfinished business to attend to. Important business. Years ago, when Sean was building his log home, he kept a massive incinerator on the property for the destruction of waste, such as scrap building materials. It had the power to turn just about anything into pure ash. This was something Porter became well aware of. Sean went to his Caravan and removed three large plastic garbage bags from the luggage storage compartment. Inside the bags were the women's track suits, running shoes, athletic socks, sports bras, spandex shorts, swim caps, and surgical gloves.

Kept hidden in Sean's home were all of the written strategic plans, progress notes, training regimens, criminal histories, photos of the targets, and the 3D polymer SIG Sauer P290s used for firearm's training. Everything even remotely connected to this operation was now moved into Sean's garage, prepared for permanent disposal. Once he got the incinerator started and heated up, the job itself was simple and quick.

All of the evidence linked to Operation Justice entered the incinerator as solid material objects but exited as weightless ash. Floating in the wind. A recent history of necessary vengeance, destroyed by the flames of justice. Any trace of evidence no longer existed. Over the next several days the microscopic ash would spread far and wide, blanketing the dry rocky terrain, like dust in the wind.

The only evidence now remaining was in Porter's possession. He had the SIG Sauer P290RS used in the operation. And five brass shell casings. Those, too, would be discarded as well, but in a much more creative manner.

WITH ONLY ENOUGH TIME to pack a few clothes into his Harley's tour pack, Danny Trask was on the move, heading south on I-15. Porter knew Trask would use the interstate to travel southwest. The interstate would be far too congested, and chock full of witnesses, for any professional assassin to try to shoot him in broad daylight. Porter was tracking his movements by cell phone and determined that he was only a few minutes away from passing right by him. The trick would be getting in behind Trask's motorcycle and following him without raising suspicion. This was paramount.

All of Trask's senses were heightened, because of Jose's phone call. He believed the anonymous caller, which meant his level of paranoia was also at an all-time high. If Danny Trask believed someone were truly out to kill him, just as they had killed Bear, Hammer and Stump, his head would be spinning. Left and right, forward, and backward, like it was on a swivel. Trask had wronged so many people. He'd have to check out every car and motorcycle that passed him by. He felt at this point that everyone who caught his eye was out to kill him. Trask tried to be cautious, but his blood pressure was too elevated. He knew he couldn't drive fast, because a biker on a Harley was like fresh meat for the California Highway Patrol. He didn't want to give the cops any excuse to pull him over.

He was heading for Riverside first. He had to try to see if he could link up with Diablo and take advantage of the offer to lay low for a while. Porter was able to monitor the GPS, so he allowed Trask to be several car lengths ahead. The goal was to follow him at least to Barstow, which was roughly one hundred fifty-two miles to the southwest. Porter knew Harley Davidson motorcycles. Trask would have to eventually stop and gas up around that area. There was nothing to do now except drive, surveil and hope that Trask did not make any sudden diversions away from I-15. To this point, Porter's predictions were accurate. He hoped that Barstow would be the end of the road for Trask.

The drive was intense, traffic was heavy, but it kept Porter alert. He was more tired than he thought and was getting concerned that Trask would drive straight past Barstow and keep heading toward Riverside. He kept following as closely as he could without being spotted and had just gone over one hundred-fifty miles. *Any time now. Any time*, he kept saying to himself.

Within minutes, Porter got his wish. His tracking software alerted him to a change in direction by Trask. He was exiting I-15. Porter sat up straight behind the wheel, shook the tiredness from his head, and tried to get his eyes fixed directly on the rear of Trask's motorcycle. There he was stopped at an intersection, about to turn into the entrance of a gas station. There were a lot of cars there pumping gas, so Porter turned in slowly, locating a place to park, keeping his distance. He watched Trask's every move.

There was one concern, and it was one of logistics. Porter knew that when this time came, he would need a lot of luck on his side. Now that Trask had pulled over to buy gas, Porter watched and waited, hoping he would walk away from his Harley, leaving it unattended for at least a few minutes. Porter had to get to that motorcycle and retrieve the GPS device. The last thing he needed was the California Highway Patrol finding a GPS device on the frame of that motorcycle and wondering who in the hell was following Trask down the highway. If Trask located the GPS himself, he would begin to suspect that the anonymous phone call he received, earlier in the morning, was nothing but a set up. That could cause him to turn right back around and return to Las Vegas in a panic. A frightening thought crossed Porter's mind. *What if Trask simply pays for his gas at the pump and gets back on his bike and heads on down the interstate?* He could drive another two hundred miles before he needed gas again, which might destroy the final phase of Operation Justice.

Porter watched Trask as he filled the tank of his motorcycle with fuel. What happened next caused Porter's heart to lodge in his throat. Trask did in fact pay at the pump, and as soon as he filled his tank, he hit the ignition switch and started it back up again. *Goddamn it!* Porter had avoided talking to God this entire trip. Especially, taking his name in vain. He needed all the help he could get. Porter didn't think it was wise to press his luck with the Almighty, which he knew he had been ignoring since the death of Ellen. But now was as good a time as any to have some divine intervention. Porter asked for only one prayer to be answered. He watched Trask pulling away from the gas station, so it seemed that the man upstairs wasn't listening. As he exited the station parking lot, Trask pointed his Harley back toward the interstate. Porter began to pull away as well, figuring he would have to continue following him, then adapt to the situation. This would challenge all of Porter's skills.

What in the hell is going on? Within seconds, Porter was slamming on his brakes. He watched as Trask stopped abruptly, making a quick turn sharply to the right. Porter was worried even more now. *What in the hell is he doing now?* Then, he realized that maybe his prayer was about to be answered. Answered in the form of a donut shop. What are the chances this guy likes donuts? Trask apparently needed a sugar fix. Nothing more, nothing less. Porter looked up and smiled. *God, you work in mysterious ways.*

He watched Trask, from a distance, pull into the donut shop parking lot. He made a flawed decision to park his motorcycle a long distance from the front door. That meant he had a long walk to the shop. This would give Porter the valuable time he needed. As soon as Trask entered the business, and was totally out of sight, Porter jumped out of his Tahoe and ran straight to the Harley, attempting to locate the magnetic GPS device. It was exactly where Jose said it would be, underneath the frame, four inches off the pavement.

With a surgical glove on his right hand, Porter recovered the GPS tracking device. He opened the left rear saddle bag of Trask's motorcycle. He located a leather pouch on the right side of the motorcycle's frame, near the gas tank. Porter had good Intel that this was where Trask carried his forty caliber Browning Hi-Power semi-automatic handgun. He removed the weapon and gently placed it inside the open rear saddle bag. Porter then removed a small plastic bag from his right front pants pocket. It was the bag that contained the five spent brass shell casings. The same casings from the rounds that had been fired from the SIG Sauer into the bodies of Carlin, Emerson and Severs. Porter dumped the casings into the open saddle bag. Finally, with the surgical glove still on his right hand, he removed the SIG Sauer P290RS from the waistband of his pants and safely placed it inside the leather pouch. The gun had only one live round left, ready to be fired. Lynn, Jen, and Angie had already fired the other seven.

Porter had to calm his racing heart and think. *Is that everything? Have I missed any evidence?* Feeling assured, he hurried back to his Tahoe to make one important, but anonymous, phone call. It was a phone call to the distinguished law enforcement agency, the California Highway Patrol. This call would be the beginning of the end of Operation Justice. One way or another, Danny Trask's day was about to be ruined. He watched as Trask came out of the donut shop and started his Harley.

Porter's 911 phone call was simple and to the point. "The killer in a triple homicide in Las Vegas is pulling out of the donut shop near Barstow on a black Harley. He's south on I-15. He's a Hell Rider named Danny Trask. He said he's willing to kill cops." Porter disconnected the call.

He followed him for another three miles, waiting for law enforcement to respond to his 911 call. He knew it wouldn't take long. He'd seen this scenario play out before, on numerous occasions. Cops come out of the woodwork if they can help catch a killer. As Porter drove south, he stayed in the right lane, driving the speed limit, waiting for the cavalry to arrive. Within minutes from his call, the response began. There was a convergence of law enforcement that communicated a sense of overwhelming force. Two California Highway Patrol motorcycle units passed him on the left. Then, a San Bernardino County squad car was entering the interstate from the west, right in front of Porter's Tahoe. There were three Barstow Police cars, two marked and one unmarked, which flew by him like he was standing still.

Porter took the next exit and got himself turned around. He knew that what was about to happen next could only end in one of two ways: Danny Trask would either give up peacefully, accept his fate, and spend the rest of his life in prison, or he would fulfill a promise he made to himself. And that was to never step foot in any prison, ever again, after all the years he spent because of the RICO case. During all the years Porter lived in the city of Las Vegas, he never considered himself a gambling man. But if he were, this would be the time he would put all his money on the latter.

Porter got his Tahoe back on the road again, now heading north on I-15, toward south Las Vegas. He kept driving, anticipating the local news on the radio to announce one of their *Breaking News* stories. Porter remained focused. Cautious and lawful driving was very important right now. As bad as he wanted to hit the accelerator and speed back to the safe house, he knew he had an anxiety-ridden one hundred fifty-eight miles to go. This would be the longest two and a half hours of his life.

Jose was at the safe house patiently waiting. With the Cessna ready to fly and the house scrubbed of any remnants of recent visitors, their hope was to be back at Porter's ranch by early to midafternoon. Porter would be flying and Jose would be driving the Tahoe. They knew that Sean was at his home in Durango, finishing his job. The three women were pacing back and forth at Porter's ranch. They were anticipating the end of this operation, praying for their safe return. It was only a matter of time now, and life for all of them would take on a whole new meaning.

When Porter pulled into the driveway of the safe house, Jose was coming out of the back door, ready to take over the driving responsibilities. Porter's Cessna waited. He exited his Tahoe and Jose entered.

"See you at the ranch," Jose said.

"Be very careful. And remember, just a leisurely drive," Porter said. "There is no rush now, my friend."

"See you soon, boss. Your plane's ready to fly," said Jose. "Are you awake? Good to pilot that thing?"

Porter was visibly dragging. He had aged. "I'll be okay. Thanks, Jose. I'll see you later."

Jose threw the SUV in reverse, swung it around and started his journey back to Porter's ranch. The women would be glad to see some sign of life in these two men. They had been out of communication now for a full day. As he prepared for his flight, Porter knew he didn't have time to be a gentleman and run into the safe house to use the restroom, so he urinated outside, right next to the old hangar. Having a full bladder, after a two-and-a-half-hour drive, with over a one-hour flight pending, was more than a little uncomfortable.

Once that was taken care of, he completed a quick walk-around, visual check of his plane. He made sure he had enough fuel to get home, then entered the cockpit. He felt safe in his Cessna. It was all he had left in his life that gave him comfort. Now, more than ever, it gave him more than pleasure. It gave him a sense of security. It gave him refuge from all of the dark places he had been taken over the last several years.

The sun was burning dim, and the skies beckoned his companionship. When his wheels lifted off the dirt runway, Porter felt relief and forced a slight grin. Just for a moment, tears welled up in his eyes. Even for a man as strong willed as Porter Steele thought he was, he could not stop his emotions from escaping. Perhaps, there was just too much pent-up frustration released all at once. Or was it the tranquility of flight. Perhaps, it was the overwhelming release of anxiety of the moment. He realized that it was the fact that a promise he had made to his daughter, had finally come to fruition.

The promise of justice opened him up to emotions that not only confused him but caused him to reevaluate his own life. Where would he go from here? How would he face his future alone? He flew toward his ranch, looking out over the vast arid land below, finally taking a moment to reflect on where he had been and where he was now going. Porter hoped God would somehow forgive his sins.

WHEN HE LANDED at his ranch, he saw three women standing at the end of the runway, waiting. He taxied his plane toward his house and parked. He exited to an emotional welcome, and they all went inside, together. Porter turned on the television. They watched as the special *Breaking News* unfolded across the southwest:

> *"The leader of the infamous Hell Riders motorcycle club has been shot and killed by law enforcement officers. In the late morning hours, right in the middle of I-15, just southwest of Barstow, Danny Trask allegedly initiated a gun battle with motorcycle units from the California Highway Patrol, Barstow Police Officers, and a deputy from the San Bernardino County Sheriff's Department. Witness accounts of what happened described Danny Trask's actions as intentional suicide by cop. He clearly provoked the deadly force brought upon him. It was learned that after a tip came in from an anonymous 911 call, which informed law enforcement that Trask was involved in the homicide of three fellow gang members of the Hell Riders, police officers from several jurisdictions attempted a traffic stop on I-15 to take him into custody. Witnesses said that Trask seemed to patiently sit on his motorcycle for a couple of minutes, making a final decision as to what he was going to do. One witness described the following: 'The guy slowly got up from the seat of his Harley, reached into some kind of pouch, grabbed a handgun, and then walked to the middle of the lanes of I-15. Once there, he faced the police officers as they tried to get him to throw down his*

weapon. He raised his gun, pointing it directly at the officers. I could have sworn I heard him fire one round at the side of a police car. Then the officers opened fire, killing the man right in the middle of the road.'"

A second reporter from a rival television station began reporting the following:

"The I-15 location is being treated as a crime scene. The interstate has been temporarily closed until investigators clear the scene. An inside source, who wishes to remain anonymous, stated that it appears the weapon Trask had in his hand may be the same weapon used to kill three fellow Hell Rider members. Early this morning, the bodies of Mike Carlin, Nick Emerson and Jake Severs were all located at their residences. They were the victims of what appears to be homicides. We were also told that shell casings from that handgun, which may have been removed from those three homicide scenes, were found inside one of the rear saddle bags of Danny Trask's motorcycle. We were informed that the one telling piece of evidence could pave the way for clearing the unsolved murders of four other rival bike members from several years ago. A similar M.O. was utilized in not only the murders of Carlin, Emerson, and Severs, but also the other four unsolved cases. The unidentified source reported that it appears that the shooter fired one bullet into the chest and one into the forehead of all seven victims, apparently in a rapid fashion. The unnamed source referred to it by using the term, double tap. Danny Trask was the primary suspect in

the original four unsolved homicides, which now, more than likely, will possibly clear all seven murders with the violent death of the Hell Rider's notorious leader. The commanding officer at the scene was asked about the next steps in the investigation. He was not able to give further details at this point but did acknowledge the lab would be testing the bullet fragments from the three deceased males to see if they matched the gun found in the hand of Danny Trask. He also revealed that there were shell casings located at the scene of at least two of the earlier homicides. And one shell casing was located in the middle of I-15 interstate, near Trask's body. All recovered casings would be compared to the firearms that Danny Trask possessed, and they would all be compared to each other. All of these findings would eventually be presented to the District Attorney's Office for review. When asked if he was confident that they would solve all seven homicides, the supervisor in charge simply stated, 'We are hopeful.'"

PORTER TURNED THE television off. He didn't want to hear anymore breaking news. He heard what he needed to hear.

"What's next, Porter?" asked Angie.

"A good night's rest and then I'm going to see to it that you guys make your flights home from Denver. I will also make sure Jose gets back home. Sean took care of everything up at his place in Durango, so I'm not worried about him."

Lynn seemed apprehensive. "Then what?"

"Then what? You three are going to get on living the lives you deserve to live," Porter replied. "No more living in the past. It's all over now. It's time to move on."

"When will we see you again?" Jen wondered.

"I'll be in touch with all three of you after things settle down around here. It may be a few months, but that's okay. You three need a much-needed break from me anyway. Wouldn't you agree?" he smiled.

"Thanks for everything," said Angie.

"You never have to thank me with words," he emphatically reminded. "Thank me by going home, living your new lives happy, healthy, and determined to find people you will love and take care of the rest of your lives. I was not able to give that gift to Kristine. If you can do it for yourselves now, I will be forever grateful."

"We will. We have to," Angie promised.

"Now, I have to get some sleep."

Porter went into his bedroom, set his phone on the nightstand, and tried to fall asleep. He was dead tired yet filled with intense energy. His cell phone startled him. *Who in the hell could this be?*

He answered.

"Porter, its Marti."

"Martina Savala?" he asked. "My God, how are you?" Porter had not spoken to Martina for years.

"I had to call you. Did you see the big news?"

"No, what's up?"

"Danny Trask is what's up."

"What do you mean?"

"He's dead."

"No shit."

"California Highway Patrol shot him dead, right on I-15, over near Barstow. He's suspected of killing three of his fellow Hell Riders."

"I'm sure he deserved it."

"I thought you'd find that quite amusing."

"It couldn't have happened to a nicer guy."

"You're right about that," she agreed. "I just wanted you to know. If you had written the script yourself for his death, that's probably the ending you would have come up with, right?"

Porter laughed. "I'm not that creative, but I'm sure it would've gone down something like that, Marti."

"Take care of yourself, Porter," she said, "and don't be a stranger if you're ever in Vegas."

"I won't. Please take care of yourself."

Porter sat quietly on the edge of his bed and shook his head. Sleep wasn't something his mind was going to allow. He laid down and stared up at the white ceiling.

TWENTY-THREE

IT WAS BRIGHT AND EARLY in the morning. Weeks had passed since Angie, Lynn and Jen had returned home. Returned to their lives. Porter warmed up a black cup of coffee that was still left over from the day before. After reading the paper he got himself dressed, pulled on his boots, and made his way out to his truck. Like every Sunday before, his chores would have to wait. He would be back soon. Porter took his cowboy hat and tossed it on the front seat of his pickup and then walked to the shed and retrieved his weed trimmer, sliding it into the bed of his old trusty Ford.

His Sunday ritual began. Six miles to go and he would be at Oak Hill. Like every Sunday since he buried his wife and daughter. On the way there he noticed some beautiful wildflowers growing along the road and stopped for a minute. Spring was a time for life. A time for rebirth. A time for renewal. He picked some newly blooming sego lilies and white poppies for Ellen and Kristine's headstones. They always loved the wildflowers that seemed to paint the brown Arizona landscape with colors so bright they must have fallen from heaven.

When he reached the cemetery, Porter parked his truck and took the flowers from the seat. He began his lonely trek up to their gravesites. What would he say today? How could he explain himself? What if what he had done was wrong? What if his heart had trumped his head? Did he throw all reasoning to the wind? His grandfather had once told him that a man must think before he acts. That a man could find himself doing all the wrong things for all the right reasons. He tried to ignore those pieces of advice. Ones he once cherished.

Porter knelt and placed the lilies and poppies on Ellen and Kristine's gravestones. He found that he couldn't stop himself from releasing his emotions. He never could. He did not have the strength to hold it in. As he stood again, and thought about his wife and daughter, he scanned the peaceful green space that surrounded him. The grass was tall.

He was glad that he remembered his weed trimmer. It was the only physical thing that he could still do for the women he loved. He walked back and opened the tailgate of his truck, reflecting on what he had done. Porter could not find any prolific words of wisdom that explained his overpowering drive to seek the justice his wife and daughter so desperately deserved. He simply remembered. He stared. He absorbed the quiet. And then, with a familiar tear streaming down his cheek, he began to clear away the tall grass.

ACKNOWLEDGMENTS

A huge debt of gratitude goes to my cover and interior designer, Christian Storm, who's creativity is second to none. I would like to thank my proofreader, Joanne Arford, who provided a much needed second pair of eyes when working on my book. I would like to thank my wife, family, and friends for their unwavering support. A big thank you goes out to all the readers who enjoy crime thrillers. Finally, I want to thank those men and women in law enforcement who fight real crime every day. This was my life for over thirty years and where I still find inspiration.